Coquelic‹

by

Allison Creal

ISBN: 9798853741898

Adult content

Adult content featuring violence, profanities and sexually explicit descriptions.

Cover image artwork by Allison Piearce from an original photograph by Raymond & Eleta Kerr. Model Charlie Thomas.

Prologue

July 2015

George Dalmano relaxed beneath a luxurious blanket of massaging bubbles in his hot tub. The frothy foam of the Jacuzzi soothed his tired muscles, as he shook the last few drops from a champagne bottle into an elegant fluted wineglass. At seventy-three years of age George was proud of his toned physique and the fact that, despite his age, he had managed to hold on to his full head of shoulder-length hair. His once glossy raven-black mane was now a little wiry with flecks of silvery-grey, but he still proudly wore it in an age-defying ponytail. George's chest and arms bore numerous faded tattoos that charted the many chapters in his colourful life. His sun-tanned skin was a little more leathery than he liked and his chin had a grey bristly five o'clock shadow, but he was still pleased with the hard muscular body that he had spent a lifetime honing and polishing. George's expensively manicured fingernails were short and perfectly shaped; he wore large diamond-encrusted signet rings on three of his strong masculine fingers. He was a self-made millionaire and enjoyed the decadent trappings of a successful businessman's lifestyle. Despite his advancing years this silver fox never spent his evenings alone. George knew his bad-boy reputation and tremendous wealth made him an attractive proposition for many young ladies.

He took a large slug of his drink, placed his half empty champagne flute into a chilled glass holder at the side of the Jacuzzi and flicked a switch to drive the hot tub bubbles to maximum power. He plunged his strong rugged hands beneath the warm frothy water and flexed his be-jewelled fingers in the foamy effervescence.

A young pretty woman with long flame-red hair sat opposite him in the water, quietly watching his every move, anticipating his next predictable demand. A devious smile stretched across George's leathery tanned face as his strong muscular arms reached further beneath the frothy surface and roughly pulled the girl closer to him. Slipping his hands between her slender

1

legs he swiftly pulled off her bikini bottoms. George pushed his face into the woman's ample cleavage as his rugged masculine grip lifted her lithe body out of the bubbles. The young woman's nipples began to harden in the sudden breeze of cool air. She felt the rasping burn of George's bristly chin scratch across her delicate skin, as he pulled her back down into the water and began to hungrily move his mouth from one breast to the other; like an excited wild animal he began sucking and licking in hot anticipation. He rolled around, shoving and pushing his quarry into a sculpted hot tub seat. His hardened exploring tongue moved ferociously across her cleavage and up over his conquest's neck, to find her mouth. With frenzied excitement, his brutal hands took firm control beneath the foaming water; he swiftly pulled the submissive young woman's thighs apart, pushed her knees up and wrapped her long slender legs around his muscular torso. He thrust his rasping tongue hard into her mouth, as she felt the stinging fullness of his hot throbbing manhood forge deep inside her.

"How hard do you want it?" hissed George into the young woman's ear. "You want it harder, don't you bitch?"

His docile prey stared back at him, too startled to speak, her face without expression.

"You want it harder, don't you? You slut," he menaced, not waiting for a reply, as his deep-blue penetrating eyes met her blank stare.

He thrust faster and faster in and out, muscles flexing, buttocks tightening; his pace quickening and deepening in time to the repetitive hum of the Jacuzzi motor. She could feel his hot eager breath panting into her ear, as his throbbing dick continued to relentlessly pulse inside her. The powerless young woman winced as George's hard bony hips fiercely jabbed against the soft insides of her thighs.

"Oh Angel-Baby," murmured George, savouring each syllable of her name, his eyes closed tightly shut. "Angel-Baby, you really are the most perfect fuck."

George could hold back no more. As he took in a sharp deep gulp of air, the young woman could feel his pulsating taut body tense up and stiffen. George held his breath for a few anxious seconds, before letting out an almost victoriously long hot gasp

2

of air across her face. As his hot climatic juices flowed deep inside his yielding conquest, a small self-congratulatory smile twitched across the old man's lips. He was proud of his achievement. His latest carnal mission had been a triumph.

Angel pushed his head away from her face, before George predictably pulled out of her sharply. He splashed back down into one of the Jacuzzi's sculpted seats to regain his composure and bask in blissful post-coital exhaustion. A tidal wave of foamy bubbles rippled across the surface of the water as George reached out for his champagne flute. The compliant flame-haired young woman took little comfort from knowing it would only be a short while before George's insatiable demands would need to be satisfied again.

Angel retrieved her bikini bottoms and pulled them back on before silently climbing out of the foaming hot tub. The sex had been rough and sudden; she was now feeling used and discarded. This was not the first time she had played the servile role in one of ageing George Dalmano's sordid sex games, but she was determined that today would be the last time. Angel hated herself for allowing the abusive pervert to fulfil his wildest lecherous fantasies with her. The seemingly endless sessions of bondage, humiliation and burning slaps across her delicate buttocks were beginning to leave their scars. She despised the millionaire businessman's sadistic fetishes and the control he had over her, but she knew that she had a job to do.

The woman was only in her mid twenties and still had a lifetime of adventure ahead of her. Angel had a secret plan in life and she was positive that one day she would achieve her ultimate goal; when all of her sleazy activities would become a buried memory. Sacrificing her innocence to dirty old men had simply been a means to an end for Angel. She had grudgingly played a convincing role in each of their depraved filthy charades for as long as it was necessary. Massaging their egos was a price she had been prepared to pay.

George was oblivious to the young woman's fermenting resentment. He relaxed back in his hot tub seat, savouring the spoils of his latest conquest as he surveyed his domain. The old man's well-toned leathery body bore testament to a hard lifetime of physical toil. In his dirty misspent youth George had been the leader of a biker gang and had violently scraped a living from the underbelly world of vehicle crime. He became an expert at hotwiring cars and stealing motorbikes; supplying them to villains higher up the criminal food chain. He earned the once insalubrious nickname of 'Sparks' from his unrivalled ability to fire any engine into life, with or without the ignition key.

Over the years he had clawed his way out of the seedy quagmire of twocking and vehicle breaking to build a more lucrative career as the local gangsters' go-to man for high end dodgy motors. On the surface his prosperous car sales business was now a legitimate dealership in the more affluent area of Hanford town, frequented by an up-market clientele; but beneath the veneer of respectability lay George Dalmano's underworld empire of luxury car stealing, dealing and smuggling. Whenever a villain needed a getaway vehicle, a clone or a luxury set of wheels to send abroad, George Dalmano's showroom was still their first port of call.

The opulent surroundings of George's home were extremely comfortable. He had carefully designed the hot tub area as the ultimate party zone and it all sat on a large decked terrace, hidden behind billowing muslin drapes, beneath the comforting protection of a large canvas gazebo. The hot tub had been lowered into the raised decking. George was a vain old man and he wanted to avoid drawing any young lady's attention to his not-so-nimble advancing years. The deliberate design detail to create a sunken Jacuzzi made it easier for George to enter the pool elegantly, rather than having to clumsily climb over a ledge. Next to the hot tub was a well-stocked bar that displayed an assortment of expensive whiskies, bourbons and brandies. Beneath the bar was a glass fronted wine chiller that housed numerous bottles of vintage champagne. A couple of sun loungers, a small glass coffee table and an upright electric patio heater completed the decadent adult play area.

George flicked a switch to return the hot tub bubbles to massaging power before lowering his silver-haired chest beneath the rippling water. In his self gratified mind he deserved the rewarding pleasure of the warm frothy water soothing his leathery tattooed body; after all he believed he'd just given his latest squeeze the best damn shag of her life and that had taken stamina. He needed to recharge his spent batteries ready for the next performance. The foam of bubbles frothed over him, a small wave of caressing warm water lapped across his ageing torso. The short silvery blanket of hairs on George's chest swayed back and forth in the water to reveal a small faded tattoo of a unicursal hexagram located just above his left nipple. The ink was an unwelcome reminder of his misspent youth and the businessman intended that one day it would be removed.

George closed his eyes and let out a small satisfied sigh of contentment; things could not possibly get any better than this. He had a successful business with a beautiful home, and now he had the ideal compliant fuck-buddy on demand to complete his perfectly decadent life.

Angel shivered as she left the heat of the Jacuzzi. She quickly wrapped herself in a fluffy white bathrobe that she retrieved from one of the sun loungers and switched on the electric patio heater. She warmed herself beneath the instant glow from the element. The young woman closed her tired eyes and allowed her mind to drift, imagining her achingly abused body was being kissed by the hot Mediterranean sun; the whooshing water in the hot tub became the lapping surf on a Spanish beach. In Angel's mind the billowing muslin drapes that hung around the gazebo were the sails of a pleasure boat fluttering in a cool ocean breeze.

"Get another bottle of champagne open while you're up," ordered George, snapping Angel out of her Mediterranean daydream. She noticed his eyes were still closed in post-coital contentment as he proudly lay back in the foaming waters.

George didn't see the slender hand that pushed the patio heater over the edge of the sunken hot tub. He had no warning of the sudden thrashing electrical torrent that would be unleashed when the three kilowatts of power hit the water. He had no escape from the burning sparks that would furiously extinguish his sordid life.

5

Chapter 1

A deafening roar of engines broke through the late night silence of the countryside. Six men rode their thunderous heavy motorbikes in strict formation through a maze of winding leafy country lanes, to reach the centre of Himley Chase. The gang of bikers were the self-proclaimed Serpent Sons of Thelema and they proudly announced their arrival to the local wildlife with an ear-splitting intrusion of clattering exhaust pipes and throbbing engines. The riotous entourage was a small and close-knit brotherhood of half-a-dozen wannabe Hell's Angels and tonight they had an important job to do; a ritual that could only be carried out beneath the cloak of darkness.

The leader of this sleazy gang of leather-clad dissidents was a thirty-two-year-old man called Sparks. He led his pack of dutiful followers proudly from the front, astride his heavy Triumph Bonneville motorcycle. Second in command of this motley crew of misfits was an overweight bearded biker with bad breath called Crusher. He had the important job of making sure all the members of the gang knew their place at all times. His steely resolve ensured everyone obediently rode their customised machines in strict formation behind the leader; no one was allowed to break free of this imposing posse and it would have been more than their life was worth for anyone to overtake the boss on the open road. Everyone knew their own respectful place in the gang's strict pecking order; everyone dutifully complied.

Zombie, Razor Fish and a man called Bullet were in third, fourth and fifth positions at the centre of the procession. They were closely followed by Yardy, the only rider with a side-car, who tucked in close behind at the rear of the grungy entourage. A twenty-year-old new recruit called Billy sat nervously riding pillion on the back of Zombie's Royal Enfield motorcycle. He was anxiously waiting to hear if he was to become the official seventh member of the Serpent Sons of Thelema.

Billy had hung around the biker gang for most of his teenage years. The miss guided youth had desperately sought the clan's acceptance and approval which had led him into a life of petty crime. He had dropped out of school just before his sixteenth birthday and he was then promptly disowned by his disappointed parents. They simply could not accept the shame of having raised such a delinquent son. With no home to go back to, Billy had grasped the chance to become the Serpent Sons' general dog's body, a gopher. In return for a roof over his head at the biker gang's headquarters, he had carried out menial tasks and seemingly endless errands for their leader. Billy had spent the last couple of years prospecting for the posse. He had eaten, drunk, slept and lived as one of the brotherhood, all in the hope of impressing Sparks, the gang's commander-in-chief. Over time, Billy's nerve had been tested by the bikers and his loyalty to the fraternity proven beyond any shadow of a doubt. Billy's only ambition in life now was to become a fully fledged member of the circle; a patch wearing Serpent Son of Thelema.

Billy had served his four-year apprenticeship faultlessly but he was still only a kid; he had only just left his teens and some of the biker gang's members had thought he was still too young to be taken seriously. As the gang's leader, Sparks had more influence than the rest of his kinsmen when it came to choosing prospectors and appointing new members. He had decided Billy should be given a chance to prove himself and tonight was going to be the young recruit's toughest test of all. It would be the most pivotal night of Billy's short life. If he had managed to successfully impress the gang as a prospector, then all of his efforts would be finally rewarded with his initiation and patching ceremony. If he had failed in his quest, then it could mean the end of his life.

The thunderous roar of the posse's engines came to an abrupt halt as the biker gang's six throbbing machines pulled onto a grass clearing at the centre of Himley Chase. Everyone switched off their engines. Sparks flipped his side stand down and slowly got off his bike. He was wearing a black open-faced helmet with a silk bandana over his mouth that had the pattern of an American Confederate flag printed on it. He pulled down the scarf and turned to face Crusher, his second-in-command.

"Over there," he barked at his loyal entourage, pointing towards the centre of the grass clearing.

Razor Fish and Bullet dutifully followed their leader's instruction. They climbed off their motorbikes and walked to the back of Yardy's machine that was parked at the end of the line. Billy remained seated on the back of Zombie's motorcycle and turned around to watch Yardy remove the plastic clip-on roof from his side-car. He could see a long pale-green tarpaulin sheet covered a very large parcel that filled the seat and foot well inside. The three men began to struggle shifting the bulky package from the seat, as Crusher moved to the rear of the side-car and pulled out a large wooden handled shovel. He returned to stand in front of the row of bikes and looked at Sparks for a nod of approval, before throwing the spade onto the moonlit grassy clearing.

Zombie ordered Billy to get off the back of his bike before pushing the new recruit over to where the shovel had landed. Sparks stared at the nervous young man who now stood before him. One by one, in a swift seemingly choreographed movement, the rest of the gang moved into place to encircle their anxious apprentice. Billy was momentarily blinded by the flickering parking lights of the gang's motorbikes as he stood at the centre of the clearing. Each member of the gang took his place in the semi circle, obediently observing the brotherhood's strict pecking order. Billy raised his right hand up to his forehead to shield his eyes, as he twisted around to look at each of the men's faces in turn.

Crusher, who proudly stood at the side of the gang's leader, stared back at Billy from behind his long bushy beard. He had large tattooed hands and began to menacingly crack his knuckles as if in excited anticipation. Zombie, a small bony man with skeletal features and greasy slicked-back Teddy Boy hair stood next to the second-in-command. Next to follow was the shiny shaven head of Razor Fish. He stood next to Bullet, a skinny man with blonde curly hair. Finally the rotund figure of Yardy stood proudly at the end of the entourage; he slowly caressed a long black drooping Mexican moustache that ran over his top lip and down both sides of his chin.

8

"Right, start digging kid," snarled Sparks, as he kicked the shovel closer to Billy's feet.

The nervous young recruit felt a sudden surge of fear pulse through his chest; it felt as if his lifeblood was going to drain down his body and out through the soles of his weather-beaten biker boots. *What the hell is this? Have I failed the test?* His mind raced.

The whole gang stared in silence as Billy slowly picked up the spade and took the wooden handle in his hands. He lifted his heavy-booted foot to press the metal head of the shovel down into the soft grass beneath to begin digging a shallow pit. The six bikers continued to stare at the ground that the young prospector was burrowing, as if silently willing him to work faster. Billy slowly came to the realisation that he must have disrespected the lawless posse in some way; he must have failed his apprenticeship and this was to be his final retribution.

With each tear of the grass Billy feared it would be his last breath; with every scratch of the earth he wondered how long he would have to endure the stressful humiliation of digging his own grave. How long would he have to wait before Crusher's powerful tattooed fists put an end to his short and futile existence?

After half an hour Billy had managed to create a shallow trench of about six feet long and a couple of feet wide. He was becoming weary and he could feel blisters beginning to swell on his hands. The anxious apprentice continued to dig, locked in the silent watchful gaze of Sparks and Crusher. The other four men left the encircled brotherhood and returned to Yardy's side-car at the rear of the procession of motorcycles. They pulled the heavy tarpaulin-wrapped parcel out of the seat of the side-car and rolled it over towards the grave that Billy was digging. Startled by the thud of the package coming to rest in front of him, Billy lost his footing and fell backwards onto a mound of small rocks. Immediately he felt a sharp piece of stone cut into the palm of his right hand. Blood began to trickle from the muddy wound.

"Come on kid, you ain't finished yet," barked an impatient Sparks. "The hole needs to be deeper than that to take this fat

9

fucker's body," he sneered, pointing at the bulky canvas-wrapped bundle that now lay in the moonlit clearing.

"What the fuck? Who the fuck is that?" gasped Billy pointing at the heavy pale-green tarpaulin package. He was clearly shocked by the lifeless mass, but his fear was quickly replaced with relief. He soon realised it wasn't his own grave he was digging after all, but the shallow pit for another unfortunate lost soul.

"You don't need to know who he was, just keep digging," replied Sparks impatiently.

"Yeah, it's just some fucker from a shit-for-brains posse who thought he could disrespect us," jeered Crusher menacingly. "Well he ain't gonna disrespect us any more is he boss?" The bearded biker loyally looked over for his leader's nod of approval.

Sparks ignored his second-in-command and continued to stare impatiently at the shallow trench in the ground. Billy pulled himself up off the mound of sharp rocks and picked up the shovel to resume digging. He felt a sudden salty sting in his hand, as blood poured from his small wound and ran into the grain of the wooden handle.

Eventually, after another hour's hard toil, Sparks and Crusher agreed that the pit was deep enough and Billy was finally allowed to rest for a short while on the grass clearing. Billy licked the blisters and cut on his hands, as the remainder of the gathered entourage unceremoniously rolled the heavy tarpaulin-wrapped bundle into the shallow grave.

"Right, get your little cock out," spat Crusher as he forcefully dragged Billy up off the ground back towards the trench.

"What the fuck do you mean man?" protested a startled Billy.

"I wanna see your bony little dick piss all over that fat fucker," ordered Sparks, as he pointed at the bulky bundle that was lying in the freshly dug earth. "I wanna see that steaming pile of shit soaked in your hot scrawny piss, so when that disrespectful bastard crawls through the gates of hell they'll feed him to the dogs for stinking like a rotting fish in a sewer."

The six leather-clad bikers closely watched the new recruit as he nervously unzipped his jeans and reached inside his fly. Could it have been his previous fear of losing his own life? Could it have been the relief that he was no longer in Sparks' line of fire? Or was it more likely to have been the three pints of brown ale he had drunk before setting out for Himley Chase? Whatever the reason, despite his imposing audience, Billy found no difficulty in summoning up a long, flowing, hard torrent that soaked through the heavy canvas tarpaulin and onto the lifeless body that lay beneath. It was the ultimate mark of disrespect for the dead rival biker gang member that would seal Billy's future with the Serpent Sons of Thelema forever.

A devious smile stretched across Sparks' narrow lips; a heavy flank of glossy raven-black hair curtained the sides of his face. He was proud of his loyal kinsmen and his instincts about Billy had been right. Their latest prospector had proved his resolve beyond any shadow of a doubt. The kid had passed his apprenticeship with flying colours and he was worthy of becoming a fully paid-up patch-wearing member of the gang. Sparks walked over to Billy who was zipping up his jeans.

"You done good kid." Sparks slapped a firm reassuring hand on Billy's back. The gang leader looked over at Crusher and nodded. Immediately the rest of the brotherhood moved together in strict formation to encircle Sparks and the new recruit. Crusher removed a large leather pouch that was bound with string from the foot well of Yardy's side-car and handed it to Sparks. Slowly the gang's leader untied the string and ceremoniously opened up the leather envelope. Inside were three pieces of white canvas material that had been hand embroidered in black and red coloured twine. One of the pieces featured an image of a unicursal hexagram at the centre, the other two semi-circular pieces, which had been designed to be displayed above and beneath the hexagram, bore the words 'Serpent Sons' and 'Thelema'.

Billy stared in awe. This was it. This was the moment he had lived his whole life for; the culmination of his misspent youth. He had reached the absolute pinnacle of his aspiration. Billy was receiving his colours; he had passed his final initiation test and he was now about to become a fully-fledged patch-wearing

11

Serpent Son of Thelema. Sparks carefully placed the embroidered pieces of cloth onto Billy's open blistered hands and began to bring the ceremony to a formal conclusion.

"Brothers," croaked Sparks, before clearing his throat with a rasping cough. "We're here tonight to welcome our new kinsman to the family." Everyone stared in awe at their leader.

"If any of you here present know of any reason why Billy Kiddo shouldn't be joined with us, then say so now," demanded Sparks as he opened a bottle of brown ale. Everyone remained motionless, as if frozen by the reverent stone-cold silence of Himley Chase. They watched their commander-in-chief raise the beer bottle above Billy's head and begin to pour its frothy brown liquid contents over the new recruit's face and hair. Billy's baptism into his new life was now complete. He knew from that day forward his biker family would always come first; betrayal of the brotherhood would never be tolerated and disloyal weasels would always be avenged.

All of the men began to cheer and welcome Billy into the fold with hearty man hugs and slaps across the new member's back. A few bottles of Tennessee whiskey were opened and numerous joints were passed among the gang, as the celebration of their new brother's initiation carried on deep into the night. Billy had eagerly sworn his oath of allegiance to his new family and wholeheartedly accepted his 'Kiddo' gang nickname, in reference to his young age.

The drug-fuelled celebrations forged on into the early hours of the morning. Gallons of brown ale and countless spliffs had mellowed the burley gang of seven bikers, as they all lay down on the grass, savouring their drunken and doped-up evening, staring up at the star-filled pre-dawn sky. Zombie moved across to sit down in the clearing next to Billy.

"You doin' okay Kiddo?" asked Zombie, as he casually rolled a matchstick thin cigarette between his bony fingers.

"Yeah man," replied Billy as he licked the salty wound and burst blisters on his hands.

"You sure mate?" probed Zombie with a small quizzical look on his skeletal face. "Cos you look like you've got the weight of some heavy shit hanging on your shoulders man." Zombie lit his spidery joint and took in a deep purposeful draw.

There was no hiding Billy Kiddo's small shiver of guilt that passed through his young body. In the back of Billy's mind he couldn't shake off the unnerving realisation that only a few hours earlier he had eagerly helped to bury the corpse of an unknown rival biker; yet he was now finding it remarkably easy to celebrate his new enhanced status that came with the protection of wearing the colours of his new family. It had been simple to blindly follow Sparks' orders without question and he felt safe among his fellow partners in crime. But there was still a nagging element of fear that gnawed at the back of Billy's mind.

"What happens to the body now?" he blurted. Six pairs of drunken and drug-fuelled eyes slowly turned to meet Billy's awkward gaze.

"I mean we can't just leave it there for some nosey dog walker to find later on in the morning can we?" he added helpfully.

"What you suggestin' then Kiddo?" rasped Crusher, as he took a deep drag of Zombie's joint. "Have you become an expert in dealing with dead fuckers now or something?" The dismissive second-in-command was clearly riled.

"No, no man," stalled the newly initiated recruit, eager not to undermine his superior. "I just meant maybe we should . . . erm . . . burn the fat bastard, just so it's not obvious who he is."

A devious smile stretched across Sparks' face, as he sat up slowly and pulled an annoying strand of his long raven-black hair from across his steely-blue eyes. He took his cigarette lighter from a small pocket on the breast of his biker's jacket and began to playfully flick the flame into life. Sparks rolled onto his back again and began to laugh.

"Yeah, let's burn the disrespectful fucker," snarled the gang's leader, as he threw his lighter in Billy's direction. "There you go Kiddo, knock yourself out."

Billy grappled around on the grass clearing, aimlessly searching for the lighter. Slowly a small flurry of giggles started to flutter through the group of leather-clad bikers; their stifled chuckles erupted into thunderous belly laughs, as the six uncontrollable men lay on the ground childishly kicking their legs up into the air with anticipating glee.

Billy looked back at the men quizzically. He couldn't understand why everyone had erupted into hysterical laughter. *What's so fucking funny?*

Eventually Crusher sat up and held his stomach, still laughing at the secret joke. "Hey man, watch what you're doing with that flame man." He stood up from the grass clearing. "Stand well back Kiddo. That stiff will go up like a fuckin' fireball if you don't watch it."

Crusher raised a heavily tattooed hand and clicked his fingers to summon Zombie to walk with him over to the shallow grave. Each of the men took an edge of the urine-soaked tarpaulin that still encased the dead body in the trench. Slowly and purposefully they lifted the soaked canvas shroud out of the pit and rolled the rotting corpse back out onto the mud. There, in the misty light of the dawn sky, the shocking contents were revealed.

Billy could clearly see the back of the old biker's tasselled jacket had been torn and stabbed mercilessly with a knife. There were darker areas in the leather where once there had been a proud set of Hell's Angels' patches. Billy took in a sharp gulp of air as he could make out the rear of a black crash helmet that looked as if it had been smashed with a claw hammer. The dead body wore dirty blue jeans that were tucked into a pair of old weather-beaten biker boots; black leather gloves hung lifelessly at the ends of the jacket's sleeves. Crusher and Zombie kicked the carcass onto its back, making it land awkwardly back down in the shallow grave. The force knocked off the black open-faced crash helmet.

Suddenly Billy let out a small shocked gasp. There was no head beneath the crushed plastic helmet, just a tight bundle of straw; there was no body inside the clothes, just a dressmaker's dummy that had been padded out with rocks and hay to make the package appear heavy and cumbersome. Billy began to smile nervously as he slowly came to the realisation he had been duped. The whole midnight burial had been a fake ritual to test his nerve. There was no dead body; there had been no rival biker who needed to be taught the ultimate lesson in respect.

Sparks smiled proudly at his prodigy and slapped a hard congratulatory hand across Billy's shoulders. The newly

14

initiated Billy Kiddo may have only buried and desecrated a stolen dressmaker's dummy, but the young new recruit had believed it was a real corpse at the time. He had then wanted to protect his new fraternity from any connection with it. He had cleverly planned in his own mind how to distance his brotherhood from the dead body in the woods. Billy had thought of nothing else for a couple of hours before suggesting the drug-fuelled posse set light to the body to conceal the dead man's identity, and ultimately shield the gang from any police investigation. Billy Kiddo had exceeded all of Sparks' expectations. He had passed his final initiation test with flying colours and had proved his unwavering loyalty to his new family.

Chapter 2

July 1976 – Two Years Later.

Sparks' girlfriend, Tracey Chambers, was a fiery red-headed cock teaser with a flame temper to match. She had caught the attention of the gang's leader two years earlier at a biker rally. Sparks had been mesmerised by the way the seductive seventeen-year-old had shaken her mane of curly auburn hair when she danced; how her slinky body had moved rhythmically to the pounding beat of Led Zeppelin's Whole Lotta Love. He had been impressed by how she knew all the lyrics to every rock song played on the rally's P.A. system.

Sparks had first spotted Tracey in the beer tent. She had provocatively teased every slavering hot blooded male that shuffled around the edge of the dance floor, by seductively running her hands all over her slinky body while miming along to Bad Company's Can't Get Enough. She had been immediately drawn to Sparks' raven-black curtain of glossy hair, and once locked onto his line of sight, she had become hypnotised by the allure of his deep Azure-blue eyes.

Tracey had always been a wild child. Her parents had despaired when she became a gym-slip mum at the tender age of fifteen. The troublesome teenager had been forced to leave Hanford Senior School with no qualifications. She had nothing to show for her bad education except the new life growing inside her belly. A couple of years after her unplanned venture into motherhood, Tracey had tried to get her life back on track by convincing a local beauty salon owner to give her a trial as a trainee hairdresser. The wayward teenager had worked hard to prove herself in her chosen career. She had even started to attend college one day a week to study for a City & Guilds qualification. It would all be for nothing though, as the young girl would soon be seduced by the false promise of a more exciting life with a gang of wannabe Hell's Angels.

At the biker rally Sparks had relentlessly pursued the fiery seventeen-year-old Tracey, until she coyly agreed to a date the following weekend. During the months that followed their first

16

meeting Tracey became totally captivated by Sparks' power; she bathed in the respect he had from the rest of the gang; she enjoyed riding pillion astride his Triumph Bonneville at the front of the bikers' formation; she was swept along with the idea that one day she could possibly become Sparks' official ol' lady. However, to be granted such an important role in the gang leader's entourage, she would first have to prove her allegiance by giving up everything from the civilian life she had known before. Sparks had often said he had no intention of taking on the responsibility of raising another man's sniffling brat; there was no room for illegitimate outsiders in his secretive nomadic world.

Tracey would have to give up her baby if she wanted to be fully accepted into the low-life world of the Serpent Sons of Thelema. The awe-struck teenager would have to leave behind the goods and chattels of her regular life if she wanted to be promoted from being the gang leader's casual fuck-buddy to become Sparks' official ol' lady. Tracey made her bad decision and chose to embrace her new and exciting unruly lifestyle. She gave up college, quit her job, left her flat and then selfishly walked out on her little girl by unceremoniously dumping the squawking toddler in her distraught parents' living room. Tracey got what she wanted; she became Sparks' ol' lady, his property. She was blissfully unaware that Sparks could then cruelly use his position of power to force the red-headed cock teaser to do anything he wanted.

In two short years their relationship had bounced and crashed from one fiery argument to another, becoming more tempestuous as the gang leader largely treated his possession like a piece of dirt stuck to the bottom of his weather-beaten boot. He had become tired of Tracey's constant mood swings; he hated her jealous sniping and bitching any time she caught him looking at other women. Sparks resented the fact that she had recently stopped being a willing submissive in his filthy perverted sex games and she had started to answer him back. She was now nineteen years old, about to turn twenty and he had noticed his ol' lady had begun to gain a little weight.

"Christ Almighty, if only the fat arsed whinging mare knew half of what I get up to when she's not around," laughed Sparks

17

incredulously, as he relaxed in the living room at the biker gang's clubhouse. "Who the hell does the moody cow think she is anyway? The fuckin' Queen of Sheba?"

The headquarters building of the Serpent Sons of Thelema was a scruffy old three-storey townhouse with blacked-out windows. The imposing property stood on a corner plot at the end of Anglesey Street, in the run down Lye Heath area of Hanford town centre. The house had been in the biker gang for a couple of decades and had once belonged to an ageing Teddy Boy called Joey Thunder. In the middle of the fifties Joey founded the Serpent Sons of Thelema and the old rocker's home became the gang's headquarters. Twenty years later, his crumbling, filthy, pebble-dashed legacy had become the keeper of thousands of sordid secrets. The dilapidated hovel still served as the posse's nerve centre and provided a general dossing space for any wannabe rock chicks and carefully vetted prospectors hoping to one-day join the gang.

Billy Kiddo sat opposite Sparks in the living room, carefully taking in everything the older leather-clad biker was saying. The gang's leader had been Billy's mentor for years. He had been the strong guiding hand that had skilfully pushed Kiddo out of puberty and into a life of petty crime and futile violence. What had started out as a simple act of teenage rebellion for Billy had now escalated into a far seedier way of life than he had ever wanted to become involved with. Unbeknown to the gang's leader, Billy had slowly begun to dislike his way of life. He had come to the painful realisation that Sparks was nothing more than a thirty-something washed-up has-been; a wannabe hard man leading a pathetic gang of misfits in an endless chaotic cycle of stealing cars, taking drugs and fighting. They were not even properly affiliated Hell's Angels.

To become a bona fide Hell's Angel motorcycle club or MC, the Serpent Sons of Thelema would have to be proposed and seconded by two other existing clubs. No other MCs felt the gang was worthy enough to be officially recognised or accepted into the larger organisation. It was clear to them that Sparks' dropouts were simply a posse of pretenders with a grudge against the whole world, who lived their lives according to their own warped interpretation of the Hell's Angels' code. Such was the other biker gangs' contempt for Sparks' entourage, they laughingly pronounced the gang's name with a mickey-taking lisp whenever the *Therpant Thons of Thelema* were mentioned.

Billy now longed to escape the clutches of his filthy dead-end existence, to get away from living in the stinking hole he shared with a dozen other low-life wasters. All Billy had ever wanted to do was ride his bikes, drink beer and shag his bird. He was not into drugs, he hated how he had to constantly hide the fact that smoking weed made him feel sick. He was becoming tired of the mayhem the gang would create in Hanford town centre every Saturday afternoon; intimidating innocent shoppers just for the hell of it. His life had become a predictably boring round of endless bravado and petty pub fights. Billy resented how he was always forced to take the rap for the gang's misdemeanours. He had spent countless nights in the cells at the local nick, whilst the rest of his posse somehow managed to evade the arresting clutches of Hanford's boys in blue. Most of all, Billy hated the way the other gang members disrespected their women. In his mind there was no need for the depths of sexual depravity the rest of the Serpent Sons of Thelema would regularly sink to.

"I'm gonna get another beer," announced Billy as he got up from his armchair. Sparks remained sprawled out on a long dralon sofa, his head of greasy black hair propped against an old sweat-stained cushion.

"Get one for me Kiddo," he belched out to Billy as he nonchalantly rolled a matchstick-thin joint between his yellowed rough fingers. Sparks lit his cigarette and inhaled hard. As he lay on his back, letting out a purposeful deep breath of smoke, he offered the spidery joint to his friend. Billy refused the offer by gently shaking his head and forcing a smile back at Sparks, as he made his way across the sticky beer-stained living room carpet.

Billy opened a small pine door that led into a galley kitchen, softly clicking the latch closed behind him. He gazed around at the scruffy interior of the squalid room. On one side was an old filthy cooker; the grill pan still contained the remnants of burnt sausages that were now encased in a solid layer of lard. The hob of the cooker looked as if it had never been cleaned. It was covered in a variety of historic mouldy spillages that had become hardened from a build up of greasy dust. A dirty tea-stained sink sat alongside the cooker, with two rusty taps that continually dripped. On the opposite side of the narrow galley kitchen, beneath a grimy open window pane, was a full-length Formica orange-coloured work surface. It was tacky on the top from a build up of cooking fat, spilled beer and whatever other fluids Billy's fellow bikers had drunkenly decided was a good idea to leave on there. A mountain of dirty saucepans, coffee-stained mugs, chipped glasses, plates and cutlery were precariously balanced in the grime; the slightest movement would have sent an avalanche of metal and broken crockery cascading onto the dirty kitchen floor. Underneath the work surface were two tatty nicotine-stained fridges; one was used to store food, the other housed a regularly re-stocked supply of super-strength beer. Both of the fridges hummed relentlessly against the sweltering air of the long summer heat-wave. At the end of the narrow galley was a grubby white painted door that led into the ground floor bathroom. Billy squatted down to take two cans of beer from the drinks fridge as Tracey, Sparks' ol' lady, opened the door from the bathroom and entered the kitchen.

"Hello Kiddo," purred the young woman as she playfully wriggled past him to get to the sink. He breathed in the scent of her heady cheap perfume as he slowly stood back up and turned around to face her.

Tracey had just washed her hair; the curly auburn damp tresses had begun to coil up into pretty red spirals that hung loosely around her sun-tanned shoulders. She was bra-less and her damp plunging vest top only just managed to stretch over her bouncy bohemian breasts. A tight pair of blue flared jeans hugged her womanly hips beneath her curvy waistline. Tracey softly placed her outstretched fingers onto Billy's shoulders, before sliding them together to gently cup his face in her hands. She pulled him towards her as he leaned in for a stolen passionate kiss.

Billy placed the two cans of lager on the kitchen countertop as Tracey lowered her right hand to reach down for the zip of his jeans. She playfully explored inside his leather waistcoat and denim shirt, frantically searching through the hot layers of material, before grasping the small metal tab that would unleash the pent up animal inside Billy's underpants. The flame-haired nymph excitedly lowered the fly zip and swiftly slid her hand inside Billy's oil-stained jeans. She grasped his heavy muscular dick in her hand and pulled it through the zip opening; gently massaging the throbbing beast into life as she dropped to her knees.

Billy held Tracey's head firmly in his hands; his strong fingers ran through her damp tousled hair in frenzied anticipation. Slowly she encircled her pout around the end of Billy's hardening cock before gently parting her lips to pull him deep into her mouth. Quickly she began sucking and licking, running her fingers up and down his beautiful strong phallus. She teasingly took his manhood deep into her throat and quickly pulled him back out again. She knew the impromptu blow-job would keep her man happy. Circling the tip of his cock with her tantalising tongue, she began to explore every inch of his beautiful, strong, caressing dick. It was a wonderfully sensitive member that she had enjoyed so many times before; a loving and caring secret wand of pleasure that he saved especially for her and no one else knew about it.

The stifling hot summer sun burned through the glass window pane above the work surface. Tracey remained kneeling on the kitchen floor as she purposefully sucked and licked Billy's hardened cock. He was momentarily lost in the pleasure of the sultry chasm of lust that eagerly swallowed his hot throbbing manhood. Tracey felt Billy's firm grip stiffen as he held her head in his hands, his whole body clenched tightly, before he let out a stifled groan of climatic contentment.

"What's happened to that beer Kiddo," barked Sparks from his sofa behind the pine kitchen door. Billy suddenly snapped back to reality and opened his eyes.

"It's as hot as fuckin' hell in here today man," continued Sparks as he took another draw on his spidery joint; seemingly oblivious to the torrid heat of passion being created behind the kitchen door just feet away.

Tracey got up off the floor and wiped the back of her hand across her salty lips, before pulling a stray wispy curl of red hair

21

from her flushed sweaty face. Billy pushed his spent cock back inside his jeans, quickly zipped up his flies and grabbed the two cans of beer off the grimy work surface. He blew a small secret kiss towards Tracey and returned to the living room. Billy handed one of the cans of beer to Sparks before slumping back down into the shabby dralon armchair. He felt as if he had the full weight of the world's problems resting on his young shoulders.

During the past few months Billy had become disillusioned with his biker lifestyle. The twenty-two-year-old had matured; he had finally 'grown a pair' as Tracey would often tease, and he now felt he needed to be his own man. He didn't want to become sucked down into the predictable spiral of violence and petty crime that his fellow gang members had. Billy wanted to make something of his life, something meaningful, before it was too late. He had recently come to the previously unthinkable realisation that he could only lead the life he truly wanted to have if he left the Serpent Sons of Thelema far behind.

His latest hot lusty session with Sparks' fiery ol' lady in the kitchen had sent a thousand thoughts buzzing through his mind. They now simply compounded the heavy burden of guilt he felt bearing down on his shoulders. Billy had fallen in love with Tracey. He wanted the two of them to escape their seedy chaotic low-life world, but would she leave with him if he asked her to?

Something that had started out as a teenage crush on his gang leader's woman had now developed into a full-blown blistering and dangerous affair. Billy had witnessed the abuse Tracey had regularly suffered at the hands of her ol' man. He remembered hearing her terrified screams echo through the whole house during Sparks' wanton bondage sessions. Billy thought about the times he had comforted the sobbing girl after she had been used as gang merchandise; when Sparks had mercilessly offered her up for sex with rival bikers, as payment when one of the gang's drug deals had gone wrong. Billy recalled how many other women he had watched Sparks shag in grubby back alleys and dirty pub toilets, whilst Tracey had loyally waited inside at the bar for her ol' man to return.

Billy was regretting ever having become embroiled in the Thelema clan and he wished with all of his heart that he had met Tracey under different circumstances. He knew he had to get away, but he also knew the strict bikers' code that Sparks used to rule over the posse meant that gang members were not usually allowed to leave the brotherhood and stay alive. Billy would have to give a highly convincing reason for leaving, before Sparks would consider allowing one of his hand-picked soldiers to break free of the sordid fraternity. Billy Kiddo knew the difficult words that he was about to say to his leader would change the course of the rest of his life.

Billy had thought long and hard about moving back to his parents' home in the West Country. His father had recently become gravely ill and his mother needed help to run the family's guesthouse. Billy churned the whole scenario around in his head, checking his facts over and over again; getting his story straight. He decided he could tell Sparks he had no choice but to help out his old family. Billy would also stress that when his parents were out of the picture in a few years' time he would inherit everything from them; the guesthouse, the land, the money in the bank, everything. He'd be a fool to turn down an opportunity like that. A blood relative with a prospective gold mine who needed Billy's help; that would be the way he would sell it to his leader.

Billy thought that maybe he could convince Sparks to regard his temporary leave as a short sabbatical; he could then return to the Thelema fold later on. Maybe his parents' bed and breakfast could become the gang's new headquarters? In time the brotherhood could expand its territory across the Midlands to the West Country. Billy could suggest the larger Hell's Angels' organisation might then take Sparks and his followers seriously and welcome the Serpent Sons of Thelema into their official circle. Billy would leave Sparks in no doubt that his proposition could be the making of the biker gang. With a plan that audacious, how could Sparks possibly refuse his loyal prodigy's request to leave?

It would be a whole new fresh start for Billy; it could be a shiny new life for him and Tracey, but would the racy cock teaser be allowed to escape the iron grip of Sparks' control?

#

August 1976 - One month later

Six leather-clad bikers huddled together around a make-shift camp fire at their favourite spot on Himley Chase. Billy Kiddo, the seventh member of the Serpent Sons of Thelema, sat alone on an adjacent grass clearing. Through the haze of yellow and orange flickering firelight, Kiddo watched Crusher pass around an upturned crash helmet.

Billy had put his plan into action. He had told Sparks that he needed a break from the gang so he could set the wheels in motion to take over his parents' bed and breakfast business. However, it was not just Sparks' who could decide whether a member could leave or not. Each fully patched brother had an equal vote on such an important decision, and it had to be put to a ballot.

The first question on that night in the woods was whether Kiddo should be allowed to leave the brotherhood. A secondary vote would decide whether he would then be allowed to remain alive after he left the fraternity.

Each man took the crash helmet and silently placed a piece of paper inside; the only sound was an occasional crackle of burning wood from the camp fire. Billy waited anxiously in the eerie silence, as the helmet was finally passed back to Sparks for his scrutiny. Slowly the gang leader removed each small piece of paper to count the results. Billy had been told that there were three options in this democratic ballot; a vote that would decide Kiddo's fate:

Stay and Repent; Leave and Die; Leave and Live.

The result had to be unanimous. If the clan failed to reach a universal verdict then the votes would be secretly cast again until everyone had reached the same decision. Each of the voting papers collected in the crash helmet had a cross that had been clumsily scribbled at the side of each gang member's choice.

Although Billy knew that his degenerate crew of wannabe Hell's Angels had only ever been involved with stealing cars

24

and cannabis dealing, he always felt there was a more sinister undercurrent running through the gang, secret deeds that he had not been privy to. He had always believed that Sparks had a psychopathic streak that was just waiting to bubble up to the surface and the gang's leader would be more than capable of killing if he put his mind to it.

Leave and die would obviously be the worst outcome for Billy, but that could be closely followed by the 'stay and repent' option. He had heard rumours all of his adult life that the repent result in the past had seen previous members who had wanted to leave the brotherhood being forced to stay in the gang. Wanting to leave the fraternity would normally be seen as an act of disrespect, and offenders were never usually given the opportunity to atone fully for their perceived disloyalty. Instead, they would be publicly degraded, bullied and abused at any opportunity and many had been driven to end their own lives rather than suffer the constant humiliation. The only outcome of the vote that Billy Kiddo wanted to hear was 'leave and live.'

"We're all agreed then?" asked Sparks, addressing his criminal entourage with a flash of his deep-blue hypnotic eyes. A watery smile grew across his thin lips as he proceeded to formally bring the ballot to a close. He remained seated and beckoned Billy to come over and kneel in front of him by the camp fire. Crusher took a firm hold of Billy's shoulders and turned him around to face the flickering flames.

"Our brother Kiddo . . ." began Sparks, emotion creaked in his voice. "Our brother has asked to leave the protection of this family, and each member has made his thoughts known by a secret ballot." Billy silently stared into the dancing firelight as the gang's leader began to spit out his denouncement behind him.

"Kiddo's sworn oath of allegiance to this family is to be tested," continued Sparks. "And now it falls to us to do what we see fit." Crusher looked over and dutifully nodded in agreement with his commander-in-chief before kneeling down behind Billy.

Crusher had earned his insalubrious nickname from a lifetime working as a bouncer at biker rallies and small rock festivals. He had led a team of door security heavies with a densely tattooed iron fist and he had a fearful reputation for always winning in any confrontation. During one particularly bloody battle with a rival gang of bikers, he had reputedly crushed another man's neck with his bare hands.

Billy heard the sound of cracking knuckles just behind his ear, as Crusher took in a deep breath and flexed his strong muscular fingers. Billy's heart throbbed loudly in his chest, its relentless beat pounding blood through his brain; he was powerless. Running away was not an option and he would have to take his punishment like a man. Crusher pulled a freshly sharpened hunting knife out of his leather ankle holster. The shiny blade glinted in the firelight as Billy remained motionless, silently staring into the pit of flames before him; his fate had been decided for him behind his head. Sparks grabbed Crusher's knife and held it threateningly at the nape of Billy's neck.

"The secrets of this family must remain with our brotherhood forever," whispered Sparks menacingly. "Our codes and secrets are never to be revealed. No one is above this law. Disloyal weasels will always be avenged."

Billy felt every joint within his body fizz with adrenaline as fear pumped through his veins. A small tear squeezed out of the corner of his right eye before he sniffed defiantly to try and stop it rolling down his cheek. *Is this how it ends? Is this really how I'm going to die?*

Sparks drew the sharp hunting knife roughly across Billy's back; tearing into his black leather jacket to ceremoniously rip away the three embroidered canvas patches. Crusher, Zombie, Razor Fish, Bullet and Yardy raised to their feet as Sparks threw Kiddo's colours onto the open fire. Billy felt Crusher's strong muscular hands grab the collar of his torn leather jacket as he pulled him to his feet. The second-in-command's vice-like grip pushed the frightened young man away from the rest of the gang, forcing Billy to trample over the flames of the camp fire and roll over onto the opposite side of the grass clearing. The oil-stained pieces of canvas sparkled into life, feeding the fire into a column of flames that stood between Billy and the rest of the fraternity. He had been physically ejected from the protection of the fold; cast out from his biking family.

The six men turned away from the fire and walked off towards their motorcycles. The gang members climbed astride their machines without looking back and kick-started their trusty steeds into life. The throaty roar and clatter of engines pierced the silent night air, before the procession rode off in strict formation behind their leader; disappearing into the dark depths of the countryside.

Billy lay on the grass listening intently to the last dying hum of motorbike engines; with that moment of growing solitude came the welcome realisation that his old fraternity had allowed him to leave and live. Alone, in the calming stillness of that hot summer's night, with nothing but his own thoughts for company, Billy began to tremble with relief; his plan had worked. For one terrifying moment he had allowed himself to believe his life was about to end. For one petrified second he had feared the gang had voted 'leave and die' and Sparks' hunting knife would be used to carry out that fateful unanimous decision. But the young biker knew that only half of his plan had been accomplished; he still had to wait for Tracey to arrive.

The secret lovers had arranged their getaway carefully, so as not to attract any attention from the unwitting Sparks. He could never know that both of them planned to leave together that night. Tracey had stayed behind at the clubhouse whilst the motley crew of bikers rode out to Himley Chase. She would pack her clothes, a few cosmetics and a couple of other precious possessions into her red leather rucksack while she waited for Sparks and his entourage to return from Kiddo's casting out ceremony. An hour or so later, once she had confirmation that Billy was still alive, she had planned to slip out of the house and take a taxi to meet her lover. She knew Billy's loving arms would be waiting for her at Himley Chase.

Once the couple were safely one hundred miles away in the West Country, Tracey would send her ol' lady patches to Sparks to annul their coupling. Billy knew the gang leader wouldn't waste any time before replacing Tracey with one of his latest fuck-buddies.

But Tracey never arrived at the woodland clearing.

After three lonely hours of intently reflecting on his young life, Billy resigned himself to the fact that Sparks' hold over his ol' lady had been much stronger than he had ever imagined. The flame-haired cock teaser had led Billy on; he had been a total fool to ever think she would leave her ol' man for him. Kiddo believed he had never stood a chance against the bond Tracey shared with the gang's leader.

Billy vowed that night would be the beginning of a new and better life for him; his re-birth as a single, free man. He slowly sat up and dusted down his torn leather jacket and muddy jeans. Billy's brothers had let him leave alive. He was free. But he was only as free as it was possible for an ex Serpent Son to be. Billy would never be allowed to forget he had sworn an oath of allegiance to the Thelema brotherhood. He knew beyond the shadow of any doubt, that if he ever betrayed that trust at any time, no matter how distant in the future, it could have far reaching fatal consequences for the young ejected ex-gang member.

The re-born Billy climbed astride his Norton Dominator motorcycle and kick-started the shiny red beast into life, before riding alone through the night, back into the welcoming embrace of his parents' West Country home.

Chapter 3

March 2004 – 28 Years Later.

Sharron Chambers nestled down on her sofa, nonchalantly flicking through the pages of a glossy magazine. The thirty-two-year-old woman had returned home from her long shift as a check-out cashier at a local supermarket, and she was now relaxing with a Chinese take-away and cheap bottle of wine in front of the television. The TV channel was running a live true-crime investigation show, although Sharron had muted the sound. She wasn't really watching the programme and she had only switched on the box for a little background company while she scanned the headlines and photos of her favourite celebrity gossip magazine. Occasionally her eyes glanced up at the rolling ticker-tape of crime stories on the television screen, before returning her attention to the idle chatter and dirty linen of tinsel-town's latest romances and break-ups.

Suddenly Sharron's gaze became transfixed by a new crime appeal story that flickered across the screen. She felt a sudden surge of pins-and-needles flutter across her chest on seeing the familiar name of a local beauty spot mentioned in the summary text. As if on automatic pilot, the startled woman picked up the TV's remote control and turned up the volume. The skeletal human remains of a female had been discovered in the Midlands. They were found in a shallow grave in woodland at Himley Chase. Sharron sat motionless, totally captivated by the television presenter's report.

"The victim has not yet been identified," announced the reporter. "We're appealing to our viewers this evening for any information about who the dead woman might be."

Sharron carefully scrutinised every small detail that the crime scene had revealed. A digger driver had made the gruesome discovery a few weeks earlier while preparing an area of woodland for the development of a new housing estate at Himley Chase. The decayed remains had been dressed in flared blue jeans, a faded black vest top, black leather platform boots and a tasselled leather biker's jacket. The skull was bound in a rotted silk bandana with the American Confederate flag printed on it, along with a pair of large plastic sunglasses. Beneath the flag's image on the scarf was a hand-embroidered unicursal hexagram. The fully-clothed body had been tightly wrapped in a pale-green tarpaulin sheet and then covered in sheets of polythene at the time of its burial. This packaging had helped to preserve the grisly contents.

The reporter continued with a final piece to camera, to explain that the remains and other items discovered at the crime scene were still undergoing extensive forensic examination. Early findings had indicated that the woman would have been in her late teens or early twenties at the time of her death, she had long auburn curly hair and the body had been buried about twenty-five to thirty years previously. The forensics team were currently checking through dental records and missing persons' files but had so far not found a match. The report ended and focus returned to the live studio.

A tall and imposing man with a wide red drinker's nose and fat stubbly chin sat at a desk in the television studio, opposite the show's anchorwoman. He was Detective Inspector Chiltern, the leading officer in charge of the investigation. The DI had enjoyed a long and distinguished career working mostly undercover in the fast-paced environment of the vice squad. At fifty-nine years old he was approaching retirement age and had secretly hoped to see out the remainder of his working life in a less stressful but equally anonymous role. Until the discovery of the woman's body at Himley Chase, his transfer to Hanford's CID had appeared to be the perfect career move. DI Chiltern knew the investigation would benefit from media exposure and he had reluctantly agreed to appear in the television appeal. The seasoned detective was not used to the limelight and he shuffled uncomfortably in front of the studio cameras as he began to share the latest piece of information he had about the case.

"We have a very strong DNA profile from the tarpaulin sheet that does not match the victim's DNA," announced the detective. "We've also discovered the same unknown DNA on the handle of a shovel discovered alongside the body."

"Are there any other clues as to this poor woman's identity?" the show's empathetic presenter enquired.

"Yes." DI Chiltern swallowed hard and repositioned himself in his chair. It was a vain attempt to escape the hot glaring heat beneath the studio lights. "From additional cartilage remains discovered within the main body, the forensic team have deduced the woman was about three months pregnant at the time of her death. She had also previously given birth to at least one other child at some point. That child could now be an adult, possibly aged somewhere between twenty-five and thirty-five."

The shocked anchorwoman took in a short audible gasp at this new revelation, before she began to wrap up the appeal by giving the telephone number for people to call with information.

"So, if anyone has any idea as to the identity of this poor woman, or if you have any information about the tragic circumstances surrounding her death, then we urge you to please come forward this evening. Let's try and get this mother back to her family."

Sharron slumped back onto the sofa in stunned silence. Her grandparents had told her that her mother, Tracey Chambers, had run away from home in the seventies after an argument. They had claimed their fiery teenager had selfishly abandoned her squawking toddler thirty years ago. That was the only carefully edited fact Sharron had been told about her mom. Mr and Mrs Chambers had chosen their words wisely. They never revealed the true nature of Tracey's heartless actions to Sharron; that she had chosen to live a dangerous nomadic lifestyle among a filthy den of low-life wannabe Hell's Angels, rather than be a responsible parent to her little girl.

Sharron's grandparents had gone to their own graves without revealing the shame and heartache they had felt when they realised their sixties' hippy idealism had raised Tracey to be such a trashy little biker slut. They had been too lenient with their moody wayward teenager and their free loving flower-power values had been a mistake. They had been determined not to make the same mistake again. After Sharron was unceremoniously dumped in their living room, Mr and Mrs Chambers cherished the second chance they had been given. Their grandchild would be brought up on a much tighter leash and she would be told nothing of her mother's attraction to the sleazy fat underbelly of sordid biker gangs.

Could that poor dead woman be my mom? Sharron began to piece together the information. It all seemed to fit. The time of her mother's disappearance, the red hair, Himley Chase was only a few miles away from where her grandparents' house had been. Sharron felt a tight knot of trepidation in her stomach as she took a large glug of wine, picked up her mobile phone and nervously began to call the number that skated across the bottom of the television screen.

#

William Weber was the proud owner of a chic little guesthouse on the outskirts of Bristol. He had recently been involved in a car accident and was recovering from a broken ankle. William sat uncomfortably in a leather armchair. The bottom half of his right leg was encased in a white plaster cast and he was trying to scratch an irritating itch that had somehow managed to escape his every attempt to reach it. The ten o'clock national news bulletin had just ended as he struggled to get up from his chair to go and refill his tumbler with Tennessee whiskey and ice.

"Bastard leg," he cursed as he pushed himself onto a wobbly pair of grey metal hospital crutches.

William Weber was a pillar of his local community; a respectable businessman. He was well-liked at his local Masonic lodge and he was held in high regard at the chamber of commerce. His comfortable West Country home was tastefully decorated and his prosperous guesthouse bore testament to decades of decent hard work.

The hotelier had loved every minute of building his small empire; he had savoured every sweet moment of success with his wife and daughter. However, the strain of running his thriving bed and breakfast was now beginning to take its toll on the fifty-year-old man. It had brought an endless rotation of repetitive house-keeping, chatting to guests, playing host in the bar each night and serving up a dozen plates of bacon, eggs and toast every morning. The businessman had recently begun to think about taking early retirement.

The private quarters of the luxury boutique guesthouse offered a calm sanctuary away from the owner's hectic day-to-day life. William limped across the living room towards a large glass-fronted drinks cabinet. He was in pain and needed to quell a stinging torrent of sadness that flowed through his heart. His world had recently been rocked to its foundations by the sudden announcement by his wife that their twenty-five-year marriage was over and she was leaving him for another man.

"Fucking bitch," he cursed, as he caught sight of his estranged wife's face smiling back at him from an ornately framed wedding photo that sat on the bookcase.

Juliette Weber had cruelly delivered her devastating news to her husband just a few months before they were due to celebrate their silver wedding anniversary.

"Cheating fucking whore," shouted William, as he angrily raised his metal crutch into the air. He slammed it hard across the bookshelf and began to smash the twenty-five-year-old photo frame. Shards of glass rained down onto the limed oak floor. William continued to hobble over to the drinks cabinet; his heavy plastered foot crunched tiny glass fragments deep into the wooden crevices.

"Jesus Christ, just give me a fucking break will ya?" he winced, gazing upwards as if praying to the gods for divine intervention. The shot of pain from William's broken ankle was a reminder of a short catalogue of events that had recently cursed his life.

A few weeks earlier William had been found guilty of drink-driving following a car crash on his way home from his Masonic lodge. The evening of his fateful accident, and subsequent arrest, should have been the night he and Juliette celebrated and partied with friends to toast their twenty-five years of wedded bliss. Instead William had drowned his sorrows over a meal for one in the Masonic restaurant, and washed it down with a couple of bottles of fine wine. The heart-broken hotelier had then stupidly climbed behind the wheel of his car for the short journey back to his guesthouse. Instead of celebrating his silver wedding anniversary with candle light and a four poster bed, his night had ended with blue flashing lights and a cold concrete police cell; meanwhile his oblivious wife had enjoyed a passion-fuelled holiday in the Caribbean with her French yoga instructor.

William and Juliette Weber's fifteen-year-old daughter had cried herself to sleep most nights since then, as she tried to come to terms with the upset of her parents' impending divorce. She had been packed off to boarding school, only to be humiliated and cruelly taunted by the classroom bullies. The cursed kid from a broken home was made to believe she was the reason for her parents' split.

William's quagmire of self-pity was rudely interrupted by a sharp persistent knocking on the front door.

"Who the hell is that?" he snorted indignantly. William had temporarily closed the bed and breakfast while he recovered from his car accident. There were no guests staying at the house that evening and his daughter was still away at school. The outside lights had been switched off in an attempt to deter any weary travellers trying to get a room for the night and the sign in the window clearly stated 'No Vacancies'. The loud heavy knocking continued. Someone outside the front door was determined to get the hotelier's attention, as they began to repeatedly rap the letter box flap and shout William's name.

"Okay, okay I'm coming," fumed the crippled man as he clumsily hobbled down the hallway towards the front entrance. William turned a big heavy metal key in the door lock; immediately the front door sprang open and half a dozen shadowy figures entered the dimly-lit hall.

"William Weber?" barked one of the unwelcome strangers. The bewildered hotelier felt a sudden tug on both of his arms, as his hands were pulled sharply behind his back.

"Who wants to know?" answered the startled man, as he felt the cold steel of a set of handcuffs bite into the skin on his wrists.

"I'm Detective Sergeant Richens," announced one of the men. "I'm arresting you on suspicion of murder."

For a couple of seconds, William could not speak. The shock of strangers bursting into his home, the pain from his broken ankle and the effects of taking painkillers with half a bottle of whiskey compounded his struggle to remain conscious.

"You do not have to say anything, but it may harm your defence if you do not mention when questioned something which you later rely on in court," continued the police officer. "Anything you do say may be given in evidence. Do you understand?"

William stared back at the policeman in total disbelief. He tried to gather his thoughts and managed to take a breath to quell the terror pounding through his brain.

"Whoa!" exclaimed William. "What the hell are you talking about, suspicion of murder?" he protested. "I haven't killed anyone."

William tried to wriggle free of DS Richens' grasp, but any attempt of escaping was futile, as two burly officers pushed him awkwardly through the open front door. William cried out in agony; a searing pain in his broken ankle shot up through his body. The determined officers were relentless in their quest to remove him from the house, as they dragged the hobbling man down the gravel driveway and frogmarched him towards a waiting police car.

One of the policemen emptied William's pockets and placed the hotelier's phone and wallet on the roof of the car before patting down his prisoner's aching body. DS Richens opened the rear door of the car, bundled his dazed suspect onto the back seat and firmly closed the door with a swift push.

"What the hell is going on?" screamed William, as he realised the extent of the police operation. He looked out through the steamed up car window and saw a large police van pull up in the road. He shouted helplessly, as half a dozen more officers stormed through the front door of the guesthouse. One-by-one he watched the lights come on at every window throughout his home, as a canine unit led two Alsatian dogs across the gravel drive towards a neat privet hedge that hugged the side of the footpath.

"This has got to be a fucking joke," growled William as he watched the whole circus of police activity unfold before his eyes. The metal handcuffs bit hard into his wrists. He felt totally powerless and began to hit the car window with his forehead to try and gain the attention of DS Richens who remained standing outside.

"What the fuck are you all searching for?" shouted a frustrated William through the closed car window.

The Sergeant calmly walked around to the front of the car and got into the front passenger seat. He turned to face his suspect. "As I just mentioned to you before Mister Weber, you are under arrest on suspicion of murder. This is a very serious crime and . . ."

"But you've got the wrong fucking man, I haven't killed anyone," protested William.

"As I was saying," continued Richens, refusing to be ruffled by the interruption. "This is a serious crime. My officers have a warrant to search your property, as it may hold further incriminating evidence." William felt a burst of adrenaline pump through his veins at the realisation that the police had made a terrible mistake.

"I can understand that this has all come as quite a shock to you, but I assure you this is all perfectly routine under such serious circumstances," added Richens in an attempt to calm down his irate prisoner. William slumped back onto the car seat. He realised that no matter how much he fought and argued with the man, the night was not going to end with his release from custody.

Chapter 4

The next morning.

Sharron Chambers walked nervously towards the austere entrance of Hanford town police station. She was a dowdy-looking plump woman with brassy home-bleached hair. Even though her appearance was the least important thing for her to worry about that day, she had still wanted to make a good impression at the police station; to be taken seriously by the investigating officer. Sharron had scraped her stripy straw-like tresses into a tight pony tail at the back of her head and hastily applied a thick layer of make-up to her tired face. A damp mist hung in the late spring air and it seemed to envelope every laboured breath, as Sharron shuffled up a flight of stone steps that led to a pair of glazed doors. The frumpy woman caught an unexpected sight of her dishevelled reflection in the glass and she became slightly embarrassed by her cheap supermarket clothes; her cotton trouser suit had creased badly on the bus trip into town and it now hung scruffily on her tubby frame.

Inside the police station, the utilitarian reception area was sparse and unwelcoming. A row of dark grey plastic chairs sat to attention on a far wall; an old coffee table covered with crime prevention leaflets lay in front. Opposite was a glass fronted reception booth. Alongside that was a large imposing grey metal door that Sharron imagined would lead to a chamber of bustling activity deep inside the building. She walked over to the reception kiosk and pushed a plastic doorbell button that had been glued to a shallow shelf in front of the window. A young policeman appeared at the counter almost immediately.

"Hi," he said with a friendly smile. "How can I help?"

Sharron took in a deep purposeful breath and let out an unexpected cough. She cursed herself for having nervously smoked a couple more cigarettes on her walk from the bus depot. It was now taking a few seconds longer than anticipated to clear her throat before she was able to speak.

"My name is Sharron Chambers," she spluttered. "I spoke to someone last night about the television appeal for information about the woman's body found at Himley Chase . . . err . . . they said I needed to see . . . Inspector Chiltern," she faltered.

The young policeman scribbled down a few notes before looking back at Sharron through the glass window.

"I'll ring through to CID to get one of his team to come and speak with you," he smiled reassuringly. "Just take a pew over there and someone will be down to see you." The young man pointed at the orderly row of grey chairs with the end of his ballpoint pen, before punching a few numbers into the reception desk phone.

#

William Weber sat on an uncomfortably hard plastic seat, behind a heavy metal table in a police interview room. It was ten o'clock in the morning and he was angrily anticipating DI Chiltern's return for another round of seemingly endless and pointless questioning. William had been dragged from his house late the previous evening and arrested for a murder he hadn't committed. He had been led away in handcuffs amid a glaring flurry of flashing blue lights and twitching neighbourhood curtains. Like a wounded wild animal he had been caged in the back of a police van. His long late-night journey from the West Country to the Midlands had concluded with his arrival at Hanford's custody suite. William had declined the offer of a duty solicitor as he believed his innocence would be the only defence he needed. The indignant removal of his belt, shoe and metal crutches, followed by a few lonely sleepless hours in a hard concrete cell, had done nothing but darken his mood. At seven-thirty in the morning, William's cell door had been unceremoniously sprung open and he had been swiftly summoned to the interview room to answer an unrelenting round of questions from Inspector Chiltern; the officer assigned to investigate the circumstances around the death of the woman whose remains had been discovered in the woods. The detective had fired his well-rehearsed unrelenting barrage of questions at the tired and angry man. Where had William been living thirty years ago? Who did he know who lived near to Himley Chase? Did he have a girlfriend at the time? Did they have an argument? Why had he left the area so suddenly after living there for so many years? Could he explain why his DNA had been discovered at a murder scene? William's answers and tired protests of innocence had been met with disbelieving glares from the detective, amid a volley of accusations and counter-attacks.

The bewildered hotelier had been given a short respite, as his inquisitor had momentarily left the interview room. The suspect was now under the ever-watchful eye of a bearded uniformed constable who stood with folded arms next to the closed interview room door. William sat back on his hard seat and crossed his arms, to emulate his guard's silent pose. He gave a small watery smile as he locked onto the policeman's poker face.

"You enjoy your work then?" asked William. The officer remained silent. "I dunno, all those years wasted at police school to become a glorified baby-sitter," he goaded, riled that his belittling of the man's duties had not raised any response. "Oooh, big scary man like me with a fuckin' broken foot. What do they think I'm gonna do? Crack open my plaster cast and make a fuckin' run for it?" The policeman simply sniffed back the urge to respond and remained silent, his gaze firmly fixed on the angry man.

"I'm telling you mate, you've all got the wrong man in the frame here. I dunno what's gone on, what they think they've found, but I haven't killed anyone," added William, resigned to the fact that it was a clear case of mistaken identity.

Suddenly the door opened and DI Chiltern entered the room. William's arresting officer, Sergeant Richens, followed closely behind his boss, dutifully carrying a small bundle of manila-coloured cardboard folders. Both men sat down opposite William, in a swift and obviously well-choreographed movement that they had probably carried out countless times before, as the uniformed constable left the room. Richens placed the manila folders on the table. Chiltern flipped a switch on an interview voice recorder at one end of the table and announced the return of the officers to the room.

William had refused the previous night's offer of legal representation when he was checked-in at the custody suite. He knew he had not killed anyone and he thought it would be pointless to waste the time of a duty solicitor. After all the only lawyer the bewildered man trusted was the bespectacled Godfrey Hathergood, the man who had handled the probate matters when William had inherited his parents' guesthouse; the same kindly and trusted legal friend who was currently helping William through his messy divorce from Juliette. If William needed any legal representation then he would ask the police to contact Godfrey later in the day. It would have been wrong to drag his elderly legal confidante out in the middle of the night when William knew he was innocent of the crime. William believed his arrest had been one hell of a huge misunderstanding, the police would spot their error and he would soon be free to leave the station. He could not see the point of wasting his hard-earned money to pay for the services of a solicitor he didn't need.

Detective Inspector Chiltern carefully scrutinised William's tired expressionless face as Sergeant Richens opened one of the manila folders and shook the contents out over the top of the metal table. There were two colour photographic prints. One was a picture of a heavily stained and faded green canvas tarpaulin; the other of a wooden handled shovel. Sergeant Richens was a tall thin man with a pinched face and a pointed tip at the end of his nose. He had only recently been promoted to his new pay grade and he was anxious to impress his new boss. He deftly turned both prints towards William; Chiltern nodded his thanks at his prodigy.

"Have you ever seen this tarpaulin before?" snapped Chiltern, tapping the end of a ballpoint pen onto the centre of the photograph of the canvas sheet. William studied the image carefully. His eyes narrowed as he took in every small detail printed on the A4 sheet of paper before him; his lips pursed together as he thought carefully about his measured response. The two detectives glanced across at each other; Chiltern began to tap the end of his pen impatiently on the metal table top. William took in a deep breath, pushed himself back onto his hard plastic seat and flicked the photograph back over to Richens.

"I can't be sure," he said dismissively.

"What do you mean you can't be sure?" quizzed Chiltern.

"Well, it just looks like any old piece of canvas to me. I've seen dozens of dust sheets that look like that over the years," he continued with a small shrug of his shoulders.

"Don't you try and get cocky with me, sunshine." The inspector was beginning to feel riled by the prisoner's lack of respect for the investigation.

"I'm not," protested William. "All I'm saying is I can't be sure if I've seen that actual tarpaulin before . . . or just a similar one."

Chiltern sat forward in his chair. Slowly the policeman took in a deep breath and brought the palms of his hands together. He raised his index fingers towards the red blotchy tip of his wide drinker's nose and tucked both of his thumbs beneath his fat bristly chin. Richens watched in awe as his boss adopted what had quickly become known at the station as Chiltern's prayer pose; it was a useful secret sign that indicated to the sergeant his senior officer's patience was wearing thin.

"What about this one then?" interrupted Richens, as he pushed the second photograph closer towards the bewildered suspect. William slowly picked up the second A4 sheet of paper and studied the glossy printed page in great detail. It was a photograph of an old metal shovel with a wooden handle. Some of the grain of the wood was stained a darker colour than the rest of the hilt. William pinched his lips tightly together and slowly shook his head.

"Nope, not something I recognise," he replied, before casually sliding the sheet of paper back to Richens.

"Right Mister Weber," announced DI Chiltern curtly. "So if you've never seen them before, can you tell me how come your DNA is crawling all over that piece of material that we found wrapped around a dead body?" barked Chiltern.

"I told you a hundred times last night and this morning, I don't know anything about any dead body," replied William as he glared back into Chiltern's accusing stare.

"How can you account for your DNA being on the handle of the suspected murder weapon then? Your blood ingrained in the wood?" probed Chiltern further.

41

"I have absolutely no fucking idea what you're talking about," William growled. "I haven't killed anyone."

Chiltern and Richens' carefully planned interrogation was interrupted by a sharp knock on the interview room door. The tall bearded PC entered the room and walked directly over to DI Chiltern. He whispered something into the inspector's ear, before Chiltern rose to his feet and swiftly followed the PC back out of the room. Sergeant Richens logged the interruption on the voice recorder and flicked the switch to pause the tape.

#

Sharron Chambers sat nervously fidgeting and fiddling with a loose piece of cotton she had snagged from the sleeve of her jacket. Her feet tapped on the linoleum floor as she stared around aimlessly at the clinically clean medical room. Sharron had agreed to a DNA test in an attempt to establish if the body of the dead woman found at Himley Chase was that of her long-lost mother. She was trying to concentrate her mind on the unbelievable events that had unravelled during the past twelve hours; the overload of information she had seen on the previous night's television crime appeal whirled around in her head as she tried to focus on the important task in hand.

The station's doctor had just finished taking a saliva swab from inside Sharron's mouth as DI Chiltern entered the room carrying two beakers of sparkling spring water. Sharron reached up to take one of the cool plastic cups and placed it on the desk in front of her. Chiltern nodded his acknowledgement to the doctor who was busily labelling up his sample vial and filling out a lab form.

"Thank you for coming in today Miss Chambers," said inspector Chiltern as he dragged over a plastic chair to sit alongside her. "You've been a tremendous help."

When Sharron had phoned the crime appeal telephone line the night before, she had been immediately transferred to the officer in charge of the investigation. She had explained to the interested voice on the other end of the line why she believed the dead body found at Himley Chase could be that of her long-disappeared mother, Tracey Chambers. Sharron's age matched the probable age of the dead woman's first child; her mother had disappeared from the family home around thirty years ago. The old photographs Sharron had of her mom featured a slender young girl with long curly auburn hair.

Sharron had always suspected that there was more to the story surrounding her mother's disappearance than her grandparents had ever told her. She could not believe that a gym-slip teenager, who must have fought so fiercely to keep her baby in the beginning, would walk out on her child so easily after a simple family argument. She couldn't help but think there was something sinister lurking in the family's past that Granddad and Grandma had not told her about. Sharron had always believed there was something suspicious about the way the old couple had refused to tell her any details about the circumstances behind Tracey leaving the family home; more worryingly they had never officially registered their daughter as a missing person. Sharron's mind had raced, filled with the knowledge that Himley Chase was not far away from her grandparents' old house. Had the couple of old hippies known more about Tracey's disappearance than they had admitted to?

DI Chiltern had already arranged a dental records check, but he had carefully suggested to Sharron that the best course of action would be to undertake a familial DNA test to establish any link. If nothing else it would eliminate Tracey Chambers' name from the murder investigation if the result came back negative.

"How long before we know?" asked Sharron as she took a sip of water.

"We can usually get preliminary results back in about twenty-four to forty-eight hours. But we'll try to fast track it at the lab to see if we can get it back sooner," replied Chiltern, fully aware that the outcome of the DNA test could potentially change the course of Sharron's life forever.

#

William Weber remained seated behind the desk in the interview room; he shuffled uneasily on his hard plastic seat. Tapping his fingernails impatiently on the metal table top, he

43

stared coldly back at DS Richens' intimidating gaze. The two men had hardly exchanged a word since DI Chiltern's departure almost half an hour earlier. Sergeant Richens patiently observed William, scrutinising every nuance of his body language. He couldn't understand how the man sat in front of him could react so calmly when shown photographs of the murder weapon that had been used to crush the life out of a young woman's skull all those years ago; how William Weber had chosen to dismiss the tarpaulin sheet as an anonymous piece of canvas; the same tarpaulin covered in his DNA that had been used to enshroud the dead woman's battered remains.

DI Chiltern came back into the room and immediately broke the stifling silence. Richens switched the pause button on the voice recorder and announced his boss's return.

"So," barked the inspector. "You still claim that you've never seen the tarpaulin or the shovel in these photographs before?" waving the A4 sheets of paper in front of William's face.

"Yes," replied William with a roll of his eyes. He had become bored of Chiltern's tiresome repetitions.

"And you have absolutely no idea how your DNA got there?" he continued.

"That's right," yawned William.

"Well, Mister Weber." Chiltern paused for a second to gather his thoughts. "I'll tell you what I think happened, shall I?"

"If you must," replied William dismissively, as he shuffled uneasily on his seat; that damn itching had returned to gnaw at his plastered broken ankle again.

"You see, I've got a copy of the police record for someone called William "Billy" Weber; it's a copy of *your* old rap sheet from back in the seventies, Mister Weber. It's a shocking bit of reading when you look into it. It's filled with lots of nasty little fights, bar room brawls and petty crime."

William allowed a small wry smile to curl up one side of his mouth as a few memories from his stupidly wayward teenage years fluttered through his mind. He knew back then he had been a wild child, but all of that was behind him now. *Christ, is that all they have? Some small-time shit I got up to when I was*

44

a kid? He knew the police had nothing to connect him to the body found in the woods, he had not killed anyone. Chiltern's whole charade was a fishing trip and the policeman's endless questions would be fruitless.

"Did that impress the birds back then?" continued Chiltern. He was clearly riled by the impertinent smile creeping across William's face. "Fancied yourself as a bit of a hard man thirty years ago, did you?" William remained silent, slightly distracted by his itching foot, as Chiltern continued his monologue.

"So, I reckon back in the seventies, when you were probably a clumsy acne-infested youth, you took an innocent young woman to the woods to have your dirty little way with her, didn't you Mister Weber?" Chiltern shot an accusing glare at William.

"When this young lady refused your spotty-faced advances you grew angry and stoved her head in with a shovel, didn't you Weber?" growled Chiltern. The inspector was clearly angered by the nonchalant reaction from the man sat opposite him.

"You wrapped her broken bones in a shroud," the inspector paused to swallow. "And then, to add insult to injury, you pissed all over her, didn't you?"

William shivered as he took in a short shocked breath. This was the first time anyone had mentioned the presence of urine on the dead body.

William's mind re-ran the climax of the most memorable night of his misspent youth. Haunting visions of his initiation into the Serpent Sons of Thelema burned through his racing brain. The long-forgotten memory of how Sparks had forced him to urinate over the pale-green tarpaulin that was wrapped around a dressmaker's dummy.

"You never expected that thirty years later there would be such a thing as DNA testing, did you Mister Weber?" continued Chiltern. The DI was encouraged by a subtle shift in his prisoner's demeanour. *Ah, something's struck a chord then?*

William remained silent, all the facts galloping through his mind, a stinging beat started to pulse deep inside his heart.

"You never imagined in your wildest dreams that one night you'd be driving back home pissed-up from an expensive night out at your snooty ministry of funny handshakes, and your darkest nightmare would come back to bite you on your posh untouchable Masonic arse, did you?" shouted Chiltern, knowing that he had taken back full control of the interview and his prisoner was now dangling on the hook.

The suspicious inspector's barrage of attack had only just begun to scratch the surface of the burning resentment he felt towards the businessman sat opposite him. During decades of working in the vice squad DI Chiltern had seen first hand how deep corruption could flow through the veins of the criminal underworld; a highly corrosive world that appeared on the surface to be hard-working and legitimate but was fuelled by drug deals, sexual exploitation and sordid depravity. He did not believe William Weber was a reformed character or an innocent man.

This was DI Chiltern's last big case before his impending retirement and he was determined to break apart the hotelier's veneer of respectability. He believed he had enough evidence to prove William was the sadistic Himley Chase murderer and he would be made to pay for his heinous crime.

"The DNA swab taken from you at your arrest for drunk driving the other month is a perfect match to the DNA found in the piss stains on the burial shroud wrapped around that poor young woman's remains and in the blood on the handle of the spade; the murder weapon."

William stared at the detective, he felt his face flush with a hot burning slap of awareness; each drop of his pumping life-blood suddenly pounding through every vessel in his brain. The presence of urine on the material was a new and unwelcome piece of information.

"So, I'll ask you once again Mister Weber; do you recognise the tarpaulin and the shovel?" pressed DI Chiltern.

William focussed on the photographs that were still held tightly in Chiltern's grasp, a sudden dawn of realisation crawled over his bewildered ashen face. That one act of stupid symbolic bravado over three decades ago was now reaching out to incriminate him in a murder investigation. Chiltern's small throw-away comments about how the tarpaulin had been *pissed over* were swiftly followed by a torrent of dark memories for the fifty-year-old guesthouse owner. How could the ridiculous mock burial of a dressmaker's dummy be coming back to incriminate him in a murder case?

A tsunami of long-lost images flooded through his brain, bringing with it the stinging awareness that the innocent William 'Billy' Weber was firmly in the frame for a thirty-year-old crime that he knew nothing about. Deep in his heart he knew the only tarpaulin that he had ever urinated over was the long-lost and forgotten one that had featured at his patching ceremony on Himley Chase. If that same piece of material had been used in a murder, then maybe Sparks and his old band of brothers had had something to do with it, but he needed to think long and hard before implicating his old fraternity.

Billy Kiddo's oath of allegiance burned through William's brain. How he had promised faithfully to never betray the secrets of the Serpent Sons of Thelema.

"Disloyal weasels will always be avenged," he whispered to himself, as Sparks' evil words beat through his every thought. *Our codes and secrets are never to be revealed. No one is above this law.* Those fateful words chanted behind his back as he knelt in front of the camp fire returned to haunt William, along with the memories of a terrified Billy Kiddo tearfully staring into the flames before being cast out from the clan.

"I'd like to speak to my solicitor," said William blankly.

Chapter 5

The Next Evening.

Godfrey Hathergood sat with his bewildered client in the over-bearing heat of the police interview room. Godfrey was a slightly-built man dressed in a pale-grey pinstripe suit. He wore a pair of thin gold-framed spectacles that constantly slid down the narrow bridge of his nose. Godfrey had been a solicitor for many decades. He was a seasoned and versatile legal professional with a soft mannered nature that was well practised in cutting to the important facts of a case. At one time, as a young and eager legal advocate, he had relished the cut and thrust of criminal law; strutting in front of circuit judges to deliver his wayward clients' defences. But there had not been much demand for such voracious legal representation in the sleepy West Country village where he had set up his practice in later life. So instead, Godfrey Hathergood had chosen to specialise in family law; the bread-and-butter cases of probate and bitter divorce. During the past few months however, he had noticed his sharp analytical brain begin to dull slightly; he was becoming old, his body and mind slowing down. Godfrey had promised his wife that he would take retirement soon and William Weber would probably be the last client he would represent.

Godfrey knew William to be a pinnacle of his local business community; a fellow member of his Masonic lodge; a professional brother some might say. As far as Godfrey was aware William was an innocent man. He believed his client knew nothing about the dead body found at Himley Chase and the whole episode had been a terrible misunderstanding built on a flimsy foundation of circumstantial forensic evidence. Godfrey sat with his arms folded, leaning back into an uncomfortably hard plastic seat. It was late in the evening and his drive up from the West Country had come at the end of a busy working day. He was now beginning to feel tired. He had advised his client to give 'no comment' responses to all of the policeman's questions, but William felt he had nothing to hide and had insisted on setting the record straight with honest answers. Godfrey allowed his heavy eyelids to close slightly as he listened patiently to his client's careful replies. Inspector Chiltern continued to unleash his relentless barrage of repetitive questions at William.

"So, you admit you used to regularly go to Himley Chase then?" quizzed Chiltern.

"Yes," replied William. "But I haven't been there for about thirty years."

Godfrey suddenly blinked open his tired eyes and frowned over the top of his round gold-rimmed spectacles. He pursed his lips together and shook his head, sucking in a small breath of air between his teeth.

"Ah," grasped Chiltern, immediately pouncing on his prime suspect's unexpected slip. "So, you're admitting to me that the last time you went to Himley Chase was around the same time as when that poor young woman's body in the piss-soaked tarpaulin was dumped there?"

"No, that's not what I'm saying," protested William, helplessly looking across at his lawyer for support. "For fuck's sake, I wasn't the only person to ever go to that godforsaken place was I?" he continued.

Godfrey Hathergood unfolded his arms and pushed his glasses back up the narrow bridge of his nose. He moved forward on his plastic seat and let out a small cough to draw William's unfiltered rant to an abrupt close.

"Inspector Chiltern," began the softly spoken elder statesman. "Do you think my client and I might have a little time alone?" Godfrey Hathergood smiled at the inspector with a presumptuous expression. Chiltern stood up from the table with a snort of exasperation. Sergeant Richens switched off the voice recorder and dutifully followed his boss out of the interview room.

"Is there anything else you want to tell me William? Something you've forgotten to mention?" asked Godfrey, scrutinising every small movement on his agitated client's face.

William looked back hopelessly at his legal confidante as he began to explain how he had once been embroiled in the seedy clutches of another life; a whole different world away from the respectable one he lived in now.

William was embarrassed as he slowly unveiled a past life of stupidly childish pranks in the woods with his ridiculous posse of wannabe Hell's Angels. How he had been party to a mock burial thirty years previously as part of his initiation into the biking fraternity. William admitted how unbelievable his idiotic anecdote sounded. How he'd sworn an oath of allegiance to impress his leader and to become accepted by the motley gang of delinquents. The futility of his life story taunted his very soul, as he described digging a shallow grave then urinating onto what he had believed at the time to be a dead man's carcass. William was adamant it had been nothing more sinister than a mock burial using a dressmaker's dummy stuffed with rocks and straw. There was no way it had been a real corpse; let alone a woman's body.

Godfrey continued to scrutinise his client's tired pained expression. Surely even if William Weber had once been the naïve disillusioned Billy Kiddo, it did not mean he had a motive to kill anyone. Godfrey needed to know if his fellow mason had any idea who could have put him in the frame. William tried to help his legal friend, but the only details he felt he could safely offer up were the useless aliases of his former gang members: Sparks, Crusher, Zombie, Razor Fish, Yardy and Bullet. He knew that the half a dozen pseudonyms from three decades ago would be of no use to the authorities as they wouldn't appear on any police databases.

Perhaps the only and best defence this seasoned lawyer could come up with at that moment was nobody could connect the body found at Himley Chase to William Weber. No one even knew the identity of the dead woman. The impressionable young Billy Kiddo had not killed anyone; the older and wiser William Weber was an innocent man. But Godfrey Hathergood feared the police would use the lack of other suspects, along with the full weight of incriminating historic DNA evidence, to convince the Crown Prosecution Service that his client deserved to be tried as a cold-hearted killer.

Inspector Chiltern returned to the police interview room, closely followed by his loyal sergeant who was carrying an A4 plastic folder. The two men sat down at the table in their well-rehearsed formation as Chiltern flicked the button on the voice recorder to resume recording the interview. The inspector drew in a deep purposeful breath and opened his mouth to speak, but Godfrey interrupted abruptly.

"Inspector Chiltern," he began. "I think my client has answered all of your questions many times. You have held him here for nearly forty-eight hours without charge, and he has still given you the same answers." Chiltern looked back at the bespectacled elder statesman momentarily, before returning to focus a steely glare at William. Godfrey resumed his defence.

"Mister Weber is an upstanding member of his local community whom I can personally vouch for. All you have is some spurious circumstantial evidence that you know any legal team worth its salt will totally rip to shreds in a court of law. You cannot connect the dead body to my client, so, unless you want to risk you and the CPS being made a laughing stock," Godfrey stood up to finish his carefully calculated statement, "then I ask my client is allowed to leave without charge."

Chiltern looked across at Richens and nodded towards the plastic folder that his sergeant had placed on the metal desk. Slowly Richens opened the wallet and passed a piece of paper to his boss. Chiltern cast his steely gaze over the printed A4 sheet, as if to make absolutely sure all of the information was accurate. The forensics lab had spent the past twenty-four hours comparing Sharron's DNA with that of the dead woman. The folder contained the preliminary fast-tracked results.

Chiltern lifted his head to meet William's blank face before delivering his verbal body blow: "Okay Mister Weber, exactly who was Tracey Chambers to you then?"

#

The Following Morning:

Sharron Chambers was rudely woken from a fitful night's sleep by the persistent ringing of her front doorbell. It was seven-thirty in the morning and she had only managed to drift off into a restless nightmare about two hours earlier. She groggily pulled back the bedroom curtains to peer outside into the burst of early morning sunshine. Sergeant Richens was standing by the porch beneath her window; next to him stood a young uniformed policewoman. Sharron stumbled across the bedroom floor, grabbing her dressing gown and slippers, before hastily making her way downstairs to open the front door.

"Morning," said Sharron, rubbing sleep from her tired eyes.

"Hello Miss Chambers," replied Richens reverently as he flipped open his wallet to display his identity card. "I'm Sergeant Richens and this is Constable Sally Garland. I am sorry to wake you so early in the morning, but we have some news about your mother, and I didn't want to break it to you over the telephone."

With those fateful words a stinging shock surged through Sharron's chest; the realisation that the dead woman discovered at Himley Chase was her long lost mom. She felt dizzy, as if all of the blood was draining out of her body and down into her slippers. A cloud of hazy mist drew a thick veil over her salty tired eyes, as she slumped backwards into the hallway.

"Hello, hello" whispered a soft voice in the blurred distance. "Hello Sharron, can you hear me?" the voice was getting closer. The shocked plump woman opened her eyes to meet the gaze of the policewoman staring down at her from above.

"Hello Sharron," soothed the calming voice of the young officer again.

"Whoa . . . what happened?" asked a bewildered Sharron.

"I'm afraid you fainted love." Sergeant Richens helped his colleague to lift Sharron up off the floor and guide her into the lounge.

"Did you say you'd found my mom?" asked Sharron wearily.

"It must be quite a shock I know," whispered Richens patiently as he helped the stumbling woman onto the sofa. "Just take it easy Sharron, while Sally goes and makes us all a nice cup of tea," he added, looking at Constable Garland with a presumptive smile.

The result from Sharron Chambers' DNA test had confirmed beyond a shadow of any doubt that the dead woman's remains discovered at Himley Chase were those of her long-disappeared mother, Tracey Chambers. The DNA that had been taken from a tiny sample of bone marrow harvested from the dead body was a maternal match to Sharron. Sergeant Richens explained that further forensic testing of Tracey's bones had revealed more details of the nature of her untimely death. Sharron was her next of kin and, as such, had a right to know how her mother had died.

Tracey had been forcibly hit across the back of her skull with a blunt object; something that matched the flat metal end of the shovel discovered at the burial site. Her skull had been smashed with what the pathologist suggested was a single blow from behind. Shards of blood-stained glass from a beer bottle had been found amongst the bones and there were signs of other trauma to the rest of the skeletal remains, including fractured ribs, a broken arm and cracked femurs. A few tiny decaying pieces of cartilage from a foetus had also been discovered at the scene, protected for decades inside the dead woman's pelvic cavity. Fat salty tears welled in Sharron's eyes at the realisation that she had never had the chance to know her mother or meet her unborn sibling.

The forensic report mentioned Tracey's body had been fully clothed at the time of its burial. Her jeans had been soaked in blood around the crotch area and unusually she had not been wearing any panties. The pathologists had discovered only two complete DNA samples at the scene; one from the victim and another one on the urine-stained tarpaulin. The same DNA profile embedded in the canvas sheet had also been found in the blood that was ingrained in the wooden handle of the shovel. A separate footnote, written in shorthand, had been hastily scribbled in pencil on a following separate page of the forensic report. It was a lab technician's observation that mentioned the condition of the other clothing found on the dead body.

Sharron sat in stony silence, taking in everything Sergeant Richens was telling her. She allowed her mind to wander as she slowly sipped a mug of hot strong tea. Had her grandparents lied to her all along? Had the family's argument all those years ago been so toxic and unforgivable that they had beaten and killed their own daughter in a fit of rage and buried her body at Himley Chase? Sharron's mind buzzed with so many thoughts

53

and scenarios; dozens of questions that she would never know the answers to flooded her brain. Had her grandparents been guilty of such a heinous crime? Had they snuffed out the life of their wayward daughter and carried their wicked secret to their graves?

"Following your help after the television crime appeal this week, I need to tell you that we do have a suspect in custody at the moment," said Sergeant Richens, snapping Sharron back out of her train of thought. "We believe he was responsible for your mother's murder nearly thirty years ago, and he was charged yesterday evening."

Sharron stared back at the officers and swallowed hard. In that one split second she realised that someone other than her grandparents had been involved with her mother's disappearance. But now she also knew she had been instrumental in helping the authorities to identify the dead woman, and that may have led to Tracey's murderer being caught. She suddenly felt sick with fear. Until now, her mother's killer had been walking around free for thirty years. She didn't know the circumstances surrounding the arrest, but the perpetrator might know who had helped the police with their investigation.

"You've got him locked up safely though, yeah?" A wave of panic knotted in Sharron's stomach as she realised the murderer might come after her seeking his revenge.

"He's in police custody at the moment," smiled PC Garland.

"Yep, he's up before the magistrates this morning and, judging by the weight of evidence we have, it's doubtful he'll be granted bail. So he should be held on remand until it comes to court," offered Richens reassuringly.

"Who is he?" asked Sharron, relieved that she was safe, also her suspicion of her grandparents could be forgotten.

"He is a man called William Weber," replied Richens. "Do you know him? Have you ever heard of him before?" Sharron looked back blankly and slowly shook her head.

"You may have known him as Billy perhaps?" added constable Garland helpfully.

Sharron scrunched her eyes together and gazed towards the ceiling, as if searching through her mind for any recollection of the accused man's name. She chided herself inwardly for having allowed her imagination to run riot and momentarily doubt her devoted grandparents' innocence, as she tried to remember if she had ever heard any mention of William Weber before. Sharron thought carefully before telling the officers his name wasn't one she recognised.

#

William Weber limped awkwardly along a concrete corridor towards his prison cell. An early morning appearance at Hanford Magistrates Court had seen Godfrey Hathergood fail to secure bail for his client. William had endured the jostling journey in a prison van, while the pain of his broken ankle had continually throbbed beneath the tatty plaster cast. He was now being escorted by a prison officer deep inside the walls of HMP Chalmoor and he was finding it difficult to keep up with the guard's striding footsteps. William winced with every pace, as he had not been given any painkillers to quell the discomfort of his broken bones. He had been forced to discard one of his metal crutches at the reception desk, as he needed a free arm to carry his prison issue towel, mug, toothbrush and a roll of toilet paper.

"This is you," barked the guard, as his marching came to an abrupt halt outside an open metal door. A dazed William shuffled inside the narrow cell, before hearing the heavy clang of the door being closed behind him.

The anxious inmate gazed around his sparsely furnished quarters. A metal bunk bed hugged the longest wall. A thin stack of scratchy woollen blankets and rough cotton sheets had been placed on the top bunk. The bed had been pushed into the corner of the room with two small metal cabinets screwed into the concrete floor at the end to secure the ensemble in place. In the opposite corner was a low dividing wall in front of a metal toilet and sink. The wall was a futile attempt to give a little privacy to anyone using the loo; but it served no real purpose other than to take up valuable floor space. The austere brick walls had once been painted white, but the acrid smoke from thousands of hard-earned cigarettes had left a thick layer of yellow nicotine clinging to every surface.

William slumped down on the bottom bunk and let out a long sigh with the welcome reprieve of resting his broken ankle. The last few days had brought a hurricane of emotion for the middle-aged businessman. He had endured a seemingly endless roller-coaster of police interviews and fretful discussions with his solicitor. The week had ended with a disastrous bail hearing that had seen William remanded in custody until his trial for murder. This was the first time the bewildered man had been left totally alone since his arrest. William now only had his own thoughts for company.

His decision to remain faithful to the Serpent Sons' oath of allegiance had come at a hefty price. He now questioned whether he had made the right decision. He knew he was an innocent man, but there was a very real prospect of him spending the rest of his life behind bars. William lay down on the bed and closed his tired eyes. He now wondered if implicating his old fraternity and facing the predictable fallout from Sparks would be a better alternative to a life in prison.

Chapter 6

December 2004 - Nine Months Later.

William Weber stood trembling in the wooden-panelled witness box at Hanford Crown Court. He had become engulfed in a wide awake nightmare, charged with the murder of the first woman he had ever loved, but he felt powerless to prove his innocence. Following William's arrest and subsequent charge, the accused man had spent nine gruelling months remanded in custody at HMP Chalmoor, so he was well aware of what life behind bars would be like should he be found guilty of Tracey's murder.

William had attended court every day for eleven torturous weeks, listening to a seemingly endless stream of experts rake over the gruesome facts behind Tracey Chambers' demise. Two imposing colonies of barristers had fought valiant vocal battles back-and-forth; just like two opposing gangs of ravenous vultures, they had scratched and clawed through the cold remains of William's life, exposing every sinew. They were all desperately trying to uncover something that would prove his innocence or guilt, beyond any reasonable doubt, to a jury of twelve independent strangers. It was now William Weber's moment to carefully answer his accusers.

The prosecution team were keen to scrutinise every small facet of the fifty-one-year-old's life; from his undeniable penchant for red-haired women, to the unfounded accusations and lies that his ex-wife had divorced him due to intolerable cruelty. The packed courtroom was told how Juliette Weber had since remarried and William's own daughter had swiftly taken her step-father's surname in an effort to escape the shame of the Crown versus Weber trial. No slimy stone was left unturned in the prosecution's attempts to sully the accused man's character.

His defence team had fought a gallant campaign, forging ahead with the fact that he was an honest businessman, a well-liked hotelier, freemason and a pinnacle of his local community. They argued that even when William had been an infatuated misguided youth, he would have had no proven motive to kill

Tracey Chambers. A returning swipe from the prosecution had suggested William's bitter divorce had brought his true personality bubbling back up to the surface of his professional persona; William was unfairly re-cast as a wild ex-Hell's Angel, an out-of-control bullying husband and hardened drunk driver who thought nothing of taking a risk to get what he wanted in life.

With the heavy weight of DNA evidence wheeled out at every possible opportunity, William knew that the prosecution would now seek to unveil any tiny hint of guilt, and they would mercilessly pounce on any small hesitation in his replies. It was all a surreal theatrical performance to convince a jury of twelve unknown adjudicators that William Weber had killed Tracey Chambers in a fit of rage when she had refused to have sex with him. Tracey would have known she was pregnant and she had probably wanted to protect her unborn child. The court was repeatedly drip-fed DI Chiltern's scenario that Billy had snatched the young woman, taken her to the woods and savagely raped her. She had put up a brave fight, breaking several bones in her attempt to escape his evil clutches. He had stabbed her in the crotch with a broken beer bottle and then hit her over the head with a shovel. He had buried her lifeless body in a shallow grave at Himley Chase, before childishly urinating over her corpse.

William Weber had admitted to fleeing to the West Country at around the same time as Tracey's death. His loyal defence team had argued this was merely a coincidence; his ailing parents had needed his help with running their guesthouse. The prosecution had claimed his leaving Hanford so suddenly was the act of a guilty man; Billy's attempt to distance himself from the crime scene.

Fiona McBride QC stood to address the packed court. She was an imposingly elegant woman with a soothing resonant voice that easily filled every cubic inch of the legal theatre when she spoke. A time-served prosecutor and a firm favourite with the Crown Prosecution Service; many had fallen in her wake over the years. She was a powerful legal force that commanded unwavering respect from all who crossed her path. This had earned her the irreverent nickname of 'The Falcon'.

Fiona McBride swiftly arose from behind a wooden-panelled desk to take her place at a lectern in front of the witness box.

"Mister Weber," she began, taking in a purposeful breath with an air of unquestionable authority. "You claim you were a member of a biker gang for almost seven years; from the end of nineteen-sixty-nine to the summer of nineteen-seventy-six," she slowly began her circling formation of attack; her petrified innocent quarry remained silent in the witness box. "The. . . ahem . . . Serpent Sons of Thelema," she added sarcastically as she turned to give a sideways glance at the jury; a wry smile twitched at the corner of her mouth.

"Yes," replied William nervously.

"So, you lived with this group of people for nearly seven years of your life?" she queried. The Falcon's words encircled her bewildered prey.

"Yes," replied William again, unsure when her line of repetitive questioning would end.

"Yet you can only give this court a handful of fictitious names of the men whom you say you shared your life with; men whom you claim were like brothers to you. How can you expect us to believe you didn't know their real identities?" Her questions slowly taunted and pecked at the scared man in front of her.

"It's just how biker gangs worked back then, no one ever used their real names," replied William sheepishly.

Fiona McBride shot a steely glare at the trembling man for a few seconds. It was as if she was mentally freezing his answer for future reference, before swiftly switching to a different line of focussed questioning.

"Mister Weber, do you drink alcohol?"

"Yes, I do." William could not keep up with the barrister's changing volley of questions.

"Ah, yes of course we all know you like alcohol, because your DNA was taken at the time of your arrest for drink driving, wasn't it?" It was a cheap attack that was merely said to blacken the accused man's reputation. William simply nodded.

"Did you regularly drink brown ale in the seventies, when you were a poor misunderstood tearaway?" added the prosecutor with a hint of sarcasm.

"Yes," replied William quizzically. *What difference does it make what I drank back then?* The Falcon was circling again and he knew he was powerless to avoid falling into her trap.

"So, Mister Weber, You claim you were in a secret relationship with your gang leader's girlfriend; Miss Tracey Chambers?" The Falcon's black silk robes billowed behind her. "The murder victim m'lord," added the prosecutor unnecessarily. She gave a cursory nod towards the judge as if the dead woman's identity needed to be clarified.

"Yes," nodded William, confused by another switch in the line of questions. "I was in a relationship with Tracey." A hard lump of sadness almost choked his voice.

"And you expect this court to believe your version of events, do you? That, when you oh so conveniently walked away from your band of brothers, Miss Chambers was alive and well?" A tearful William simply nodded back at the fearsome woman as she continued her measured verbal attack.

"And so Mister Weber, you also expect us to believe it must have been your gang's leader, Mister Sparks, who killed his girlfriend after he found out about your grubby little love affair?" The barrister mockingly highlighted the biker's pseudonym with a prefix that made it sound as if he was a fictitious character from a child's story book.

William just nodded his head as he blinked back a fat salty tear in his right eye that was threatening to break free and roll down his hot cheek. After all the months that had passed following his arrest, he still could not relate the dead woman's remains found at Himley Chase to the beautifully vibrant and fiery woman he had fallen in love with all those years ago.

"So, tell me, why is your gang leader not here today? Why are your so-called brothers, with their quite frankly ridiculous made-up names, not here today to set the record straight Mister Weber?" continued Miss McBride, still pecking at her quarry. William stared back and opened his mouth to speak, but he was unable to answer the barrage of questions fired at him.

"Why aren't the elusive Mister Sparks and Mister Crusher standing in that witness box and answering my questions instead of you?" A few members of the jury started to cough in an attempt to stifle their giggles that followed the comically sounding name of Mr Crusher. The barrister gave a reverent nod of her head towards the Judge.

"M'lord, even the defendant's own legal team have been unable to track down the men that Mister Weber claims are responsible for this despicable act," she added incredulously.

The imposing Falcon was carefully manipulating her enthralled courtroom audience to believe that the Serpent Sons of Thelema had only ever existed in William's childish imagination; he had invented the names of his supposed fraternity in an attempt to mislead the court and waste everyone's time. Fiona McBride continued her relentless verbal attack before elegantly swooping in for the kill.

"I put it to you Mister Weber that you became infatuated with Tracey Chambers to the point of stalking her, didn't you?"

"No, you've got it all wrong. I loved her," cried William.

"I don't doubt that Mister Weber, but she didn't love you back, did she? She was a stranger who you stalked from afar and when you made your move she turned you down, didn't she?"

"No!" he screamed.

"Admit it Mister Weber, you were drunk on brown ale, weren't you? Tracey refused your advances, didn't she? So you relentlessly pursued her, abducted her, raped her and stabbed her with your beer bottle when you were finished. Then, just for good measure, you smashed her skull with a shovel and buried her, before soaking her cold lifeless body in your urine. You then skulked away from the scene, leaving Tracey to rot away in a shallow grave on Himley Chase. Didn't you Mister Weber?" The Falcon had masterfully dealt the final blow that would help to seal the tearful man's fate.

William felt powerless. He had no more answers for the eloquently over-bearing prosecutor. He had first realised long ago in DI Chiltern's interview room that Billy Kiddo had been firmly pushed into the frame for the murder of Sparks' ol' lady. He knew that his beloved Tracey hadn't joined him as planned at Himley Chase following his release from the biker gang. Instead Billy had waited alone at the woodland clearing for three hours before reluctantly admitting defeat; Tracey would not be leaving Hanford with him. He had sombrely climbed astride his motorcycle without his lover. A torrent of tears had flooded into his eyes as he had ridden blindly into the night, towards the comforting West Country embrace of his parents' guesthouse.

Tracey never telephoned Billy to explain why she had not joined him at Himley Chase. He had heard nothing from her and reluctantly accepted that she had chosen the nomadic lifestyle with Sparks over a more sedate way of life away from the Serpent Sons. In line with the conditions of his release from the motley crew of misfits, Billy had not been allowed any contact with his former fraternity. He had slowly accepted that he would have to live the rest of his life without the woman he loved.

Almost thirty years later, he now knew that the lawless gang of bikers had killed her and framed him for the murder, probably in retribution for his leaving; but he could never tell the police. He knew that even though the Thelema brotherhood had unanimously agreed to let him 'leave and live,' they would never forgive him for turning his back on them. They would always regard his action as disloyalty and, as a consequence, he would remain in their debt and under their control.

During the nine months he had been held on remand, William had endured numerous unwelcome encounters with some of Sparks' underworld associates. Billy had been given every horrifying detail about Tracey's murder. He had been sent a very clear message. The accused man was made to understand that if he ever revealed the true identities of his old biker gang to the authorities, then his ex-wife Juliette and their innocent young daughter would be hunted down by the sordid fraternity. He knew that he couldn't risk his own child being made to suffer the same torturous demise as his beloved Tracey had endured at the hands of the depraved gang of misfits. He would soon learn that proving his own innocence whilst protecting the true identities of his old kinsmen would be an impossible task.

William had told his solicitor that he believed Sparks could have found out about his affair with Tracey; his gang leader had probably murdered the red-haired cock teaser in a furiously jealous rage. Maybe Tracey's spurned ol' man had hit her across the back of her skull with the same shovel that Billy had bled onto at his initiation ceremony. Sparks could have then wrapped Tracey's corpse in the tarpaulin that had been safely stored in the garage at the gang's headquarters; the old piece of faded green canvas from the dressmaker's dummy used in the mock burial; the shroud that contained Billy's incriminating DNA.

William's evidence had been ripped into tiny fragments by the gnarling claws of Fiona 'Falcon' McBride. The accused man had trembled in the witness box as his words were twisted into legal knots. He had insisted he had been in a relationship with Tracey Chambers, but he had also admitted the last time he had visited Himley Chase was around thirty years previously; the same time that it had been estimated the murdered woman's body had been buried there. He was unable to give the real names of the members in the biker gang; instead he could only offer pseudonyms. His version of events as to how his DNA had become so embedded in the tarpaulin and shovel handle were completely dismissed by the prosecution.

Fiona McBride had described William as a stalker and his explanation as total fabrication; a tissue of lies that had begun to unravel at the Falcon's first battering round of questions. The old squalid clubhouse on Anglesey Street no longer existed. All of the old pebble dashed properties in the road had been demolished a couple of decades earlier to make way for more social housing; no one living on the street could remember the Serpent Sons of Thelema. Back in the seventies all police records were manually written onto a card indexing system; thirty years later the information was being painstakingly transferred onto a computer database. However, there were no listings on any police spreadsheets to confirm the identities of Sparks, Crusher, Razor Fish, Zombie, Bullet or Yardy; pseudonyms or otherwise. Furthermore, Sharron Chambers had absolutely no knowledge of her mother having ever been involved with a biker gang.

William knew that the cards were firmly stacked against him. Despite the impending guilty verdict and the undoubted prospect of spending the rest of his life in prison, he could never break his sworn oath of allegiance to the brotherhood. No matter how misjudged William's bad decision had been, he knew betraying Sparks and the Serpent Sons of Thelema would have far worse and wider reaching consequences for his daughter and ex-wife. He could never give the gang members' true identities to the authorities. Instead, William would protect his blood family by remaining faithful to his misguided vow and take his punishment like a man.

Chapter 7

April 2005 – Four Months Later.

Sharron Chambers stood in the garden of remembrance outside Hanford Town Crematorium. The court case to bring her mother's killer to justice had attracted a constantly buzzing swarm of unwelcome media attention; daily court reports had been presented on the national television news to reach into the hearts and souls of its judgmental audience. Newspapers across the country had graphically reconstructed the last tormented moments of Tracey Chambers' life. There had been no escape from the constantly intrusive reporters' questions. Since William Weber's conviction, Sharron had begun to re-build her life and the past few quieter months had brought a small reprieve from the constant media intrusion. But today, at her mother's memorial service, a new storm of jostling camera crews and jabbing microphones would invade Sharron's life.

Tracey's funeral had been a very intimate affair, attended only by her daughter and a couple of the police officers who had befriended Sharron early on in the investigation. Six months later, the memorial service was proving to be a far more public event. A group of well-wishers had gathered to attend the ceremony, all eager to bid their fond farewells to the tragically murdered young woman. From mature ladies with blue-rinsed tresses who affectionately remembered the bubbly young trainee hairdresser, to a couple of retired school teachers from Hanford Senior School who chose to reverently describe the wayward teenager as a spirited young girl; everyone seemingly only had good memories of the dead gym-slip mum. The fact that their attendance at the service could buy them fifteen minutes of fame on the lunchtime TV news, or get their photographs in the local rag, was an opportunity too good to miss.

Sharron slowly walked away from the group of mourners, making her way towards a chubby teenage girl who had just placed a small posy of flowers beneath an engraved wooden plaque bearing Tracey's name. The girl wore a smart school uniform of grey knee-length skirt, white blouse, grey tie, maroon blazer, straw boater hat and grey silk gloves. Her long strawberry-blonde hair hung in two neat plaits that swayed at either side of her plump yet pretty freckled face.

"Hello," said Sharron, smiling down at the kneeling schoolgirl. "Are those flowers for my Mom?"

"Yes," replied the well-spoken girl. She shyly smiled back at Sharron. "They're from my friends and I." She pointed over towards a small group of other girls who all wore the same unfamiliar school uniform and stood chatting to whom Sharron assumed to be a couple of their teachers. The tubby schoolgirl explained how she attended an academy in Oxford and was studying for a GCSE in forensic science. The Tracey Chambers' murder case had captivated her and her fellow classmates. Every fascinating detail of the investigation had been picked over and scrutinised in the classroom; they had debated the subject extensively and even carried out their own mock trial of William Weber based on the forensic evidence, before making the final edits to their end-of-term dissertations. Tracey Chambers' murder had brought so much real-life interest to their otherwise dull studies, that the well-educated young ladies now believed the victim's family should receive a small token of their appreciation. It was the only right and proper thing to do.

Sharron paused for a moment in front of Tracey's plaque as she read a few of the messages of condolence that had been tied to a mountainous collection of floral arrangements from unknown well-wishers. She realised just how far her mother's story had travelled and how it must have impacted on many strangers' lives.

During the past six months Sharron's face had been emblazoned on the front covers of countless newspapers and magazines, she had become the latest target at the centre of that month's juicy gossip columns. She was the innocent daughter of a blameless misguided mother. No news editor could resist the story of an orphaned child who sat at the heart of a grisly murder story. Sharron shook her head in realisation that the fascinating and powerful headlines had even managed to leave their indelible stain on one school's curriculum almost a hundred miles away from Hanford.

"We're having a small gathering at a pub down the road after the service, in the Huntsman's Arms. Would you and your teachers like to join us for a cola or an orange juice or something?" offered Sharron to the chubby young schoolgirl who was still kneeling next to the flowers. "You can tell me more about your course work then."

"Yes please, an orange juice would be great. Thank you." The young teenager smiled warmly at Sharron, excited at the prospect of being invited to spend a little time with Tracey Chambers' daughter. "I'll go and ask our teachers if we have enough time before we catch our train back to Oxford. We'll see you in there."

Sharron smiled back, turned away from the girl and slowly walked towards the heavy wrought iron entrance gates of the garden of remembrance. She took in a deep purposeful breath before greeting the waiting posse of clicking paparazzi cameras and quick fire questions.

The schoolgirl remained kneeling in front of Tracey's plaque. She took a small pad of paper and a stubby pencil out of her blazer pocket and started to quickly jot down all of the unfamiliar names written at the bottom of each message of condolence. She knew her fellow classmates would be interested in adding the details to the final chapter of their school project.

"Do come along girls," shouted an impatient voice. "I think we've spent quite enough time dawdling around here as it is." It was the high-pitched tone of Miss Winbrook, the girl's form teacher who had begrudgingly accompanied her pupils to the memorial service. The elderly mistress had not really cared for the contemporary slant given to lessons at the academy. Miss Winbrook firmly believed in a more traditional education for the young ladies in her care. She had been strongly opposed to the field trip. She had felt it was too morbid for the girls to attend the memorial service and take part in the final chapter of the Tracey Chambers' story. Such immersive experiences were not the type of thing she was used to or appreciated. The sooner she could round up her charges and get them on their way home

to Oxford the better. All of the schoolgirls dutifully gathered up
their belongings, stood in line and boarded a minibus back to
the train station.

#

The smoke-filled acrid air of the public bar in the
Huntsman's Arms bore testament to its long history of public
service. It had been the central meeting place of the town's beer
swilling wheelers and dealers since the beginning of Queen
Victoria's reign. Today this noisy, smokey drinking den was
hosting a small wake after Tracey Chambers' memorial service.
The long narrow room was filled with a sporadic arrangement
of mismatched wooden tables and chairs. The nicotine stained
walls featured rough cast plasterwork that had aged badly; the
threadbare red tartan carpet had also seen better days. A heavy
dark oak bar dominated one side of the smoke-filled galley. An
overweight moustachioed barman stood behind the bar. He was
busily cleaning glasses and continually checked his watch for
the time. Behind the barman, amid groaning shelves of spirits
and liquors, a small collection of dusty yard-of-ale glasses hung
precariously on the wall. A large group of loud lager-fuelled
men and women stood at the far end of the room; their raucous
language immediately fell to a hushed silence as Sharron
Chambers entered the bar through a glazed wooden door. The
barman immediately turned and smiled a warm, welcoming
smile at Sharron. She nervously giggled inside as she thought
the man's long black Mexican moustache made him resemble
an ageing seventies' porn star.

Colin Lawson was the proud owner of the Huntsman's
Arms. Like so many of his regulars, he had followed the case of
the murdered woman discovered at Himley Chase with great
interest. Tracey Chambers had once been a local girl, a spirited
teenager, her young life mercilessly slain almost thirty years
previously. The town's newspaper had delivered the guilty
verdict of William Weber's trial and then announced Tracey's
memorial service would take place at Hanford Crematorium a
few months later. Colin Lawson was a local pub landlord, and
he had been quick to offer his premises as a venue for the main

gathering afterwards. There would be no charge to the grieving family; it was the least he could do for one of the community's poor lost souls.

The jolly barman was a rotund figure who ruled his domain with an iron fist. His long seventies' porn star's moustache made him an instantly recognisable character of the town. The scruffy town centre boozer had previously endured a salacious reputation as the local pick-up joint for touting prostitutes. The relatively new landlord was working hard to transform the fortunes of his drinking den. At fifty-three years old Colin Lawson had grafted hard for his money and his regular clientele knew they had to behave. Gone were the bawdy back-room brawls; the seedy deals in the gents' toilets and old slappers plying their trade in the bar. The only focus of attention in Colin's mind was how to get more customers to drink more booze and spend more money with him. He knew that, for the cost of a few sandwiches and sausage rolls, today's seemingly generous act of kindness towards the family of an infamous murder victim would bring him limitless publicity and goodwill in the area.

Sharron pulled a wooden stool out from beneath the bar and perched uncomfortably on the seat. She smiled back at the barman and ordered a large glass of white wine for herself and an orange juice, in anticipation of the arrival of the plump schoolgirl she had just met in the garden of remembrance.

A muscular man with a bushy beard stood at the other end of the bar, carefully watching Sharron as she took a sip of wine. She saw he had gaps in his teeth when he smiled. What remained of his teeth looked like crooked tombstones rising up from a blackened pit of hell. She noticed his hands were very large, his fingers clumsily tattooed with the words LOVE and HATE. Sharron allowed a small shudder to flicker through her body at the thought of what heinous acts those fists had probably been responsible for in the past.

"They're a bit of a characterful bunch aren't they," interrupted the jolly landlord who had noticed Sharron's obvious disdain for the customer standing at the opposite end of the bar. "But they're okay when you get to know them, I mean they're all here to pay their respects to Tracey Chambers today." The barman wiped over the bar with a damp rag and started to polish some glasses as he talked.

"Take Brian there, for example," he said, pointing at the bearded man with bad teeth and love-hate hands. "He runs the local boxing club. He certainly knows how to keep the young'uns under control if you know what I mean, but he's a bit of a softy at heart." Colin winked at Sharron while tapping the side of his nose.

The customer was Brian Walsh, the fifty-eight-year-old owner of a boxing gym. Colin regaled Sharron with a colourful account of how Brian had built a fearsome reputation as a no-nonsense fighter in his early years working as a doorman. It was rumoured Brian had once crushed someone's neck with his bare hands. The moustachioed barman went on to reassure Sharron that she had no reason to fear the bearded hulk sitting at the end of the bar as, despite his outwardly intimidating appearance, he was a bit of a pussycat when it came to looking after the ladies.

Sharron took a large nervous gulp of her wine. The barman dutifully re-filled her glass and began to introduce the rest of the group of men who were gathered around Brian Walsh.

Dave Corden was Brian Walsh's best friend. The sixty-two-year-old bald-headed man ran a barber's shop and tattoo parlour above Brian's boxing gym; the two men were often seen together in the Huntsman's Arms. They had been joined by a slightly older man with greying blonde curly hair called Peter Crowther. He was carrying a shiny full-faced crash helmet and was dressed in a smart set of red and white racing leathers with matching red motorcycle boots. Peter Crowther owned the bike shop next door to Colin's pub.

A fourth member of the group had returned to a booth to sit down and roll a cigarette. He was about the same age as most of the other men but appeared to suffer from a nervous tremor. Sharron gazed pitifully at the fretful looking man as he shakily opened his tobacco tin, spilling most of its contents onto the table in front of him. Colin explained that he was Patrick O'Doyle, an ex-junkie who had recently been released from another spell in rehab. He always found it hard to adjust to a life outside without his white powders and blue pills; but it was obvious to Sharron that the rest of Brian Walsh's entourage were all highly supportive of their ailing friend.

Sharron finished off her second large glass of wine and summoned Colin to pour her another measure. She heard the glazed door behind her open; a cool breeze of fresh air drifted into the smokey atmosphere before instantly disappearing into the acrid stench of cigarettes and stale beer. Everyone in the bar fell silent once more as a menacing presence seemed to envelope the gathered crowd. George Dalmano had entered the room.

George was a tall imposing figure with chiselled features and sun-tanned skin. He wore a thick head of raven-black hair in a glossy ponytail that swished around the upturned collar of his heavy black overcoat. Underneath he wore a stylish blue pin-striped three-piece suit over a crisp white cotton shirt. His heavy cloud of expensive aftershave filled Sharron's nostrils as he turned to greet her. His deep Azure-blue eyes flashed a devious smile and she noticed his expensively manicured fingernails were short and perfectly shaped. The large diamond-encrusted signet rings that he wore on three of his strong masculine fingers glinted in the afternoon sunlight, as he held out his hand to introduce himself.

"Hello, you're Miss Chambers aren't you?" began George as he reached to gallantly pull her hand to his mouth for a small kiss. "I recognise you from the news reports."

"Yes, I am. And you are?" Sharron smiled nervously. She was a little startled by his old-fashioned introductory kiss of her hand.

"Err, this is George Dalmano," Colin quickly interrupted from behind the bar. "The owner of Dalmano's Motors?" he added helpfully with a raised inflection at the end, trying to impress upon the young woman just how important a man George was.

Sharron got up from the uncomfortable wooden bar stool; immediately she felt light headed and began to regret having quickly drunk two large glasses of wine on an empty stomach. She had embarrassingly snagged the stiletto heel of her shoe on the threadbare red tartan carpet. George reached out to steady Sharron's clumsy small stagger as she stumbled into his chest.

She looked up at his face to thank him and felt the unwavering focus of his Azure-blue eyes penetrate deep into her soul. Sharron couldn't understand the confused feelings she had of overwhelming instant attraction to this striking man, whilst also being a little afraid of him.

"You must excuse me," she said nervously. "I was waiting for a friend, but I don't think she's coming now." Sharron glanced across at the untouched glass of orange juice that she had ordered for the absent schoolgirl she had met outside the crematorium. George continued to fix his steely glare onto Sharron. She handed the barman a ten pound note to pay for her drinks, before making her way through the smoke-filled room. A devious smile stretched across George's sun-tanned face as he watched her open the glazed door and walk out into the fresh spring air of the outside world.

"Well, she ain't as willing as her mother used to be, is she?" laughed George as he turned around to face Colin. The barman had begun to nervously stroke his porn star's moustache with his thumb and forefinger; it was as if he was trying to coax the black caterpillar of facial hair to grow a little longer on demand. George reached into the inside pocket of his heavy black overcoat and took out a thick bundle of crisp twenty-pound notes. He nodded at the landlord and placed the cash on the bar, before sitting down on Sharron's vacated wooden bar stool.

"That's for Tracey," announced George. "Let's give my ol' lady the send off she deserves," he quietly whispered.

Brian Walsh's entourage simultaneously raised their glasses in respect, as Colin Lawson placed the money inside the till and poured George a double measure of Tennessee whiskey over ice.

The landlord was relieved that his old gang leader had arrived. He had worried all afternoon that some of the gathered old gang members might cause a scene when faced with the daughter of Sparks' ol' lady. Colin knew how unpredictable Patrick 'Zombie' O'Doyle could be, especially if he hadn't taken his medication. Everyone had tried to keep news of the wake a secret from Patrick, but he had heard about the event when he visited the local bookies. The whole group had promised to keep the fretful old man in check if he began to ramble too much about Tracey's murder. The old Serpent Sons of Thelema were all acutely aware of the risk that their thirty-year-old buried secret could be revealed. Everyone knew it was only George Dalmano who had any real control over the loose-lipped junkie, so Sparks' arrival at the bar had been largely welcomed.

Chapter 8

June 2014 – Nine Years Later.

William Weber sat impatiently waiting for his new solicitor to arrive. He watched five circuits of the thin second hand click around the circular white face of the clock on the wall. William carefully counted every second ticking by; just as he had through every day for the past ten years. But today would be different. Today he had a new reason for counting time.

The small room at Chalmoor Prison was sparsely appointed with minimal furnishings. It was a tiny space reserved for private meetings between prisoners and their legal representatives; a small escape from the prying eyes and ears of prison guards and other inmates. There were no windows and the room was only illuminated by a blinding fluorescent strip light that continually buzzed and hummed high up on the ceiling. The roof, walls and floor of this airless concrete box were coated in a pale utilitarian grey paint. William sat alone on a pressed metal chair at one side of an old wooden table; his impatient glare firmly locked onto the clinical clock that hung above a solid metal door. Next to the door was a wall mounted handset for a two-way intercom; it was the only method of communication with people on the other side of this austere sound-proofed chamber.

The hands on the clock reached their target time of two-thirty, as the heavy metal door squealed open and an efficient-looking slim young woman was ushered into the room by a uniformed prison guard.

"Good afternoon Mister Weber;" announced the eloquent stranger. "I am Miss Tisserand, one of your new legal representatives." She smiled warmly at William and held out her hand, before turning back to nod at the prison guard. The dutiful uniformed man backed out of the room and pulled the heavy metal door firmly shut behind him.

Lin Tisserand was a trainee lawyer with what remained of Godfrey Hathergood's legal practice. Old man Hathergood retired soon after William's trial had ended. He never recovered from the abject disappointment he felt after his last and very public court case had ended in total failure for his fellow mason. Almost two years after the guilty verdict, Godfrey Hathergood had suffered a fatal heart attack during a sunny afternoon's stroll on the golf course. His West Country legal firm was swiftly taken over by a new dynamic team of high fliers who now specialised in criminal defence. The young trainee solicitor that visited William Weber today was on a fact finding mission to establish any missing evidence that could be used to rebuild the wrongfully imprisoned man's defence. She was confident the law firm could construct a good case for a successful appeal against Billy's life sentence.

Lin was an attractive yet boyish-looking young woman. She was a law student from Switzerland and had come to England to finish her post graduate degree. She had taken up a vocational internship with Godfrey's old firm in anticipation of studying for her bar examinations. The pretty young woman had pale skin and elfin-like features. Her short glossy blue-black hair had been chopped bluntly into a no-nonsense, business-like bob. She wore a smart linen knee-length shift dress with a matching slate grey jacket and she carried a new graphite coloured leather briefcase in one hand. Every facet of her demeanour was that of a professional executive who had a very long and rewarding legal career ahead of her.

During his incarceration William had become frail. His gaunt expression and sallow skin made him appear much older than his sixty years. A decade spent locked-up behind Chalmoor's cold prison walls had taken its toll. William's small greying body seemed to hug itself together in a vain effort to keep warm as he huddled on the pressed metal chair. Lin was quick to notice the hopeless old man had a small tear that was threatening to crawl out of his eye and roll down his cheek. She gazed back at William with a supportive smile, as the broken, weak and fragile man that sat in front of her began to deliver his sad news. He had just learned he had an inoperable tumour. The Cancer was his second life sentence.

Despite her professional veneer, the youthful Miss Tisserand demonstrated a highly compassionate attitude towards her client. She was a warm and caring young woman who was obviously sympathetic to Billy's seemingly lost cause. Lin reached a supportive hand across the wooden table to gently stroke Billy's frail arm. There and then, in the cold silence of that airless concrete meeting room, she realised that Billy was quickly running out of time. She believed his only chance of ever tasting the air of freedom again rested firmly on her young shoulders.

A couple of hours passed as Lin wrote down everything William said. He gave her all the information he could possibly remember about the Serpent Sons of Thelema. Real names, places, times, dates; no slimy rock was left unturned. He was happy to give his new legal counsel all the ammunition she needed to strengthen his court appeal; to secure his release; to give him one precious day as a free man. With his wife and daughter being so far removed from his life these days, William gave Lin far more information than he had ever felt was safe to give to the authorities a decade earlier.

The police and the whole justice system had only ever failed William Weber. Ten years previously the condemned man knew that if he had told Inspector Chiltern and Sergeant Richens everything he knew about the sordid underbelly of his previous life, then the police would not have been able to protect him or his family against Sparks' revenge. Billy would have been dealt a far worse hand than life imprisonment by the brotherhood. At best he would have been branded a grass; at worst his ex-wife and innocent young daughter would have suffered the uncontrollable wrath of a betrayed gang of ruthless, lawless outcasts.

William had not seen his family for ten years; his estranged relatives now had new identities. They had begun a whole new life with Juliette's new husband; they had managed to escape the shame of being branded as the murderer's family. More importantly they had managed to elude the vengeful clutches of salacious Sparks and his sordid disciples. William was now a dying man. He had nothing left to lose. He felt safe entrusting his secrets to his new legal confidante, he only prayed she would know the most effective way to use the information he gave her.

At the end of the meeting Lin picked up the intercom handset and summoned the prison guard to open the door.

"Don't worry Mister Weber," said the young woman looking back over her shoulder. "Where I come from in Switzerland, we have a very strong sense of justice and we pride ourselves on being able to protect confidential information. You can be assured I will do all in my power to help you in your case. Your secrets will be safe with me."

William watched the young elfin-like woman walk through the doorway as she carried her heavy graphite-grey leather briefcase loaded with his explosive revelations. William gazed back up at the clock face on the wall. Today he had a different reason for counting time. He would no longer calculate the years until his release from prison; instead he would begin ticking down the months until the end of his life.

Chapter 9

Peter Crowther zipped up the front of his weather-beaten red and white racing leathers then slowly climbed astride his powerful motorcycle. The ageing biker was the owner of a chain of motorcycle shops called Ammo's Cycles. His company specialised in supplying Pro Stock bikes; the category of two-wheeled machines that were mostly used at motorcycle drag racing events. Peter had made his name on the drag racing circuit in the eighties and his motorcycle supply company now regularly sponsored events at Hell's Angels' rallies and illegal race meetings across the country. Despite his advancing years, Peter was still a very agile man; his grey-blonde curly hair and nimble physique belied his sixty-five-years. He sat proudly astride his trusted machine and blew a good luck kiss at his giggling young girlfriend, before pulling on his shiny red and white full-faced crash helmet.

The latest object of Peter's affection was a young woman called Angie, or Angel as she was nicknamed by her friends. Peter was pleased to see she had turned up to watch him ride. Angel had casually walked into Peter's motorcycle shop on Hanford High Street a couple of months previously. She had been looking for a part-time Saturday job as a shop assistant and quite fancied trying her hand at selling bikes. A bit of a vintage chick at heart, she had impressed the old lecherous shop owner with an ample braless bosom that bounced beneath her favourite tight black vest top. She had seductively sashayed her hips between the rows of bikes in his shop before handing over her curriculum vitae. Peter had been instantly attracted to the flame-haired young woman with captivating green eyes.

During the weeks that followed he had been more than willing to forgive Angel's obvious lack of sales experience in return for countless gropes of her bouncing bosom behind the counter, or stolen cheeky kisses in the back of the store room. Over the months their playful sexual chemistry had continually simmered beneath the surface. Peter had become totally infatuated with Angel's bohemian outlook on life, and she had confessed to him that she had a growing fond affection for the old rocker. The sultry temptress had wanted to know all about Peter Crowther, how he had ever become involved with the motorcycle drag racing circuit; where the name Ammo had come from and what his life on the road as a racer had been like. He had willingly spilled the secrets of his misspent youth to the seemingly impressionable young woman.

Peter Crowther had named his business Ammo's in secret reverence to his nickname from his earlier life riding with the Serpent Sons of Thelema. He had earned the pseudonym 'Bullet' in the early seventies as, just like a bullet out of a gun, he was always the fastest away on his bike after a punch-up with rival gangs in the local boozer. At biker rallies he had won hundreds of standing start races and time trials; especially on his home turf at the old Hanford Cross airfield. Tears of pride had welled up in the elderly rocker's eyes as he regaled countless anecdotes from his by-gone drag racer's life; the sex, drugs and rock 'n' roll before sprinting down the track to victory. When his old biker gang had disbanded he was forced to stop using his Bullet nickname. Angel was one of only a handful of people who knew about his sordid past.

The red-headed temptress had grown close to the bike shop owner and the more she heard about his misspent youth the more she was convinced the old man still had that same fire in his belly. Angel knew that a racer's adrenaline-fuelled passion for fast bikes can never be extinguished; she just needed to re-kindle that flame in Peter Crowther. He may have been a few decades older but he wasn't finished yet; there was still plenty of life left in the shaggy old dog. He could be the Bullet once again if he really wanted to be.

Angel had teasingly massaged his ego and playfully egged the old biker on at any opportunity she could find. It was during one of their stockroom fumbles that Peter had realised the only route into the nubile young woman's knickers would be to convince her he still had that old Bullet fire. His red hot temptress had made it quite clear that he needed to prove he could be as strong, fast and agile as any young man, before she would surrender to him totally. After all, she wasn't a tramp who would sleep with just any old biker who had a few stories to tell; she had laughingly insisted her men had to be fit enough to go the distance.

Peter had arranged to meet his young trophy girlfriend at Hanford's old abandoned airfield. Alone at the edge of the track, in the dusky light of the setting sun, the two of them each had their own motive for being there. He would re-live his heyday. He would show her how to smash a time trial. Afterwards Angel would let him reap his reward with her in any way he saw fit. On that late warm summer evening, bathed in moonlight, Angel's free-love spirit and months of tantalising sexual teasing had brought Peter to the cusp of sexual fulfilment; his dream of steamy hot passion beneath the stars would be realised. But first he had to demonstrate his championship winning motorcycle prowess. Angel's promise of lusty hot sex on the scorched tarmac of glory was too much of a temptation for Peter to resist. He would once more become the Bullet; he would once more thunder across the sprint line; she would willingly give him his reward. Peter knew the flame-haired vixen would be made to swallow down his glorious victory; just like the biker slut from hell she was.

Hanford Cross had started its life as an RAF airfield, serving the great and the glorious of World War Two. It had once been a noble base from which Spitfires and Lancaster bombers were launched; their young brave pilots valiantly fighting for king and country, to retain the freedom and proud values of a great nation. The airfield had been abandoned by the government in the early fifties, its illustrious heritage soon to be forgotten. In the sixties the vast span of grassland and central concrete runway strip became a popular proving ground for café racers to vie for the position as leader of the pack. The following decades brought a host of biker rallies and illegal drag racing events where Bullet had made his name. During the nineties the Cross became a popular hangout for a generation of chavvy wannabe weekend rally car kings. They were a new breed of idiotic tyre squealers who proudly paraded their big exhausts and little pricks up and down the tarmac on a Saturday night. Decades later, lines of burned-out wrecked cars and motorcycles still lay strewn along the edges of the neglected runway; the pieces of rusting scrap metal bore testament to many a failed boy racer's dream of glory.

Peter Crowther kissed Angel hard on the lips, before flipping down the visor on his crash helmet. He pulled on his leather gloves and fired up his trusted iron steed. The deafening throb of the bike's powerful engine pierced the still night air as it shook the ground beneath Angel's feet. The Bullet was back in the chamber, ready to be fired. He gave his nubile nymph a small salute and kicked his motorcycle into first gear. Angel set her stop watch and raised a small silk bandana in front of Bullet's bike. Three-two-one, she dropped the scarf and his machine screamed off the start line.

She squealed with childish delight as his bike thundered down the tarmac, leaving a choking cloud of heavy oily smoke in its wake. Angel excitedly jumped up and down as she watched the speed of Bullet's take off in awe-struck amazement. The young woman shook her head and laughed as she focussed on his machine's red tail light as it grew smaller and dimmer. Suddenly the red glow began to flicker before it zigzagged down to the ground in the distance. Angel watched as a bright shower of burning sparks danced up into the still night air; the scraping metal of Bullet's steel throbbing beast had hit the road and was grinding to a shuddering halt. The young woman stared blankly into the darkness and waited to hear the sickening thud of Peter Crowther's crash helmet hit the runway.

Angel quickly walked towards the hazardous scene; a feeling of immense trepidation quickened her stride. The noise from Bullet's motorbike still thundered through her ears as she could clearly see Peter's headless leather-clad body twitching in the moonlight. The bike and rider lay horizontally on the grazed runway. Bullet's legs remained astride the wreckage of his revving machine, but his decapitated head had been thrown to one side, the visor on his helmet snapped wide open. A large pool of blood began to collect around the back of his head, as Peter's lifeless open eyes stared up at his stunned girlfriend. Adrenaline surged through Angel's body as she felt a wave of vomit begin to rise in the pit of her stomach. She had not been fully prepared for such a gruesome sight. The shocked young woman took in a deep breath of night air to quell her sickness,

81

she then kicked Peter's separated head to one side, sending the shiny red and white crash helmet rolling into the gutter at the edge of the litter-strewn tarmac. Bullet's bike's engine gave one last roar before spluttering to a halt. Angel bent down over Peter's body, taking care not to stand in the blood that had pumped across the tarmac. The venomous vixen smiled to herself as she placed a small piece of cardboard into the breast pocket of his racing leathers.

Bullet was dead.

Angel took out a small torch from her pocket and switched it on so she could survey the grisly scene. A thin metal wire with razor sharp edges had been stretched across the tarmac. It was tied to two burnt out cars on either side of the runway. The lethal cheese wire had remained in place after the accident; it glinted in the moonlight but now dripped with Peter Crowther's blood.

Angel shivered and quickly got up to walk away from the airstrip. She crossed over a grassy embankment towards her own motorcycle. The young woman zipped up her tasselled scarlet leather biker's jacket and covered her face with an American Confederate flag bandana, before pulling on a crash helmet. The fiery red-head climbed astride her crimson-coloured motorbike and fired it into life, before turning around to take one last look down the runway towards Peter Crowther's corpse. Angel quickly rode away, leaving the lecherous Bullet's evil soul to burn in hell.

#

The Next Day.

Lin Tisserand sat behind an antique leather-bound desk in the clerk's office at the legal practice where she worked. The organisation that had taken over Godfrey Hathergood's West Country law firm had many satellite offices across the Midlands. Lin had taken up residency in one sited not far from Hanford town centre, so she could be closer to her client as she carried out her background research on the Weber case.

She had spent most of the day poring over the mountainous stack of archived files from William's trial and previous appeals against his conviction. The Tracey Chambers murder case was an infamous crime story that had stretched over forty years. Billy Weber's guilt had been decided beyond the shadow of any doubt a decade previously. The jury of twelve strangers at Hanford Crown Court had all been satisfied that their unanimous verdict was safe.

Godfrey Hathergood had been a meticulous man and every small facet of information that William had given him was accurately documented; however, Lin's fresh pair of eyes couldn't help but notice how little information her client had actually given to his old legal confidante. Ten years ago there had not been much substance to William's story; he had been unwilling or unable to reveal the true identities of his former fellow bikers. A decade later, behind the locked metal door of the sparsely furnished meeting room at Chalmoor Prison, Miss Tisserand had convinced a dying William Weber to divulge all the sleazy secrets of his misspent youth.

The young trainee advocate had been searching for a juicy case to sink her teeth into. Nothing would be better than a successful miscarriage of justice appeal. If she could become instrumental in getting William Weber's conviction overturned, then her professional future would be set. Lin's debut on the legal stage would be covered by the local TV news. Suited and booted she would proudly stand shoulder-to-shoulder with her exonerated client outside the Court of Appeal. She would efficiently answer questions on behalf of a dazed William Weber. Reporters would jostle and jab their microphones in front of her, paparazzi cameras would click and roll; photographs of her elfin face and boyishly cropped glossy blue-black hair would grace the covers of legal journals and gossip magazines alike. This would be the launch pad to catapult Lin into a long and rewarding career as a fully fledged defence barrister. She sat aimlessly chewing the end of a ballpoint pen as a short knock at the office door interrupted the law student's self indulgent daydream. Her four o'clock appointment had arrived.

Sharron Chambers entered the office and sat down on a leather seat opposite Miss Tisserand. The past ten years had been kind to this once bingo-winged check-out worker. A publisher had been quick to grasp the rights to ghost-write Sharron's life story; the subject of her mother's sinister murder had since become a successful true-life crime novel and film. A sharp-suited public relations team had helped Sharron to take full advantage of every money-spinning opportunity that had rolled in her direction. Gone were the ill-fitting supermarket clothes, untidy home-bleached hair and hastily applied make-up. Instead Sharron had been carefully groomed, polished and stage-managed into an elegant middle-aged woman. She wore a slimline powder blue skirt and jacket over a crisp white linen blouse. Her re-coloured glossy auburn hair had been expertly pulled into a sleek chignon at the back of her head. Sharron gracefully crossed her ankles, gently placed her hands in her lap and sat poised at the edge of her seat, patiently waiting to hear what the young legal intern had to say.

"Thank you for coming in to see me today Ms Chambers," Lin warmly welcomed her visitor into the clerk's office.

"Nice to meet you too," replied Sharron. "I was unsure what you needed to speak to me about though. My publisher said you were looking into something about my mother's murder and I should bring my old notepads and diaries with me." Her response was well-practiced.

"Well," began Lin, in an equally well-rehearsed tone. "Our law firm has been asked to look into the possibility of launching an appeal against the conviction of William Weber."

Sharron swallowed hard, raised her eyebrows and stared back in fear at the young legal advocate. This was the first time anyone had seriously suggested to her that William Weber was an innocent man. Sharron firmly believed he was guilty of her mother's murder. A wave of panic arose in her chest at the thought of what revenge he might reap on his victim's daughter. Sharron often thought had she not come forward to help identify the remains found at Himley Chase all those years ago, it would have been more difficult for the police to associate William with the dead woman. They may not have been able to build a strong enough case to secure his conviction. Furthermore,

84

Sharron knew that if she inadvertently helped Lin to secure William's release from prison, then the whole foundation she had built her shiny new haut couture life upon could crumble to dust beneath her expensively pedicured feet. Slowly, Sharron sat forward and leaned on the leather-clad desk; she studied the fresh face of the twenty-five-year-old sat across from her.

"You do appreciate how scary for me the prospect of my mother's murderer being released from jail is, don't you? Apart from it changing absolutely everything I've worked for over the past ten years, William Weber will obviously come after me seeking revenge, or even compensation." Sharron sat back in her chair, grateful that she had been given the chance to raise her objection to the appeal.

The boyish Miss Tisserand smiled back at her.

"Ms Chambers," she began, flicking back a chunk of glossy short bobbed hair that persistently fell over her eyes. "It's not a question of your mother's murderer being released from prison. We believe that the person who really killed her has never been brought to justice and he, or she, could still be roaming free."

Lin had read Sharron's autobiography in advance of their meeting. She knew the successful book had transformed the former check-out worker's life. The story had highlighted Sharron's life growing up and focussed on how she had been cruelly robbed of a mother's love. Sharron had been resentful of the very strict upbringing imposed by her grandparents, but the book made no mention of how they had needed to protect her from following the same wayward path that Tracey had gone down. Lin had gained a good understanding of how the middle-aged woman had felt at the time when told her estranged mother had in fact been murdered. The writer's account fiercely protected Tracey's reputation and it firmly laid the blame for the young woman's death at William Weber's door; Sharron believed that Tracey had been the victim of a hard drinking rapist whose rampant hormones would not take no for an answer. Sharron's account never acknowledged William's relationship with her mother or the claim that fiery cock-teasing Tracey had been involved with the Serpent Sons of Thelema.

Although Lin understood Sharron would be reluctant to admit the virtuous portrayal of her mother had been somewhat

85

embellished, she was keen to establish if there was anything else related to the case that had not been mentioned in the memoir; something which the writer may not have thought was important enough to include.

Over the next couple of hours Sharron listened intently to the young law student's arguments in favour of William Weber's innocence. Lin slowly and purposefully planted seeds of doubt into each and every facet of the prosecution's circumstantial and forensic evidence; she expertly threw a variety of new and different scenarios into the conversation to cast more doubt over the safety of William Weber's conviction. The trainee advocate convinced Sharron that if there had been a miscarriage of justice, William Weber should be released from prison immediately. Sharron agreed that she owed it to her mother's memory to ensure the real perpetrator was found and made to pay for his heinous crime.

The young woman gave Sharron multiple assurances that William did not blame her for his wrongful incarceration; Lin guaranteed that he was not a vengeful man and she managed to extinguish any fears Sharron had of the convicted man's retaliation. Despite those promises, Sharron was in no doubt that establishing William Weber's innocence would have a dramatic effect on her story. However, the fact that a juicy sequel book to set the record straight, with another possible film deal on the horizon, was an appealing prospect in the middle-aged woman's calculating mind. She agreed to help with the appeal and willingly gave Miss Tisserand all of the facts as she remembered them.

Sharron recalled how, on the first day the national press had discovered she was the daughter of the dead woman in the woods, she had been mercilessly hounded by a paparazzi pack. Sharron had been swiftly approached by a public relations company who said they could help her to handle the sudden and unwelcome media intrusion on her life. Sharron's newly appointed PR manager had been keen to ensure his client capitalised on the notoriety; after all it wasn't every day that an orphaned child discovered that their mother had been so brutally murdered.

A few months later, at the start of William Weber's trial, Tracey Chambers' remains were released for burial and there had been a small private funeral. The PR agent had been annoyed by the loss of the marketing opportunity to cover the ceremony in the press. Following William Weber's conviction it became clear that the media's coverage of the Chambers' case had begun to wane. The PR man knew his client was about to publish her autobiography to detail her side of the story and he was keen to capitalise on any available column inches to promote it. To generate a new spark of interest, the PR expert had suggested a separate memorial service should be held as a mark of respect for the dead woman. He said a group of business owners from the Hanford area had been deeply touched by Sharron's tragic story. One of the businessmen, the landlord of the local pub, had been keen to offer his premises as a venue for the event a few months later.

Lin continually took meticulous notes, as Sharron described the people who had been present to pay their last respects to the murdered woman; the memorial service had been well attended. Sharron had been so proud that her mother had been fondly remembered and respected by the locals that she had made a note of who had been there in her diary that evening. From the old ladies with blue-rinsed hair and retired teachers at Tracey's senior school, to respectful shop owners and the young chubby schoolgirl representing her classmates; everyone was dutifully mentioned in the list of names.

Sharron said Colin, the moustachioed landlord at the Huntsman's Arms, had introduced her to a few of the locals who were at the event. There was a scary looking bearded man called Brian; he owned a boxing gym next door to the pub. His friend, a bald headed man called Dave, ran the barber's shop and tattoo parlour upstairs. Another man called Pete, who was dressed in motorcycle leathers, ran the local bike shop. The group of men had also demonstrated warm support for another one of their friends who had just come out of rehab; he suffered from a very bad nervous tremor. She wasn't sure but his name was something like Paddy or Pat. Sharron had never met the men before but she was touched by how the local business community had rallied around to show their respects at her mother's memorial service. Sharron told Miss Tisserand that she had felt fairly comfortable in the bar of the Huntsman's Arms, until local car dealer George Dalmano had entered the room. She remembered feeling unnerved by the imposing man and she had been keen to leave the wake soon after meeting him.

Sharron said she had returned to the pub a couple of days later, to thank Colin Lawson for the memorial service arrangements and to ensure she didn't owe him any money for the refreshments. Colin had said there was no charge as George Dalmano had been more than happy to foot the bill. Sharron didn't know why the local businessman had insisted on paying and she had simply assumed it was a charitable act of kindness.

At the end of the meeting, Lin closed her notepad and got up from behind her leather-bound desk. She shook Sharron's hand warmly and thanked her for the information, before watching the well groomed middle-aged author leave the clerk's office.

Chapter 10

October 2014 – One Month Later.

The Huntsman's Arms had witnessed major changes under Colin Lawson's watchful guardianship. The once sleazy back-street boozer had been transformed into a trendy vintage seventies-themed bar called Hunter's. Gone were the mismatched wooden tables and chairs, long dark wooden bar and sticky threadbare tartan carpet from a decade before. Instead, the re-branding re-fit had brought in a long shiny mirror-backed marble counter and lava lamps. An array of multi-coloured leather bean bags and hammock chairs had been scattered artistically on a newly-laid wooden laminate floor. Large posters featuring seventies' pop stars and sporting legends adorned the freshly re-plastered walls and ceilings. It was an elegant homage to a colourfully gauche era.

The sixty-three-year-old moustachioed bar owner was undeniably proud of his achievement and he would seize any opportunity to regale his rags-to-riches tale to anyone who would listen. The stack of vintage yard-of-ale glasses still took pride of place behind the bar; they bore secret testament to Colin's rough-and-ready misspent youth.

In his earlier life, Colin had been the undisputed champion at swilling back a yard of ale in the quickest time at endless biker rallies. Colin's reputation for winning the drinking game had soon earned him the nickname 'Yardy.' However, amid all his anecdotes and tales regularly spun out to his enthralled clientele at Hunter's Bar, the Yardy nickname had always been carefully omitted. It was a small detail from his seedy past that had remained a secret for almost four decades while he built his new re-branded life.

Colin Lawson's moderate wealth and growing reputation as a wild party animal always attracted a bevy of beauties to his watering hole. They were all keen to grab any gold they could sink their manicured finger nails into. Over the years Colin had expanded his pub into a few of the neighbouring properties in the block. His swish converted loft apartment above the bar was regularly used and abused by the salacious landlord. On countless occasions its sound-proofed rooms had been the venue for seemingly endless nights of carnal debauchery; its polished marble floors and soft leather furnishings had borne witness to a depraved carousel of drinking games, drugs and sordid sex with a parade of submissive wide-eyed young women.

Now, in his autumn age, Colin was only a couple of years away from his well-earned retirement. He was beginning to enjoy winding down a little. He planned that after pulling his final pint at Hunter's he would sell the bar; pack his worldly goods into a couple of panniers and begin a whole new final adventure. He would explore all the continental pleasures of Europe from astride his Harley Davidson motorcycle. Until that long-awaited day arrived, Colin's highly polished, chrome-plated two-wheeled pride and joy sat patiently waiting in his garage. He constantly dreamed of re-living the freedom of the open road but, for the time being, Colin had a more pressing idea in his mind. How could he get into the knickers of the flame-haired young woman sat in front of him?

Angel had applied for an evening job at the newly refurbished Hunter's Bar. She was currently being interviewed in the lounge of Colin's loft apartment for the position of part-time barmaid. Angel had said she desperately needed the job since she had been made redundant when Ammo's Cycles had closed down following the owner's fatal accident a month earlier. The young woman had pulled out all the stops to impress her prospective new boss. She had thoroughly researched her potential employer and had chosen her clothes for the interview with great care. She knew men like Colin Lawson were always attracted to leather thigh boots, a deep plunging cleavage and hip-hugging jeans, and that was the look she had gone for. Angel let her waist-length red hair hang loosely beneath a bandana and large sunglasses to complement her retro biker-chick style. She knew her subtle seventies' garb would evoke powerful feelings in the randy old bar owner. He would be unable to resist her.

Colin had been instantly attracted to the beautiful red head who now sat opposite him at one end of a sumptuous leather sofa in his loft apartment. The overweight barman studied Angel's pretty face as she talked sweetly about her previous work experience; he watched every curve of her nubile body sway, as she reached into a red leather rucksack to retrieve her curriculum vitae. Colin gently stroked his seventies' Mexican porn star's moustache; slowly opening his thumb and forefinger along his top lip and running them down either side of his chin. He wasn't really listening to what the young woman sat in front of him was saying; instead he simply watched Angel's beautiful pouting lips open and close; imagining how sensual that soft chasm of loveliness would feel wrapped around his aching cock.

Lost in his own sordid fantasy, he continued to caress his caterpillar of facial hair as he looked into Angel's captivating green eyes. He was trying to visualise how arousing her terrified gaze would be, when she was forced to yield to his throbbing, hot dick. In Colin's warped mind this young fire-cracker was just another slutty biker chick who would deserve everything she had coming to her; after all, she was like all the other women he had ever known; she was gagging for it.

Following Peter Crowther's untimely death at Hanford Cross Airfield, most of the staff at his bike shop knew they would soon be out of a job, and many of them had applied for work at Hunter's. The lecherous landlord had heard all about Angel on Hanford's grapevine, and what she had been like when she worked at Ammo's Cycles. By all accounts the alluring vixen Angel had been more than willing to let the ageing Bullet give her boobs a good grope behind the counter, and she wasn't averse to the odd stock-room fumble either. Colin had met her briefly at Bullet's funeral, but she had spent most of her time talking to Brian Walsh, another old biker at the wake. Colin hadn't wanted to muscle in on his old mate Crusher's action, but his fantasy of ensnaring Angel had festered. If she had a reputation for offering it up on a plate to older men, then he would be a fool not to act on the opportunity if he ever managed to get her alone. Here was his chance. The slimy bar owner could no longer resist the beautiful woman's charm. He decided to make his move.

91

Colin clumsily lunged over and grabbed Angel's shoulders, pushing her down into the leather sofa with his rough strong hands. It wouldn't be the first time a petrified woman's screams would resonate around the sound-proofed walls of his plush loft apartment. Angel felt the unwelcome damp hairs of Colin's thick black moustache envelope her mouth as he began to kiss her hard on the lips. He started to grunt and pant as he became more aroused, safe in the knowledge that no one would hear her desperate cries; no one would hear her beg him to stop.

"Hold on, hold on, you naughty man," teased Angel, as she managed to pull one of her hands free and playfully wag a finger in Colin's face. He smiled back at her in pleasant surprise that the nubile young woman hadn't recoiled from his sudden ham-fisted advances. Colin loosened his grip of her shoulders. Angel gently pushed back and wriggled free from beneath his sweating rotund body. She rolled off the leather settee onto a cream coloured rug on the floor in front.

"Let's have a drink first," said Angel breathlessly, as she slowly crawled away from the sofa. Colin was mesmerised and excited by such an encouraging reaction from the beautiful young woman. She had definitely said a drink would be *first*. In his mind that could only mean something else would be second. *Christ Almighty, the rumours are true, she's absolutely gagging for it.* Colin couldn't believe his luck.

"After all, this is a job interview," mewed Angel, as she got up from the floor. "I'm supposed to be here to show you how good a barmaid I'll be. Let me show you how good I am at pouring drinks." Angel made her way over towards a heavily laden glass drinks trolley that stood in the corner of the room. "Now then, let me guess what your favourite poison is," she purred.

Colin remained sprawled across the sofa, totally captivated by the alluring beauty. *She really is panting for it.* Colin felt his dick tingle. She was going to be absolutely perfect, so long as he could get hard.

Slowly but surely Angel purposefully perused a collection of decanters and bottles of spirits gathered on top of the drinks trolley; a spotlessly clean yard-of-ale glass hung on the wall above. She carefully caressed each bottle in turn, seductively running her fingers up and down the glass necks.

"Tennessee Whiskey would it be by any chance?" soothed Angel as she turned away and secretly pulled a small piece of folded paper from her jeans pocket. The crude little envelope contained a couple of crushed sedative tablets inside, and it was carefully kept hidden from Colin's view. "Over Ice?" asked Angel looking back over her shoulder, as she covertly emptied the powdered drug into a cut glass whiskey tumbler.

The awe-struck bar owner nodded eagerly as he waited for the gorgeous woman to return to the sofa with his drink.

#

Detective Inspector Alexander Richens settled in behind his office desk. He had recently been promoted to his new pay grade and was making himself comfortable in a new leather swivel chair that had just been delivered to his office. He twiddled the adjustment buttons on the side of the seat for a minute, before finding the height position he liked best. Richens' office was a small square room, next door to the main CID suite, at the end of a corridor deep inside Hanford town police station. The small office was neutrally decorated with magnolia painted walls and a cream tiled floor. Two metal desks were pushed back-to-back against each other on one side of the symmetrically furnished room; two small filing cabinets squeezed into the wall space opposite. Inspector Richens shared this utilitarian space with his new deputy and right-hand-man, Detective Sergeant Jonathan Duke.

"Yo Duchess!" announced Richens as his sergeant entered the room. DS Duke hated the irreverent nickname that his boss was so fond of using. To Richens it was a term of endearment; a bit of friendly coppers' banter. To Duke it felt like a bullying hangover from the men's time spent together at Hendon Police College fifteen years before. It grated on the sergeant's nerves each time he heard it. Fortunately no one else at the station used Duke's annoyingly derisive moniker to his face, but Richens was now his senior officer and, as such, got away with many irritating habits.

93

DS Duke placed two steaming mugs of tea on Richens' desk and glanced down at his boss's laptop computer. A fatal incident report into the gruesome death of local motorbike shop owner Peter Crowther was open on the screen.

"Bit of a grisly way to meet your maker isn't it?" said Richens as he picked up his mug to blow across the top of the rim, before noisily slurping a small sip of tea from the edge. Sergeant Duke ignored his governor's irritating ritual as he read through the summary report into the old biker's death.

A local man walking his dogs had taken his daily trek over Hanford Cross Airfield. He had discovered Peter Crowther's headless body astride a crashed motorcycle in the centre of the old runway. The shocked and trembling dog walker told the police that groups of teenagers on BMX bikes regularly used the abandoned airfield and landing strip to practice acrobatics and stunt riding skills. A foolhardy and childish game played by the cyclists was called Chicken Run. This involved a wire twine being pulled taut across the track. Two opposing riders would race head-on towards the twine; whoever reached the wire first had to remember to duck beneath it to avoid being pulled from their pushbike. They would then successfully be crowned the race winner; but if they stopped short of the obstacle, then they would be deemed to be a chicken.

For the time being Inspector Richens had decided to withhold many of the horrifying details of Peter Crowther's death from the media. The local press had been quick to speculate, but he wasn't sure whether it was an accident or a deliberate act. The detective's gut instinct had been to keep the finer points of the biker's decapitation out of the press until he had more answers. Was it simply death by misadventure? Had the doddery fool stupidly failed to check that the runway was clear before charging down the centre like a bullet from a gun?

"The old timer didn't stand a chance, did he? Poor sod," muttered Richens.

Sergeant Duke returned to his own desk opposite Richens and clicked his laptop into life. The photographs from Peter Crowther's post mortem examination came into full view. After a couple of minutes Duke began to rub his open fingers over his eyelids, as if trying to wipe his memory clean of the gruesomely graphic images he had just witnessed. The full colour photo of a lifeless headless torso would be difficult for the sergeant to erase from his mind. He quickly clicked to a second image that was a close-up photograph of the dead man's chest. The sun-tanned skin was wrinkled and covered in grey chest hairs. Duke observed that Peter Crowther's physique had been quite athletic. He zoomed in to a small dark blue patch that was on the skin just above the dead man's left nipple.

"What do you reckon to this Sir?" Duke turned his screen around to face Richens. The two men scrutinised the image and read the accompanying pathology report. It described the anonymous looking image as a small faded tattoo of a unicursal hexagram, approximately three centimetres wide and two centimetres high. The old metal-based blue tattoo ink had been in the dead man's skin for many years, probably since the nineteen-sixties or seventies, suggesting he had been tattooed when he was a much younger man.

Duke continued to read through the other reports inside the forensics folder, as Richens looked at the photograph of the dead man's torso once again. The inspector was unsure of the significance of the tattoo, but he couldn't help feeling that, in the back of his deep and enquiring mind, he had seen an image just like that somewhere before.

"This is a bit strange too," announced Duke, snapping Richens out of his train of thought. A small piece of cardboard had been discovered on the body at the scene. It was an old faded card of condolence.

"It looks like the sort of thing people tie to flowers at funerals and the like," observed Richens. The front of the card had a slightly shiny finish to it and featured a faded picture of a lily. On the back a pre-printed line of text read: With deepest sympathy. Beneath, in almost illegible scrawled ballpoint pen, someone had written the word 'Bullet'. The old piece of card was scuffed around the edges. It had been found in the blood soaked breast pocket of Peter Crowther's racing leathers. Richens and Duke looked at each other quizzically, each hoping the other would be able to cast light on the significance of the unexpected find.

The initial pathologist's report suggested it was death by misadventure, although it would be up to the coroner to give an absolute verdict. Investigations at the scene had established that Peter Crowther had accelerated his powerful motorcycle on the abandoned runway at Hanford Cross Airfield. He had ridden it recklessly at full power into a steel wire that had been stretched across the airstrip between two rows of old burned out cars. The cause of death was decapitation. It was fair to assume his demise had been instantaneous. A foolhardy mistake made by an elderly thrill seeker who should have known better. Attached to the bottom of the document was a coroner's court inquest form. It asked the police to officially confirm whether or not they had any evidence to suggest the circumstances surrounding the death were suspicious. Duke closed the file, clicked away the forensics folder and shut down his laptop. His boss would send the coroner his considered reply in the morning.

#

Colin Lawson groggily opened his sore eyes. His mouth was dry; his tongue felt like a rasping piece of sandpaper helplessly trying to moisten his cracked, arid lips. Slowly he raised his heavy head up off his chest, to bring himself around from his drug-induced sleep. He blinked his eyes several times and shook his head in a vain attempt to escape the reality of the menacing scene unfolding before him.

The licentious landlord had been tethered to a kitchen chair. Metres of duct tape held his arms securely at his sides; more strips bound his legs to the chair. His whole rotund body had been encased in sticky silver tape. He looked like a baby elephant that had been tightly wrapped in swaddling clothes; his movements were totally restricted. Angel sat at the end of the leather sofa opposite her bewildered prey; watching every movement on his moustachioed face.

"You're awake then? Yardy," she said coldly. Colin opened his eyes wide with shock and stared back at the young woman.

"What the fuck is this?" he shouted. *And how the fuck does she know my old gang nickname?* He felt a wave of panic knot deep inside his stomach.

96

Angel kept her gaze firmly on the frightened man's face, as she purposefully opened her leather rucksack in front of him and pulled out a small decanting funnel and a new roll of duct tape.

"Let me the fuck out of here, bitch!" Colin furiously wriggled on the kitchen chair. He could only imagine what excruciating abuse she was going to inflict on him with her instruments of torture.

Angel calmly got up off the settee and walked behind the angry bar owner as he continued to shout and scream at his captor. He was utterly powerless to pull free of the sticky silver-coloured bindings.

"Would you like another drink then? Yardy?" whispered Angel menacingly as she stood behind her scared quarry.

"Let me out of here now, you fucking bitch," he spat.

Angel snapped on a pair of latex gloves before deftly ripping off a new piece of duct tape to place over Colin's nostrils. The terrified man instinctively opened his mouth and began to pant frantically.

"You can't do this! You can't do this, you stupid bint." The knot of fear in Colin's stomach crawled through the muscles in his lower body.

"I think you'll find that I can," smiled Angel as she bent down next to the panic-stricken man and breathed into his ear. "Just ask your friend Bullet what I'm capable of."

Colin felt the sudden heat of his bowels loosen in the stinging realisation that he was going to die. With one well-rehearsed manoeuvre Angel put her left arm around Colin's neck. She held his chin in the crook of her elbow and forced his head back, pulling him and the kitchen chair downwards onto the marble tiled floor with an un-relenting crash. Angel mounted Colin's tethered torso and plunged the funnel into his gasping mouth. She squeezed his flushed cheeks together to seal his moustachioed lips around the plastic tube. Angel kept a tight hold of her tethered quarry's face; her captivating green eyes flashed menacingly as she began to pour a bottle of neat Tennessee whiskey into the funnel. Colin began to choke on the liquid as it burned down the back of his throat; he shook his head in a vain attempt to escape Angel's firm grasp. He tried to roll his rotund strapped body from side-to-side, but his bid to escape was futile. Angel calmly gripped her fingers tighter around Colin's lips, and pushed the funnel deeper inside his mouth. He gurgled and twitched as the unstoppable stinging flood of whiskey continued to wash down his gullet.

Colin tried to push away on the floor and furiously shook his head in a desperate attempt to dislodge the plastic tube from his mouth; but Angel remained astride his chest and firmly pulled her knees together to tighten her grip. His thick black caterpillar of facial hair was now dripping with sweat and saliva as Angel carried on, relentlessly pouring a second bottle of whiskey into the back of the bar owner's throat. The more violently he swayed on the floor, the firmer her grasp became. There was no escape as he started to choke on a torrent of vomit that began to rise from the pit of his stomach.

The hazy sight of Angel's ample cleavage and her curtain of long curly red hair swaying over his face was the last thing Colin saw through his petrified, tear-filled eyes. His poisoned body gave one last convulsed jerk as he took his final drowning breath.

Yardy was dead.

Angel carefully cut Colin's limp body from the duct tape bindings that tethered him to the kitchen chair; his dead weight slumped over onto the plush cream rug in the centre of the lounge floor. The young woman took a pack of cleaning cloths and a bottle of concentrated solvent cleaner from her leather rucksack. Next she removed Colin's T-shirt and jeans before soaking one of the cleaning cloths in the solvent; she began to carefully wipe away all traces of sticky duct tape from the skin on Colin's arms and the kitchen chair.

Colin had been forced to swallow almost two bottles of neat whiskey; the young woman had thought it a fitting send off for the lecherous hard-drinking Yardy. Angel took the yard-of-ale glass from the wall above the drinks trolley and poured the remaining dregs of Tennessee Whiskey out of the second bottle into the bottom of the yard glass. She swished the dark golden liquid around inside the bulb at the end of the tube, before placing the long vessel in Colin's cold, dead hands. She firmly pressed the rim of the glass between his blue lifeless lips, before allowing it to roll over his rotund torso and fall casually at his side.

Angel took a used wineglass from her rucksack and placed it on the rug in front of the leather sofa. She had taken the glass from a table in the bar downstairs earlier; a clever move she thought, that would add confusion to the crime scene as it carried an unknown woman's DNA and finger prints. Next Angel gathered up Colin's sweaty T-shirt and soiled jeans and stuffed them into her rucksack with the discarded duct tape, empty solvent bottle and cleaning cloths. Finally, she carefully washed away all traces of the sedative from the cut glass whiskey tumbler, wiped her fingerprints off the decanters and spirits bottles on the drinks trolley and returned the kitchen chair to its rightful place beneath the breakfast bar. With all of her belongings safely stowed inside her bag, Angel checked her appearance in the hall mirror and let herself out of the apartment. She pulled off her latex gloves and smiled a satisfied smile, as she made her way out towards the stairwell. She was happy in the knowledge that Colin's frantic cries would be the last petrified screams to be heard within the sound-proofed walls of the landlord's sumptuous loft apartment. Angel was pleased she had sent Yardy's evil lecherous soul crawling through the gates of hell.

Chapter 11

The Next Day.

Inspector Richens and Sergeant Duke stood in the lounge of Colin Lawson's loft apartment. Both men were trying hard to ignore the overwhelming smell of faeces; they held thick cotton handkerchiefs up to their noses in a vain attempt to hold the stench at bay. The bar owner's lifeless body had been discovered at nine o'clock in the morning by Mildred Brown, his unsuspecting cleaner. She told the detectives when she had first arrived for work she assumed her employer was asleep in one of his regular drunken stupors. It was quite normal for him to crash out in his underpants on a sofa in the lounge after one of his all night party sessions. When Mrs Brown had entered the apartment that morning she had seen Colin was laid out on the floor in the lounge; she had called out his name a few times before walking over to try and wake him up. She had noticed a pungent whiff in the air, as if someone had suffered a bad case of Diarrhoea. She said she had never known Colin to *shit himself* before, and it was only when she had touched him and felt the coldness of his stiff chest that she realised he was dead. Mildred shakily said she had dialled nine-nine-nine immediately and then gone outside for a cigarette to calm her nerves while she waited for the police and paramedics to arrive.

Sergeant Duke held his breath as he frantically wrote down Mildred's gabbling account, while Inspector Richens cast his steely gaze over the unexplained death scene. At first glance it appeared to be a drinking game that had gone badly wrong for Colin Lawson. The dead man's half naked body lay on the floor on top of a large cream coloured rug; a yard-of-ale glass at his side contained a few dregs of liquid that smelled like whiskey inside. Two empty bottles of Tennessee whiskey lay nearby.

Richens quickly tested a couple of probable theories in his own mind to try and establish what had led to Colin's death. *Would this man have stupidly drunk a yard of spirits showing off in a drinking game and expect to survive? Or maybe it was suicide?*

"Is this exactly how everything was when you first turned up this morning," asked Richens, still scrutinising every detail of the room.

"Yes," replied Mildred. "I ain't not moved nothin' officer."

Richens winced at the ill-educated woman's lack of good grammar and pronunciation.

"Is this how the flat normally looks? I mean nothing looks like it's out of place or missing?"

Mildred thought for a few seconds, her mouth scrunched up to beneath her nose; the smoker's crevices above her top lip pulled together like a concertina as she gazed around the room.

"I can't see anyfink's missing," she offered. "In fact it looks a right load tidier than what it normally does after one of Colin's parties."

Mildred explained that she regularly found the apartment in utter disarray after her employer had spent the evening entertaining young ladies. Many of her mornings were spent washing up champagne flutes or wineglasses and emptying dozens of take-away cartons into plastic bin liners, whilst giggling groups of naked young women darted about the apartment trying to retrieve their previously discarded underwear. But that morning Colin had been found alone in the flat. There was only the yard-of-ale glass and one wineglass to wash up, nothing else was out of place and everything else in the apartment seemed immaculate; everything except for the bad smell and lifeless corpse lying on the lounge rug.

"Can I let a bit of fresh air in 'ere? 'cos it don't half stink," asked Mildred as she made her way towards a set of balcony doors to open them up.

"No!" shouted Richens and Duke. Despite the overwhelming odour, both men were mindful how a refreshing breeze could send crucial evidence literally flying out of the window before SOCO had a chance to gather all of the evidence. Neither man wanted to suffer the wrath of the pathologist or be held responsible for any contamination of the scene.

Sergeant Duke bent down to carefully inspect the used wineglass that had been left near to Colin's body. He noticed a faint smear of pink lipstick was smudged around the rim.

"It looks like the victim had female company last night then sir," said Duke.

"Maybe," replied Richens, deep in thought. "Log it for SOCO to bag up and get it off to the lab. You can check later if there are any prints or DNA that turn up anyone we know . . ." Richens' voice trailed off, as he suddenly spotted something on the dead man's body. It was a small faded tattoo of a unicursal hexagram, approximately three centimetres wide and two centimetres high, located just above the dead man's left nipple.

#

Lin Tisserand had spent most of the previous evening typing up the very detailed hand written notes she had taken during her meeting with Sharron Chambers. During the past month, she had carefully scrutinised every facet of her informative conversation with the murder victim's daughter. It was now time to update the office case files with the list of names of people who had been at Tracey Chambers' memorial service.

Another line of enquiry that the legal intern had been keen to follow up was if there were any records at the Land Registry office that confirmed the existence of the bikers' old clubhouse in Anglesey Street. Furthermore, if the property had existed, who had owned it forty years previously? So far, she had received no reply from the records office. She had found a clerk who was willing to manually search through the hundreds of historic files for her, however, such a task would be extremely time-consuming. Lin knew she would have to be patient, but time was a luxury her client was running out of.

It had been a long late night, followed by a particularly tiresome journey into work that morning, which had seen the law student battle through driving rain and a queuing snake of stop-start traffic. The young woman now sat in her office before the official start of her working day and uploaded her file to the company's network PC. She hovered over the icon on the computer's desktop screen to open up a folder and check that her document had copied over successfully.

Lin noticed a new pdf scan had been added to the folder by one of the legal secretaries the previous evening. The scanned image was a copy of Tracey Chambers' original pathologist's report; the one that had been written at the time of the first examination of the human remains discovered at Himley Chase. Lin yawned loudly, as she lazily clicked the pdf file to open it up and check if the scan quality was clear enough; she knew from bitter past experience that some legal secretaries were not as diligent as her when it came to scanning in archived material.

The eagle-eyed trainee solicitor read through the scanned A4 pages, the typed text was clearly visible. Then, quite by chance, Lin noticed what appeared to be a series of shorthand marks written in faded pencil, jotted at the bottom of the second page of the forensic report. The scan wasn't very clear and the faint abbreviated notes were difficult to read at first glance. Lin quickly adjusted the brightness and contrast of the computer screen display, in an attempt to make the faded pencil-written symbols appear more clearly. Slowly, after a couple of focussed adjustments, the marks came into view. It was a lab technician's note of their observations.

The young law student recognised the symbols instantly. She had learned shorthand during her time at college which had enabled her to take more descriptive notes during legal seminars at university. Although she had used it as an invaluable tool for recording detailed information during lectures, the ever efficient Lin Tisserand could never have imagined how useful such an old fashioned secretarial skill would be in later life. She picked up a pen and a piece of paper and began to translate the wiggly lines, dots and abbreviations jotted down by the lab technician. It was an unexpected piece of information that mentioned the condition of the clothing found on Tracey Chambers' dead body; most importantly it failed to mention the presence of any urine.

"That means the urine may have only been present on the tarpaulin sheet," gasped Lin. The excited law student flicked back a chunk of her glossy blue-black fringe that persistently fell over her eyes, before she raised a triumphant fist into the air.

The important point about the absence of urine on the murder victim's clothes had not been noticed by Godfrey Hathergood; the lab assistant's shorthand notes had never been typed up, consequentially they had been completely overlooked and dismissed as scribble. The point was never raised by William's defence barrister at the time of his trial. Lin realised it was a piece of new evidence that could be used to significantly speed up William's appeal application. In the midst of that miserable damp morning, surrounded by leather-bound desks and dusty antique books, Lin had discovered a crucial piece of information that could lead to William Weber's conviction being over-turned. It could prove that Billy's urine was on the tarpaulin long before the canvas sheet was wrapped around Tracey Chambers' body. This could corroborate William's explanation for how his DNA had got there; it would demonstrate that what he had said in court about his initiation into the Serpent Sons of Thelema had been true.

#

Inspector Richens and Sergeant Duke sat opposite each other in their small magnolia painted office at Hanford town police station. Sergeant Duke's laptop computer was positioned in between the two men, astride a small gap where their metal desks backed onto one another. The detectives were carefully scrutinising the grainy CCTV footage taken from the communal landing and stairwell that led to Colin Lawson's loft apartment. They noticed the bar owner had entered his apartment at approximately eight p.m. the previous evening. He had been accompanied by a woman with long curly red hair. She had carried a red leather rucksack and wore seventies' vintage style clothing, a bandana, large sunglasses and a red leather tasselled biker's jacket. The footage showed the woman leave the building three hours later. She had appeared to be drunk as she staggered out of the apartment and down the stairwell.

"She looks pretty plastered whoever she is," commented Duke as Richens paused the CCTV recording.

"Do you reckon so Duchess, or is she just pretending?" asked Richens. "It could be a drinking sex game gone wrong, but I've got a funny feeling it could be something else." Richens continued to stare at the paused screen. Slowly the inspector took in a deep breath and brought the palms of his hands together. He raised his index fingers towards the fine pointed tip of his thin nose and tucked both of his thumbs beneath his bristled chiselled chin. Duke watched his boss adopt the same infamous pose inherited from his predecessor Inspector Chiltern; a tribute stance that would now become affectionately known at the station as Richens' prayer pose.

The two men were trying to find any clue to the mystery woman's identity from the CCTV footage, but it had been a largely fruitless exercise. Her face was obscured by a pair of large retro sunglasses; neither man could make out any distinguishing features. Her biker's jacket obscured the shape of her frame. Sergeant Duke was working on the theory that she was Colin Lawson's latest squeeze and the ageing bar owner had taken her back to his apartment for drinks.

"Maybe he thought pulling out his yard-of-ale party piece would impress her?" said Duke.

"Yeah, but an experienced landlord like Lawson would have known it's deadly to play that game with spirits," replied Richens dismissively. The inspector opened up his own laptop screen and began scrolling through a collection of pathology files in Colin Lawson's case notes. There was something nagging at the back of his mind; a mental itch that he just couldn't scratch. There was something that just didn't fit.

"Hold on a second! Here's something that puts a whole new light on the case," said Richens. Duke looked quizzically across the desk at his boss as he saw the inspector's mouth motion the word he was reading off the screen for the second time; as if practising the pronunciation in his head.

"Flunitrazepam!" exclaimed Richens.

"What?" queried his young sergeant, resisting the childish urge to say *bless you*. "Do you mean a date-rape drug like Rohypnol or something?"

"Yes! Exactly that." Richens was thankful that his sergeant was taking the case seriously and had refrained from cracking an immature joke about sneezing. "It says here they found traces of Flunitrazepam in Lawson's blood. So we can assume our Miss Scarlet isn't as innocent as one might assume."

A tidal wave of scenarios ran through the inspector's analytical mind as to how Colin Lawson would have been incapacitated and then forced to swallow nearly two bottles of neat whiskey. *I guess a tranquiliser would be the only way a small woman like Miss Scarlet could over-power a burly bloke like him?* Richens read through the remainder of the pathologist's examination notes searching for any other unexpected findings, before returning to the forensic scene of crime report.

"It says in the file that only the DNA and fingerprints belonging to the victim were found on the yard-of-ale glass, no one else's."

"Right," responded Duke, trying desperately to come up to speed.

"So, if the mystery woman didn't drink anything from the yard glass it wouldn't be a proper drinking game would it?" probed Richens. Duke was still none the wiser.

"Maybe she doesn't like whiskey?" offered the bemused sergeant.

"Look here, Duchess." Richens impatiently tapped his ballpoint pen on the plasma screen. "The only other used glass found in the apartment is one wineglass that had smudges of lipstick and a set of as yet unidentified prints on it." Richens looked questioningly at Duke, like a headmaster scolding an errant schoolboy.

"But . . . what else did we discover?" urged Richens, hoping his prodigy would grasp his train of thought. "There was no bottle in the flat that contained the same house wine as the dregs in the glass, and his cleaner told me he never had cheap plonk upstairs." The whole scenario that had so clearly shot through Richens' enquiring mind slowly began to filter into Duke's brain.

"So Miss Scarlet arrives at eight p.m. looking sober; leaves a few hours later looking smashed, but obviously hasn't drunk anything else or taken part in the yard-of-ale contest in between," surmised Duke.

"Yes, finally, you've got it in one!" agreed Richens a little sarcastically. "She wasn't carrying a drink with her when she arrived at the apartment either, and the glass only contained wine from the bar downstairs, so that's why I reckon the wineglass wasn't hers but one she just planted there to put us off the scent."

"Maybe she took her own wine in her rucksack?" offered Duke.

"Nah, I don't buy it," replied Richens. "Who would take their own booze to a pub?"

The DNA and finger prints found on the wineglass didn't match any others found anywhere else in the flat and Lawson's apartment had been meticulously cleaned. Those facts had aroused Richens' suspicions, and he now firmly believed the wineglass had been deliberately planted. Mildred Brown had confirmed she hadn't done any housework on the morning when Colin's body had been discovered, yet the flat had been spotless; even the empty whiskey bottles had all been wiped clean. The inspector believed any young woman who had been drinking inside the apartment for three hours would probably have needed to use the bathroom at some point and she would have left her prints on a door handle or surface somewhere. An innocent, seemingly drunken woman would not have bothered to wipe all of the surfaces, booze bottles and door handles clean with solvent. Additionally, Colin Lawson would not have needed to be given a date rape drug to get him to comply. His licentious reputation suggested he would have been more than willing and able to take part in any sex game that had been offered; so he must have been incapacitated with the sedative for another reason.

It was becoming clear to the two detectives that the crime had not been committed on the spur of the moment. Whoever helped the lecherous landlord to meet his maker must have had some pretty cold-hearted reason to plan the whole thing. Sergeant Duke opened the folder containing the photographs that had been taken at the scene.

"Do you remember this too?" Duke showed Richens a photograph of Colin Lawson's chest and zoomed in to the small faded tattoo of a unicursal hexagram just above the dead man's left nipple.

"Yes!" exclaimed Richens, thoughts sparking through his brain. "Yes! That's the same as that thing on the headless biker's chest. Do you remember I said at the time that I'd seen something like that before?" The perplexed sergeant shook his head.

"Well Duchess, I've also just remembered where I saw it the first time." Duke looked at his boss quizzically.

"I worked the Tracey Chambers' murder case about ten years ago with old Chiltern, and that same shape was embroidered on a scarf that was found among the dead woman's remains," Richens announced triumphantly. He was relieved he had been able to scratch at least one mental itch today.

"Also," added Duke a little dismissively of his boss's new revelation and slightly riled by his interruption. "You'll never guess what else SOCO found in Colin Lawson's apartment." Duke opened up another image on the screen.

When Colin Lawson's dead body had been discovered, it was dressed only in a pair of soiled boxer shorts. The T-shirt and jeans he had been seen wearing in the CCTV were missing. A small piece of card had been tucked inside the waistband of the victim's booze soaked underpants. On the front of the card was a faded picture of a lily. On the back a pre-printed line of text read: With deepest sympathy. Beneath, in scruffily scrawled ballpoint pen, was the word 'Yardy'.

Colin Lawson's death was most definitely suspicious and the discovery of a condolence card on a second body made Richens believe it was almost certainly connected to Peter Crowther's earlier misadventure. The small thing that had been niggling at the back of Inspector Richens' mind raised up to teasingly slap the forefront of his brain. Richens had a new bothersome mental itch that desperately needed to be scratched. *How were the words Bullet and Yardy connected to the dead men? What did they mean?* Was someone taunting the inspector with the start of an elaborate word game? Richens knew the words together rang a distant bell in his memory but he couldn't quite put his finger on why.

\#

Lin Tisserand was curled up on a sofa in her living room; her trusty laptop computer lay open beside her. She was busily checking the typed-up report she had written from the notes taken during her meeting with Sharron Chambers. The young law student momentarily flicked her eyes up at a plasma TV that hung on the wall opposite to read the scrolling tape that danced across the bottom of the screen. The early evening regional news report was covering a breaking story. Local businessman Colin Lawson, the owner of Hunter's Bar, had been found dead in his loft apartment. His death was reported as being unexplained while police investigations were ongoing.

Lin picked up her laptop and looked at the list of the people Sharron has said attended Tracey Chambers' wake. It was probably going to be a long shot that any of them would have anything helpful to say. It was doubtful that Tracey's teachers or customers from the hairdressers would have known if Tracey had been in a biker gang all those years ago. But Lin was prepared to track down anyone who had known the young gym-slip mum when she was alive, as talking to them could give her a little more insight into what Tracey had been like as a person.

There was a separate window open on her laptop screen that had a short list of names that the trainee solicitor had intended to follow up. Slowly, Lin drew her cursor over the document and deleted Colin Lawson's name from the top of the list. That was one avenue of information that she could no longer visit.

Deep in thought, she picked up a ballpoint pen and aimlessly began to chew the end of it. Following the deaths of Peter Crowther and Colin Lawson she was quickly running out of people she wanted to talk to about the Tracey Chambers case. Two of the men from the dead woman's memorial service had both passed away recently. Lin hoped that the scary looking bearded man called Brian Walsh was still alive and still owned the boxing gym that was now down the road from Colin Lawson's pub. Lin wondered if Sharron's ten-year-old hazy recollections of her encounters at the Huntsman's Arms had been accurate. Had she given the information to anyone else and could Sharron's memory of those names have any bearing on the two recent deaths? She wondered if the police were also aware of the list of names.

#

Sharron Chambers picked up a pair of long-nosed scissors and carefully clipped around an article in her local newspaper. It was a report about the demise of Colin Lawson. A suspicious death was a rare event in the town and the Hanford Recorder's front page had been dominated by the story. Photographs and feature articles about the late landlord's business had been carried over onto a few pages inside. His legendary sex parties had been swiftly re-branded and were reverently described as fundraising events for local charities. Many of Hunter's regulars had taken to social media to offer their condolences to the benevolent bar owner's family and friends. A collection of their tributes were printed at the end of the article.

Following her meeting with Miss Tisserand, Sharron had realised if William Weber's conviction was overturned, then it would open up a new avenue of inquiry into her mother's murder. Doubt could be cast over the substance of her autobiography if Billy's courtroom account of the Serpent Sons of Thelema was proved to be correct. Her mother would no longer be regarded as a blameless young girl lured to the woods and slain by an evil spurned stalker; consequentially Sharron would lose her reputation as being the innocent orphaned child of the woman murdered at Himley Chase. Instead, the media could quickly re-cast her as the vengeful daughter of a biker slut from hell. She needed a back up plan should that unthinkable scenario happen.

Sharron's enquiring mind had been ignited by Lin Tisserand's interest in the mourners at her mother's funeral. Did the legal advocate think any of them were involved with Tracey's murder? Memories of the group of local businessmen sat at the end of the bar in the Huntsman's Arms had flooded through Sharron's brain. When reports of Peter Crowther's accident and Colin Lawson's death appeared in the news, she recognised their names as being two of the men who had been at her mother's wake.

Sharron smiled as she carefully placed her newspaper cuttings about the lecherous landlord's death inside an A4 cellophane wallet. She opened a large ring binder and clipped it safely inside, next to a collection of articles about the bike shop owner's accident. Their deaths may have appeared to be unconnected, but the middle-aged author decided she would build her own dossier in anticipation of a juicy sequel to her autobiography.

Chapter 12

George Dalmano relaxed in the private sanctuary of his plush car sales office. He sat in an oversized leather swivel chair, behind a curved walnut cantilever desk. An espresso machine purred seductively in the corner of the room, as the imposing businessman waited for his morning cup of coffee to brew. George was a smartly dressed man, donning a double-breasted blue pinstriped suit over a pale-pink elegantly tailored shirt. He wore his glossy mane of silvery-grey hair in a sleek ponytail. Three diamond-encrusted platinum rings were majestically displayed on his fingers. Cocooned in a sanctuary of decadent soft leather and beautiful dark, rich wood, George Dalmano took a sip of his first cappuccino of the day. As he savoured the rich flavour of creamy coffee dancing across his taste buds, he looked through a sparkling plate glass window to proudly survey the activity in his sumptuous car showroom.

A fleet of expensive shiny limousines bathed in shafts of coloured rays from overhead recessed halogen lamps. Speckles of light danced on the gleaming bonnets of Jaguars, Aston Martins and Mercedes cars, before cascading onto the highly polished Italian stone floor beneath. George allowed himself a small self-satisfied smile as he watched his gaggle of competing car salesmen hover around the showroom's water cooler. They all jostled for pole position, eagerly waiting to pounce on the next wealthy customer to enter their domain.

Suddenly, George's attention was drawn towards a small scruffy elderly man who had burst into the car dealership through a pair of highly reflective glass doors. The unwelcome visitor was dressed in tatty drainpipe trousers and an old grey trench coat, the collar was turned up to cover the back of his heavily tattooed neck. He had greased-back white hair that fell into a messy fifties' D.A. style. The bony fretful Teddy Boy strode past the group of salesmen and hurriedly made his way towards their boss's office. George Dalmano's haven of peace and tranquillity was about to be rudely interrupted by a frantic Patrick O'Doyle; the piece of low-life drug-pedalling scum who was well-known to the businessman as Zombie.

"They've killed Yardy," shouted Patrick. "First Bullet and now Yardy," he rambled, as George opened his office door and quickly ushered the trembling man inside.

"Calm the fuck down," shouted George, as he returned to sit behind his desk. "Just get a grip of yourself and tell me, calmly, what the fuck has happened?" He took a large glug of his cappuccino to prepare himself for what Patrick had to say, as the bony frail visitor reached a trembling hand into his coat pocket to retrieve his tobacco tin. George patiently watched the weasel of an old man hastily roll a matchstick-thin joint between his skeletal fingers.

Years of drug-fuelled street deals had taken their toll on Patrick. Sallow skin hugged the sunken features of his tired face. George couldn't help but notice the biker's weak body had withered to an emaciated shadow of a man; his spindly drainpipe legs looked as if they may shatter beneath the weight of his trench coat when he walked. Patrick sat down and lit his cigarette, spitting out a tiny piece of tobacco that had escaped from the end of the spidery spliff. George's piercing blue eyes burned into Patrick's quivering gaze, as he reached into one of the drawers of his walnut desk to pull out an old glass ashtray. In disgust at the sight of the dishevelled old Teddy Boy sat before him, George slid the ashtray across the desk towards the shaking man.

"What the fuck has happened to you, Zombie?" asked George. "You're back on that Columbian powdered shit again, aren't you?"

Patrick had no answer. Instead he remained seated, shivering silently in the corner of the sales office; he was grateful for the small opportunity to give his weary bones a rest in the comforting aromatic leather of an office chair. George took in a deep purposeful breath, catching an unwelcome whiff of his visitor's stale body odour. He locked his steely glare onto Patrick's sallow face and shook his head. The suited businessman could feel a deep torrent of anger begin to build within his veins. He could hold back no longer.

"Right you little twat," he began his tirade, a startled Patrick shot back into his chair.

"Stop being so fucking paranoid Zombie. Have you been taking your meds?" George's steely-blue eyes locked onto Patrick's tearful stare; his visitor's skeletal body began to tremble in the chair.

"Fucking hell Zombie, I've lost count of the number of times I've paid good money to get you sorted out and off that shit, so the least I can expect is a bit of fucking respect from you." The car dealer was incandescent with rage, his voice menacingly loud. "But instead you swan in here shouting the odds about a couple of old-time losers, as if it's got fuck all to do with me." George arose from his leather swivel chair. "Go home Patrick." The businessman strode out from behind his desk. "Take your fucking stinking carcass and shitty tin of weed back to your squalid little shit-hole flat and wait for me to call you."

Patrick was petrified by the outburst. He could smell George's hot coffee breath crawl across his face, as the angry man grabbed the collar of his trench coat to drag his bony body out of the chair.

"In the meantime keep your fucking scrawny junkie's arse out of my showroom, you snivelling little cretin," screamed George as he roughly shoved Patrick towards the office door.

Three of George Dalmano's salesmen had heard the commotion that was quickly escalating behind the plate glass window. They swiftly ran to their boss's aid. A couple of the men sprung the door open and pulled Patrick out of the office; his feet barely touched the shiny stone floor beneath him, as they dragged the weak old man through the showroom. The three burly salesmen ejected the fragile bag of bones out onto the street and firmly closed the highly polished doors behind him.

George returned to his office desk and sat back down in his leather chair. He picked up his mobile phone and angrily punched in a saved number. The businessman decided Patrick O'Doyle had become a liability. Zombie was a loose tongued coke-head that could jeopardise everything George had worked for. The drug-pedalling waste of space would have to be dealt with once and for all.

#

114

Early November 2014 – One Month Later.

Brian Walsh flexed his taut muscles; he was admiring the reflection of his ageing six-pack in a full-length mirror in his deserted gym. He always preferred to exercise alone. His skin was leathery following too many sessions on a sun bed, but he had kept himself in good shape. Brian had a cleanly waxed chest and the muscles in his powerful arms and legs were well defined. His whole body was toned and moisturised, ready for any action. A small pair of tight Lycra gym shorts held his twitching hard buttocks firmly in place as he practised a few moves in front of the mirror. Images of oiled sculpted bodies and steroid-pumped men filled dozens of posters that adorned the walls of his gym. Brian turned and posed to emulate the models' pectoral perfection. The sixty-eight-year-old gym owner looked at a clock on the wall to check the time. He smiled widely in anticipation of how he had planned the evening would progress. He was still able to pull the birds, and tonight he was determined he would be flexing more than his biceps when his latest fuck-buddy arrived.

Brian had met his latest squeeze, a sexy little shop assistant with long red hair called Angel, at Bullet's funeral. She had cried convincingly at the dead biker's graveside as she watched the coffin lower into a pit in the ground. She had taken refuge in Brian's strong arms, as she shuddered at the tales from his friends when they discussed how Peter Crowther had decapitated himself.

The old bikers had all lamented Bullet's stupidly impetuous behaviour. He would have known Hanford Cross was used by BMX riders at weekends and they were always pulling stunts on the tarmac. Stretching a twine across the road was a favourite prank to dismount their rivals from their mountain bikes. Bullet should have checked to see if the runway on the abandoned airfield was clear before speeding away from the sprint line. The coroner had seen no other evidence to suggest anyone had intentionally caused the tragedy and she had recorded a verdict of death by misadventure.

115

Angel had been magnetically drawn towards Brian Walsh at Peter Crowther's funeral. The gym owner had worked hard to improve his personal appearance over the years. Brian's once wayward beard was now closely clipped into a smart long goatee. Following a punishing regimen in a cosmetic dentist's chair, he was now the proud owner of a full set of pearlescent veneers; his crooked tombstone teeth and bad breath were a long forgotten memory. Angel had admired how proudly Brian had stood to deliver his impromptu eulogy at Bullet's wake, as his obviously muscle-bound physique had rippled beneath a black denim shirt. The sultry temptress had known all about Brian's nasty reputation. She had endured dozens of flirtatious fumbles in Peter Crowther's stock room as the bike shop owner had been keen to impress her with tales about his old biker gang. Brian Walsh's strong love-hate tattooed hands had gesticulated wildly at the appreciative congregation at Bullet's funeral, as he regaled many entertaining anecdotes of his dearly departed friend.

"Always one for a misadventure was our Bullet," Brian had said, with all the affection expected from an old fellow gang member. "The old tosser was probably following his dick, trying to impress some stupid bint that he was still the fastest arsehole off the starting blocks." Angel had watched Brian's animated delivery as she knew his hands were the same strong love-hate hands that had once crushed the life out of a rival biker's windpipe many decades before.

Brian heard the heavy metal door to the gym swing open. He checked the clock for the time again before turning to greet Angel who was standing in the doorway. The beautiful woman wore a bosom-hugging black vest top. Brian smiled as he thought her bouncing ample breasts looked like two bowling balls desperately trying to break free from the black stretchy cotton. He noticed her left arm was sporting a new large tattoo; the image featured a string of red roses, held together with barbed wire. The ink wound around the whole sleeve of her arm. A smaller repetition of the pattern carried on up over her shoulder towards the left hand side of her neck. Angel's long slender legs donned skinny vintage blue Levi jeans that had been tucked into a pair of ridiculously high shiny-black

116

platform boots. She was wearing large plastic sunglasses with a bandana and carried a small rucksack. Her red leather tasselled biker's jacket was loosely slung over her right shoulder.

"Excellent timing," panted Brian as he gazed over at the beautiful woman. "I've just finished working out." Angel slowly pulled the solid metal door closed behind her and casually hung her rucksack and jacket on the locking door handle.

"You'll be needing a little light refreshment then?" She giggled, as she took a couple of small bottles of pre-mixed Tennessee whiskey and cola out of her bag's side pouch. She knew it was Brian's favourite tipple and she hoped that the one laced with a sedative would help her evening run as planned. The alluring young woman removed her sunglasses and bandana and placed them on top of her bag. She picked up the two drinks before seductively sashaying between various benches, cross trainers, multi-gyms and discarded dumbbells that were scattered across the sisal-carpeted floor of the gym. Finally she reached Brian Walsh's hot and sweaty enveloping hug.

"That's a nice piece of body art," he said, admiring Angel's tattoo.

"Well, it will be when I get it done properly," she purred, as she unscrewed the cap off one of the bottles of whiskey and cola and passed it to him. "It's just a fake tattoo at the moment, until I get used to it being there."

Brian grabbed the drink from her but immediately put it down on the floor before drawing Angel into his bare, cleanly waxed chest. His huge muscular hands gripped around her tiny waist as he breathed in the young woman's heady perfume. He felt her delicately scented body tremble slightly beneath her plunging black vest top, as he stroked his strong fingers teasingly up and down her spine. Angel felt powerless as his strong thumbs quickly reached beneath her T-shirt. Brian's rough muscular fingers pulled at the cotton material, swiftly lifting the vest upwards to expose the full roundness of her braless bouncing breasts. He slapped his Lycra-clad buttocks down hard to sit astride a weights bench, as he pulled Angel

117

down onto the bench, nuzzling his scratchy goatee beard into the warm soft sanctuary of her ample cleavage.

Angel felt a sudden surge of panic rise in her chest as she quickly realised she was in danger of losing control of the situation.

"Hey, big bear, how about a drink first?" She tried to reach down for one of the bottles on the floor. *Slow down you fuckin' hairy beast, just have a drink, will you?* Her hand flailed beneath the bench aimlessly searching for the bottle, but it was no use, she could smell that the sugary spiked contents had spilled out over the carpet. Fear buzzed through her veins as she realised she would have no chance of taming Brian's ardour now.

"You ain't trying to get me drunk, are ya Sugar-Tits?" murmured Brian as he licked her nipples. "I don't need no booze to get me in the mood."

Angel felt him suddenly pull her arms up and clasp her wrists together in one of his over-sized hands. His rough nails scratched across her bosom as his other hand voraciously ripped her vest top over her head. She began to panic as the heavy weight of his sweating muscular torso pinned her down, pushing her backwards onto the bench. His strong, punishing love-hate hands tore at the small cotton garment. Angel fought back a petrified scream, she knew she had to conceal her disgust of Brian's impending sexual assault. He probably thought she was loving it, but Angel knew he would become more violent if he realised that was not the case.

He pulled Angel's wrists behind her head and tethered them to the end of an adjacent multi-gym. In hot anticipation of his next move Brian began to knead her pounding breasts. Angel took in a terrified breath as she tried to wriggle free. He hovered over his powerless quarry and pushed his hot eager tongue hard into her mouth to silence her cries. Quickly his clumsy groping fingers clawed down Angel's body towards the zip of her jeans. She froze in terror as adrenaline coursed through her body. Brian frantically grappled with a small metal button on the waistband; impatiently tearing the button hole. His cumbersome leathery fingers gripped the zipper tab and pulled it down to yank open Angel's jeans. She knew she was powerless to escape as she felt one of his strong grasping fists lift her buttocks off the bench. His other hand snatched her Levi's and panties down to her knees. Angel knew her only route to get through the ordeal alive would be to play along with his depravity. She turned her head to the side to watch the whole scene of wanton debauchery unfold in the reflection of a full height mirror.

Through tear-filled green eyes she watched as Brian roughly pulled off her platform boots. He furiously tugged her skinny jeans and lacy underwear down her slender legs, before unceremoniously discarding the clothes on the carpeted floor. Brian stood up and proudly released his hardened dick from his Lycra shorts. He forced Angel's legs astride the weights bench and bent her knees upwards. The heaving beast of muscle-bound testosterone mounted the bench; he was about to unleash the full power of his voracious member on the flame-haired temptress and there was nothing she could do to stop him.

She felt sick as his fat sweaty cock tore into her dry unyielding chasm. He was an over-sized muscular man with a wide powerful throbbing dick and all the ignorance of an over-heated rutting stag. It was useless her trying to escape. Angel knew if she wanted to survive this nightmare, then she would have to take her punishment; just like the biker slut from hell she had become.

Angel feared Brian's display of vicious lust would never end. His unflagging stamina had terrified the red-headed vixen, as his selfish heavy manhood furiously jabbed inside her for seemingly endless hours. Brian had continuously lunged and poked; jerked and panted as he repeatedly stoked her sore, burning furnace. His frantically mauling crushing hands had pummelled her breasts; his suffocating grip had felt as if his love-hate fingers would squeeze the last gasp of air out of her chest. Suddenly, his onslaught came to an abrupt halt as Angel felt him slide out of her. But the respite was short-lived; the insatiable barbarian was not finished with her yet. He swiftly stood up astride the weights bench, grasped Angel around the hips and flipped her over to face away from him. His thick leathery thumbs wrenched her buttocks apart as she felt the hot thrust and stab of his relentless cock burn inside her again.

Angel let out an uncontrollable whimper. *No! Please god, not that!*

"Ooh, you like it like that, don't ya," said Brian, proudly mistaking her cries of terror for those of arousal. "You've never had it in the back door before, have you Sugar-Tits?" From her shocked expression in the mirror he realised he was the first man ever to have explored her body in that way. "Don't tense up on me Sugar-Tits, just relax, don't be scared." He tried to calm her down. He wanted to get his pulsating cock deeper inside, but her terrified clenching resistance was making it difficult for him. In frustration, he delivered a stinging slap hard across her buttocks. "Come on, just relax bitch. I promise ya, everything will be okay."

He was wrong. Angel knew that nothing would ever be okay, ever again.

She felt his hot breath across the nape of her neck as he selfishly poked and panted, relentlessly chaffing her dry delicate skin as he bore deep inside her. Angel silently winced in agony as she anxiously prayed for the sordid session to reach its end.

#

Sergeant Duke had spent a couple of hours visiting local florists and stationery shops to see if any of them sold the same condolence cards as the ones discovered inside Peter Crowther's blood-stained leather jacket and Colin Lawson's underpants. His boss believed that if they could track down who had sold the cards, then maybe there would be some CCTV somewhere to identify who had bought them. However, the search had been fruitless as none of the shop owners recognised the design on the front of the cards. The weary policeman's final call of the day was to a small printing company tucked away on an industrial estate at the edge of town. Duke entered the reception area and walked over to a young man who was sat at a bench behind an Apple Mac.

"Hello, I'm Sergeant Duke from Hanford CID," he began, flipping open his warrant card. He noticed a small plastic badge on the young man's tee-shirt had the name Bruno engraved on it.

"So Bruno, I wondered if you could help me in identifying the design on these condolence cards?" asked Duke, as he slid a photograph of the two cards onto Bruno's desk. The young man studied the images for a few seconds before looking back up to meet Duke's stare.

"Hmm, it's nothing I recognise as being printed here I'm afraid, and I guess you've already done a reverse image look-up on the internet?" he smiled. Duke nodded proudly, as that was one of the first things he had done as part of his investigation into the cards.

"Well, the design looks quite old-fashioned to me, especially the font used for the pre-printed message on the back," said Bruno, as he took out a magnifying glass to take a closer look. "Also, depending on how good your photograph is, I'd say they've been four-colour printed which is how things used to be done in the old days."

"How can you tell?" asked Duke, intrigued by the printer's expertise.

"Well, all full-colour printing used to use what we call a four-colour process, so you'd print the yellow layer of the image first, then magenta on top, then cyan and finally black. So the sheets of card would be run through the machine four times to apply each layer of colour to make up the full colour image. Sometimes the paper wouldn't be lined up exactly on one of the runs through, so you could get blurred edges. So if you look closely enough at your photograph here, you'll see very tiny areas where the overprinted bit wasn't quite lined up properly." He handed the photograph back to the policeman. "Also, what do the fronts of the cards feel like? Are they a shiny finish or like dull cardboard?" Bruno offered his eye glass to Duke so he could take a closer look.

"It's a little bit shiny," replied Duke.

"Ah, it was probably laminated then, which was an old trick that used to be used on more expensive cards to protect the image in case it got wet in the rain." Duke jotted down a few notes. He smiled back warmly at Bruno as this was the first piece of useful information he had heard all day.

"Things do still get printed using the four-colour process, but nowadays lots of stuff like this gets laser printed instead, it just gives a much sharper result and they're cheaper to produce in small batches. Also funeral directors or florists usually include their own logo on them these days, so I reckon you could be looking at something that was printed at least ten years ago, maybe even older," added Bruno helpfully.

#

Brian Walsh drew in a long purposeful breath; the whole of his testosterone pumped body stiffened above Angel as his eyes rolled up towards the ceiling. His brutally savage rear entry had pegged his victim to the weights bench. Angel's muscles had remained tense which had given his lumbering dick a satisfyingly tighter fit. The excruciating pain was etched across Angel's face, but knowing this was the young woman's first time had only prolonged Brian's sadistic enjoyment. Brian held his gasp for a couple of seconds before letting out an almost victoriously long hot breath across the nape of the young woman's neck. He slipped out of her and flipped his tethered conquest over to lie on her back, before triumphantly slumping down onto her, as his hot sweaty waxed torso slid over Angel's chest. Brian smiled a self-satisfied smile of fulfilment and lay on top of Angel, nuzzling his face into her ample cleavage. He was totally oblivious to the denigration his violent abuse had inflicted.

The panting lothario's spent cock withered and returned to its familiar flaccid state, as his discarded quarry remained awkwardly bound to the weights bench. Unable to move beneath the hefty bulk of the dozing man that lay on top of her, Angel stared at the ceiling as silent tears streamed down her flushed face. Her whole body ached, everywhere inside of her throbbed; as a steady flow of the evil rapist's hot climatic juices began to tauntingly dribble out over her sore skin. She felt sick and desperately wanted to scream; she needed to get away. But Angel knew there would be no escape until she had fulfilled her mission.

Brian lay in selfish post coital contentment. *Those little blue pills had been worth every penny.* If only he could have captured this hot steamy session on tape. His mates down at Hunter's Bar would never believe that someone of his age had managed to pull such a fabulously willing and nubile hotty.

Brian had decided long ago that whatever happened inside his gym stayed within its mirror-clad boundaries. The dealing, the cheating, the assaults and torturous beatings, none of it could ever be witnessed outside of the shiny reflective walls; nothing could ever be captured on video tape. There would be no CCTV evidence crawling out of the woodwork to come back and bite Brian Walsh on his muscular arse. What happened in the gym would remain a secret, but Brian wished with all his heart he could have filmed this evening's particularly torrid sexual epic. In his mind he had been a prize winning stallion siring his willing fiery conquest. Unfortunately for Brian's ego, no one would ever be able to witness his performance.

Eventually Brian released Angel's tethered wrists from their bindings; her black cotton vest top had been stretched and torn beyond recognition. The elderly gym owner rolled off her and heaved his taut muscular body onto the rough scratchy carpeted floor to rest.

Angel got up off the weights bench and leaned over to pick up her discarded underwear. Her body felt heavy, her muscles still throbbed inside, the dry, chaffed skin between her legs burned and she had pins-and-needles in her arms and hands. Yet through the agony and shame of having been so brutally abused, Angel still managed to feign a small smile towards her bearded predator. She took in a deep breath, pulled on her panties and sat back down at the end of the weights bench.

Angel looked around the room and noticed a weightlifter's bar was placed on a holding rack at the opposite end of the bench. A cluster of iron weighted discs were attached to each end of the bar.

"How many of those can you lift then, big bear?" she purred, concealing her true disdain for the sweating bearded bully flopped out on the floor beneath her. *Come on you vicious bastard, get up. I'm going to teach you the lesson of your fucking life.* Angel's plan was slowly getting back on track.

"I regularly lift at least forty kilos," replied Brian proudly.

"What?" Angel pretended to be impressed by the old man's claim. "Forty kilograms? Above your head?" she goaded.

"Easy," he replied, keen to impress. "I'll show you how us old-timers do it, if you like."

Angel smiled back. *That's it, you fucking filthy rapist, come to mamma for your just desserts.*

Brian lifted his naked muscular body off the rough carpet and slid back up onto the weights bench. He pulled his legs astride the long narrow seat and lay down with his head and shoulders beneath the weightlifter's bar. His heavy flaccid dick flopped to one side. Angel climbed on top of the weakened body-builder; her long slender legs straddled his powerful thighs. Slowly Brian raised his arms and grabbed the metal bar above his head, positioning his thick leathery love-hate fingers around the pole as he took in a deep lung-expanding breath. His veins swelled into action as they pumped energy to his flexing biceps, his torso tightened in anticipation of the lift. Brian straightened his arms and raised the heavy weights bar off the supporting cradle, lifting it high into the air. Angel felt sick as his spent cock began to wriggle back into life beneath her.

"Make your willy dance for me, big bear" she giggled teasingly, as she gave a seductive flash of her captivating green eyes.

Brian obligingly strained beneath the heavy weight of the lifting bar, as he held his bulging arms straight above his head. His lumbering dick began to harden in excited anticipation of another performance. Angel peeled her aching body off Brian's sweating panting torso and moved towards the back of the bench, behind his head. Slowly she reached down and released the brake on the support frame that had held the weighted lifting bar, before purposefully wheeling the cradle just out of Brian's reach.

"Hey baby, that's not fair;" grunted Brian as his flexing muscles desperately fought to keep the heavy bar aloft.

"What do you mean it's not fair?" teased Angel as she smiled back down at the bearded man beneath her.

"Come on baby, that's enough now, let me drop it back," his voice raised in fear, as his stinging muscles began to burn. Angel bent over the man and breathed into his ear.

"What's the matter, Crusher?" she whispered. Brian's face began to redden as blood rushed through his brain at the mention of his long-abandoned nickname.

"What the fuck? I can't hold it any longer you bitch," he squealed.

"Don't worry," soothed Angel. "I'm sure Bullet and Yardy will be happy to see you on the other side."

What felt like a sudden cramping surge of electricity stung through Brian's chest and shot down his left arm. He became breathless as his biceps weakened and a crushing pain emanated across his muscular torso. He could hold on no longer. The sight of Angel's bouncing bare breasts and her mane of tousled red hair hovering above his head was the last vision Brian saw through his frightened, sweat-filled eyes. His exhausted body took in one last frantic gasp of air before his arms buckled beneath the groaning weight of the lifting bar. The hefty forty kilogram load landed forcefully across his neck, pinning his burned-out naked body to the bench.

Crusher was dead.

Angel limped over towards the door to retrieve her rucksack, before returning to stare into the lifeless open eyes of her slain predator. She summoned every ounce of pent up fury that now forged through her body, as she slapped the lifeless man's face hard with the back of her hand. Angel pulled on a pair of latex gloves and, one-by-one, carefully removed the weights from the ends of the lifting bar, before placing it back in the cradle. Next she shuffled Brian's heavy body to the far end of the weights bench. She took a couple of cleaning cloths and a bottle of concentrated surgical spirit from her bag and wiped over the area where she had been forced to lay during her terrifying ordeal. She fastidiously removed all traces of her fingerprints and sweat from the gym equipment, before dragging Brian's heavy corpse back down to the centre of the bench.

Angel was angry with herself. The evening hadn't gone exactly to plan. It was an infuriating fact that she had stupidly put herself in a vulnerable position. A small lapse in concentration had put her in danger. She had failed to incapacitate the beast and she had allowed herself to be tied up like a suckling hog, ready for Brian to wrench apart and use to fulfil his most depraved fantasies with in any way he had seen fit. The fiery-haired vixen was livid. She poured the remainder of the cleaning fluid over his lifeless genitals and furiously rubbed between the folds of his skin with a rough cloth; as if physically trying to erase the cruel memory of that evening's torment. Next, she repositioned the lifting bar across Brian's neck and replaced the weights on the ends, before gently pushing the holding cradle back into position just behind Brian's head.

She winced at the pain between her legs, as she slowly pulled on her jeans, boots and leather jacket before carefully tying the bandana on top of her head and slipping on her sunglasses. Angel gathered up Brian's Lycra gym shorts along with the rest of her own belongings and placed everything into her rucksack. She turned around to take one last look at the dead sadistic beast that lay slain across the weights bench. A small smile of consolation twitched across her lips as she walked out of the gym, leaving Brian's savage soul to rot in hell.

#

Angel arrived at her house just before ten o'clock in the evening. She ran into the hallway and hastily bolted the front door behind her. She leant her exhausted body against the door, panting with adrenaline, relieved that she had managed to reach the warm comforting sanctuary of her own home. Angel took in a deep steadying breath before pulling off her crash helmet to survey her reflection in the hall mirror. Her eyes were bloodshot from crying; her tears had dried, leaving dark track marks of mascara down her flushed hot face. The hairline around Angel's forehead was damp with sweat and a few wayward strands of hair persistently dangled over her eyes. Every muscle in her body ached; her tired legs felt as if they would collapse beneath her as she gripped onto a handrail and slowly climbed a short flight of stairs to the landing. She made her way to the

126

bathroom and switched on the shower's hot jets to full power. Angel kicked off her platform boots and removed all of her clothes, before ripping off the fake nylon sleeve tattoo that encased the top half of her left arm. Small speckled blood blisters were beginning to form on her wrists from where she had been tethered to the weights bench; two purplish-blue bruises bore testament to where Colin's brutish thumbs had dug into the delicate skin around her neck.

The tormented young woman stood in the shower cubicle and welcomed the steamy torrent of water that began to wash over her aching body. Angel filled a rough exfoliating sponge with shower cream and began to scrub all over her arms and legs; trying to expel every trace of Brian Walsh's brutal attack. But, no matter how much she scoured soap into her battered and bruised limbs, memories of the excruciating pain and terror she had endured that evening could never be washed away. She slid down to her knees onto the shower cubicle floor and began to sob uncontrollably.

Almost an hour later, Angel noticed the skin on her fingers had wrinkled from over exposure to the water, so she switched off the jets and slowly climbed out of the shower. She wrapped her hair in a towel and enveloped herself in a soft fluffy bath robe and sat down on the closed toilet seat next to the cubicle. Angel watched the last few soapy remnants wash down the drain; relieved that her body was now clear of the temporary rose and barbed wire artwork that had adorned her neck and shoulder. She began to slowly rock back and forth as fat salty tears started to fall down her flushed face. Deep down, Angel knew any attempt to remove the stench of Crusher from her sore skin was futile; the burning pain of his rutting dick inside her would be forever etched on her memory.

Chapter 13

Inspector Richens and Sergeant Duke stood at the scene of another unexplained death. Brian Walsh, an ageing fitness fanatic and owner of a popular boxing gym, had apparently been crushed by his own weight-training equipment. His lifeless body had been discovered spread-eagled and naked on a work-out bench, trapped beneath the forty kilogram weight of a lifting bar. It appeared as if the bar had landed across his neck, crushing his windpipe. The pathologist had suggested he could have suffered a fatal heart attack prior to the accident as he was an old man and it was a heavy weight to lift. A young personal trainer called Lewis Myers had found Brian's dead body when he arrived for work earlier that morning. Lewis now sat shivering on a receptionist's chair, hugging a mug of hot, strong coffee. The inspector walked out of the gymnasium and made his way towards Lewis in the foyer to ask his well-rehearsed questions.

"Was it normal for your boss to exercise alone?" began Richens.

"Yes, Mister Walsh usually waited until everyone had left the gym before he started his weights routine." The shocked young man looked back at the detective's expressionless face.

"Why was that do you think?" queried Richens.

"I don't know really. I suppose he just liked a bit of peace and quiet while he exercised." Lewis took a comforting sip of hot coffee.

"Did he normally exercise in the nude?" probed Richens. The young man looked back perplexed. He pursed his lips together and shrugged his shoulders. He knew that randy old Brian Walsh could be a bit of a pervert sometimes, but he wasn't aware of any naked gym sessions. Then again Lewis wouldn't put anything past his old egotistical boss.

Sergeant Duke beckoned over the scene of crime photographer who was busily snapping background pictures of the mirror-clad room.

"Can you get a good focus on that for me please?" asked Duke, as he pointed at a small faded tattoo of a unicursal hexagram that lay in the shrivelled skin just above Brian Walsh's left nipple. The photographer obediently began clicking away taking numerous shots of Brian's chest from various angles. Duke nodded his appreciation at the photographer.

"Did anyone take any swabs of that damp patch on the floor?" asked Richens as he came back into the room. "It smells like whiskey and cola to me which seems a bit out of place for a gym."

"Yes, I got a tech to do that earlier," replied Duke. He had also noted that there was no bottle or glass anywhere near the spilled drink.

"We must be thankful for small mercies I guess," added Richens. "At least it doesn't stink of shit like the last one." The inspector instinctively wiped his nose at the vivid memory of the pungent odour in Colin Lawson's apartment.

The pathologist had already given her permission for the body to be removed from the scene, so Duke asked a small group of police officers to help move the cadaver onto a black plastic body bag that lay opened on the floor. Brian's lifeless arms and legs flopped clumsily into the men's grasp as they carefully lifted him off the weights bench.

Suddenly something caught Duke's attention. Out of the corner of his eye he spotted a small piece of card wedged within a plastic fold on the padded seat. It had been lying beneath the body, having been flattened and crushed into the sweaty crease between Brian's prostrate buttocks. Sergeant Duke's latex-gloved hand picked up the card and he swiftly placed it into a polythene evidence bag. On the front of the card was a faded picture of a lily. On the rear, a pre-printed line of text read: With deepest sympathy. Beneath, in childish hand-written ballpoint pen was the pseudonym 'Crusher'.

#

A few days later

George Dalmano stood in a marble-lined luxury en-suite bathroom and casually picked up his mobile phone. It was the

129

fifth time in as many minutes that he had seen Patrick O'Doyle's name appear in the caller display.

"I wonder what the dozy smack head wants now?" muttered George as he dismissively pressed the decline button on the phone's screen. George flushed the lavatory and quickly washed his hands. He wasn't in the mood for baby sitting Patrick Zombie O'Doyle. George had paid good money for his five-star hotel room and he had a far more exciting proposition waiting for him between the satin sheets of the luxury king-size bed. He had just taken a little blue tablet, so whatever the paranoid Zombie wanted, it would have to wait. The businessman would eventually reply to the fretful old man's messages, but only after he had given the nubile young red head who wriggled beneath him the best fuck of her life.

George Dalmano had first met his Angel Baby when she walked through the sparkling doors of his showroom looking for a job. She had worn her red curly hair up in a sleek no-nonsense bun on the top of her head; the crowning glory to her smart red business suit and scarlet stiletto-heeled shoes. He had briefly scanned over her CV and remembered her name from Peter Crowther. How his old biker mate had crowed about his wicked red-haired temptress who worked in the shop at Ammo's Cycles. Bullet had regaled tales of how the flame-haired beauty had not been averse to the odd stock room fumble and he had firmly intended to break her in properly, as soon as the opportunity arose. George had been instantly attracted to the beautiful woman the moment she had graced the forecourt of his car dealership. He had thought how, back in the day, she would have made a perfect showroom dolly; a pretty face to lure in middle-aged men looking for a new sports car. But George had bigger plans for her. He knew Peter Crowther had never managed to get inside her knickers, and now his old friend was dead, he would take up the challenge himself.

This was the first time he had managed to get Angel all to himself and he had assumed it wouldn't be too difficult to get her into bed. The old lothario's favourite tactic was to use the opulent setting of an anonymous five-star penthouse to ensnare his conquests and impress them into submission. Today would be Angel's turn. George had become aroused by a couple of old bruises and fading friction burns he had noticed on the young woman's body while he undressed her. *So, she likes it a bit rough then.* He didn't really care what Angel had endured to get so many physical scars; he knew her emotional baggage would never be his problem. Today would be a test-drive to see how she performed in the sack. If she didn't make the grade then he knew he had a brace of other willing young ladies he could choose from, all eagerly waiting in the wings and just a simple text message away. George had no idea just how perfectly compliant his new fuck-buddy would turn out to be.

"Sparks, you gotta listen to me man . . . another one's gone Sparks, another one. First Bullet, then Yardy and now fucking Crusher man. Have you seen the news? It's your fucking ol' lady Tracey, man. She's coming for us all and I'm fucking shitting myself here. I ain't got Razor Fish's number to warn him. Come on Sparks, you've gotta help us out here man."

The fear in Zombie's frantic voicemail message was clear; the terrified coke-head had just seen the TV report of Brian Walsh's accident in his gym. The death of another member of Zombie's old biker gang, coupled with the CCTV footage of a mysterious woman seen leaving Yardy's apartment, had sent his drug-induced brain into overdrive. He was convinced that it couldn't just be a coincidence. It had to be Tracey Chambers' ghost. Zombie's building paranoia welled deep inside the pit of his stomach as he allowed his imagination to run amok. *What if she'd already got to Sparks? Who would save him now?* Patrick O'Doyle swayed restlessly back-and-forth on a hard plastic kitchen chair, hugging his trench coat into his fretful bony body, as he nervously waited for George Dalmano to return his call.

#

Sharron Chambers sat at one end of an elegant oak table in her dining room. She had carefully cut out a collection of articles about the death of local gym owner Brian Walsh. A small wry smile stretched across her lips as she remembered the large man with a bushy beard and love-hate hands who had dominated the space at the end of the bar at her mother's wake.

Sharron took out her notepad that contained a list of the names of the men who had been in Hunter's Bar that afternoon. Peter Crowther and Colin Lawson's names had small red crosses alongside. She wondered how long it would be before other names on the list would be in the news, as she placed a cross alongside Brian Walsh's name. The formation of a storyline for the sequel to her book was already beginning to take shape, but she still needed to ensure that her late mother's reputation remained in tact.

Slowly, Sharron placed the newspaper cuttings into four cellophane wallets, taking care not to crease the thin sheets of paper. Next she clipped the plastic envelopes safely inside a ring binder. They were the latest addition to her dossier on the local businessmen who had attended Tracey Chambers' memorial service.

#

Sergeant Duke sat at his desk watching a CCTV recording from Brian Walsh's gym. The young detective was highly frustrated as there had only been security footage of the foyer leading into the gymnasium; there were no recordings of any activity inside the mirror-clad exercise room. Duke returned the short burst of footage to the beginning to give it one final run through.

The grainy black-and-white video recording showed a long-haired, heavily tattooed woman enter the reception area to Brian's gym at just after six p.m. She wore sunglasses with a bandana and was dressed in a short dark vest top, jeans and platform boots. She carried a rucksack and a retro leather tasselled biker's jacket over one shoulder. The tattoo on the left hand side of her neck, shoulder and sleeve of her bare arm, featured an image that resembled roses entwined with barbed wire.

Three hours later the same woman opened the door and walked out of the gym back into the foyer. She appeared to be limping and was now wearing the vintage tasselled leather jacket zipped up over her jeans; her rucksack hung heavily between her shoulder blades, as she walked away from the camera and out through the entrance doors, before disappearing into the crowded street outside.

"What happened in between Duchess?" Inspector Richens stood behind Duke, peering over his sergeant's shoulder.

"It's hard to say sir. There's no footage from behind that door in the foyer. Apparently Lewis Myers said there were loads of rumours that the victim was into all kinds of shady stuff, and I guess it wouldn't have been good business practice to have any of his dodgy dealings turn up on a CCTV tape somewhere."

"Hmmm, that masterful plan backfired on him big time then," mused Richens.

"She does look very similar to that woman who was at Colin Lawson's apartment, although I don't remember her having a tattoo," replied Duke. "Mind you, I suppose it could have been underneath her jacket all the time? I'll do some digging around the tattoo parlours in town and see if anyone remembers creating that particular piece of body art."

Richens picked up a marker pen off Duke's desk and confidently turned to face a free-standing white incident board that had been propped against one of the metal filing cabinets. He pulled the cap off the top of the marker pen with his teeth and began to write a few notes across the freshly cleaned sheet of melamine. He started off three short columns of text by writing the names of the three recently discovered dead men across the top of the board. Beneath each of the victims' names he jotted down the corresponding pseudonym written on the cards of condolence found at the three separate scenes, along with the nature of their deaths and when the bodies had been discovered. Underneath each column, Richens tacked a small post mortem photograph of each man's chest tattoo.

The inspector drew a long horizontal line, splitting the melamine board into two sections. Beneath the line he wrote the summary descriptions of the women who had been seen at the last two scenes. Both of the women had long hair, one had been a red head; the other looked like she could have been too, but it was impossible to distinguish her colouring from the monochrome recording. Both women had been dressed in seventies' style clothes and each carried a rucksack.

"Damn this shit quality recording," shouted Duke in exasperation. "What's the point in having CCTV if you can't make out colours or people's faces clearly?"

Richens returned to sit down behind his own desk. He printed off Brian Walsh's post mortem report and another document that contained details about items discovered at the scene in the gym. He meticulously studied all the neatly printed text on the A4 sheets before him.

The pathologist had found Sildenafil Citrate in Brian Walsh's body. The report suggested that the gym owner may have used the drug to enhance his sexual performance and it could have contributed to his fatal heart attack. Consequentially his windpipe had then been crushed by the weightlifter's bar when it had fallen across his neck.

"There's no chance of him needing to be knocked out by a date-rape drug then. Sounds like he'd have been well up for any sexual encounter, especially if he'd taken a little blue soldier to help him get his strength up," observed Duke.

"You're right," agreed Richens. "There was no trace of any date-rape drug in his body, but interestingly you know that sticky brown carpet stain that you asked someone to take a sample of? Well, the lab found Flunitrazepam in it." Richens gave his prodigy a nod of appreciation, it was a small reward for his quick thinking at the scene. Although both men knew that the whiskey and cola had been out of place at the gym, neither of them could work out how the spiked drink featured in the scenario.

Richens and Duke stared blankly at the reports, re-reading every line. No trace of the mysterious woman had been found anywhere inside the room; she had meticulously covered her tracks extremely well. The gym equipment and weights bench where Brian's body had been found had been wiped down with solvent cleaner.

"Well Duchess," began Richens as he faced his young sergeant sat at the opposite desk. "Just like the woman who had been in Colin Lawson's apartment during the bar owner's final hours, the woman at Brian Walsh's gym didn't forensically exist either."

The pathologist had reported an unusually high trace of isopropyl alcohol on Brian Walsh's body. She had concluded the victim's genitals must have been soaked in the cleaning fluid.

"That was hopefully done post mortem," suggested Richens, wincing at the thought of how much such an act would sting his skin. "I know he was a bit of a pervert, but surely no bloke would willingly stick his cock into a jar of surgical spirit, would he?"

Duke's mind began to race. He remembered reading that chemical's name somewhere before. Richens stood up and stepped back over to the incident board to make a note of the unusual finding underneath Brian's name.

"Hold on sir," interrupted Duke. "It says here in Colin Lawson's post mortem report that a cleaning solvent was present on his body and on the waistband of his underpants," Duke tapped his ballpoint pen on his laptop screen.

The fact that alcohol had been discovered on Colin Lawson's underwear had gone largely unnoticed by the two detectives; after all, the pathologist's report had concluded that the bar owner's death had been caused by alcohol induced vomit aspiration. He had swallowed a couple of bottles of Tennessee whiskey before choking to death. But isopropyl alcohol was different from whiskey. This was an unusual factor that was common in two of the three recent deaths. Richens and Duke continued their examination of the details from all three scenes; trying to establish any other connections between the three cases. The hexagonal chest tattoos and condolence cards were obvious links, but what did they mean?

Background checks into the three dead men's businesses had revealed that Ammo's Cycles and Walsh's Gym had once occupied properties in the same block as Hunter's Bar. Brian Walsh had moved his boxing club to larger premises at the other end of Hanford High Street approximately five years earlier.

Peter Crowther had successfully expanded his drag racing empire and the businessman had owned a small chain of shops all over the Midlands. Richens and Duke believed that the three men must have known each other when their businesses were starting out. Maybe that fact could also connect their deaths in some way. But there was something else nagging at the back of Richens' mind; a niggling mental itch that he just couldn't scratch. Why did the words Bullet, Yardy and Crusher that were written on the condolence cards ring a distant bell in Richens' mind?

"What about a gang turf war?" blurted Duke suddenly from behind his laptop screen. "That could go some way to explain the strange tattoos on their chests. They could be some sort of old man's gang insignia perhaps?" he added, hoping to back up his new theory.

Richens leaned his head onto the back of his swivel chair. He closed his eyes and adopted the now familiar prayer pose inherited from his predecessor. Suddenly he opened his eyes and jolted forwards in his seat.

"That's it!" he exclaimed, quickly grabbing the mouse for his computer. "Duchess, you're bloody brilliant sometimes. Those words written on the cards aren't just random words, they're nicknames, bloody nicknames." Richens furiously clicked his mouse. "Christ Almighty how could I have forgotten about that? How could I have been so stupid? . . . it must have been about ten years ago," he muttered.

Duke watched in slight frustration as his techno-phobic boss aimlessly searched through a list of folders on his laptop.

"You remember I mentioned something about the Tracey Chambers' murder case a few weeks ago . . . there was a hexagonal thingy-mu-jig embroidered on the scarf found with her remains," Duke watched his boss impatiently click away at numerous icons on his computer screen.

"Well the old rocker who was sent down for her murder said he'd been in a biker gang in the seventies. I'm sure Crusher and Yardy were a couple of the gang members' nicknames. Come to think of it I think Bullet might have been one of them too," the inspector continued to ramble.

"No one believed the bloke on trial 'cos he wouldn't cough up any real names. But it might be worth checking him out."

"When exactly was this sir?" asked Duke patiently.

"Well Duchess, I'd only just become a sergeant myself and it was my first big case under old Chiltern, so it must have been somewhere around two-thousand and four."

"The same era the condolence cards were from then?" asked the sergeant.

Following his informative visit to the printer's shop, Duke had submitted the pieces of cardboard for even greater forensic testing. The lab had confirmed they had been four colour printed and they were still undergoing tests to determine the age of the ink used. Just as Bruno the printer had suggested, the cards had been laminated when they were produced. That thin layer of protection had collected numerous fingerprints. One of the most unexpected results confirmed that the top layer of fingerprints on each of the cards were those of each victim. There were also partial matches to Peter Crowther, Colin Lawson and Brian Walsh on all three cards. It was as if someone had bought a pack of particularly expensive condolence cards and each of the dead men had passed them to each other at some point. This case was becoming more baffling by the day.

Brian Walsh's demise was Hanford town's third suspicious death in as many months. The tattoos on all three victims contained the same very old metallic based ink, suggesting they had all been tattooed at least thirty years previously. That fact, coupled with the condolence cards discovered at each scene, made Richens suspect the deaths were connected in some way. The lack of forensic evidence at the scenes and fastidious cleaning of the two later bodies had suggested to him that those deaths were not accidental. Richens was beginning to come to the conclusion that Hanford had a serial killer. *Either someone is going around bumping off the town's old men for a laugh or they have a heavy score to settle.*

Duke trawled through the archived files on his laptop before triumphantly announcing the name of the man locked away for Tracey Chambers' murder.

"William Weber, sir."

Richens recognised the name in an instant; a torrent of memories flooded through his brain. Pictures of the young woman's disintegrated remains discovered at Himley Chase raced through his mind, closely followed by images of the urine-soaked tarpaulin and blood-stained wooden shovel handle; William Weber continually screaming his protests of innocence from the dock at Hanford Crown Court.

"He's still doing time at her Majesty's pleasure," interrupted Duke.

"I don't suppose his sticky fingerprints are on any of the condolence cards are they?" asked Richens hopefully.

"Nah, none identified as his yet, although I guess, as he's still safely tucked up in Chalmoor Prison, he can't possibly be our man, sir."

Chapter 14

Mid November 2014.

George Dalmano sat inside the cosseting leather interior of his Jaguar sports car. He had parked his trusted steed in a quiet residential street, just around the corner from Patrick O'Doyle's bed-sit flat. Deep in thought, George checked the car windows were all closed and anything of any value inside the car was securely locked away in the glove box, out of view of any passing low-life. He felt particularly uncomfortable in this badly run-down neighbourhood. George had a good view of the front of the bookies that Zombie always visited to pedal his drugs. He tapped his fingers impatiently on the steering wheel of his car as he could see Patrick's bony hand lift up the receiver on the payphone inside the shop; presumably to make another dirty drug deal. All George had to do was patiently wait for his former fellow gang member to leave the betting shop and walk a few paces back to his own front door. George pulled on a pair of tight-fitting black leather gloves before peering out through the car windows to take a good look at his surroundings.

The Lye Heath Estate was a particularly degraded area of Hanford that had suffered badly from a regular barrage of drugs raids, battering rams and riots. The drab pebble-dashed buildings bore testament to a seventies' town planner's misguided ideas of what modern living should be. This dystopian den of depravity had been filled with Hanford's lost souls; the cesspool of society, where homeless people were unceremoniously dumped by a council that could no longer afford to care.

As dusk began to fall over the feral corridor of concrete terraced houses, George saw a familiar figure emerge from the bookies' shop. Patrick O'Doyle's skeletal body shuffled along the paving slabs as he made his way home. George swiftly got out of his car, buttoned up his overcoat and quickly paced across the road to quietly follow his ex-fellow gang member along the pavement. Patrick's white greased-back Teddy Boy hair brushed the top of the turned up collar of his dirty grey trench coat. He didn't notice the man catching up behind him. The bony fretful Zombie turned to walk up a path towards the filthy chipped wooden front door of his ground floor flat; his fragile emaciated fingers shook uncontrollably as he fought to jab his key into the lock.

"Hello Patrick," announced George, as he peered down at his nervously twitching friend. Patrick spun around in shock and gazed back up into the steely glare of George's piercing blue eyes.

"Wha . . . what do you want Sparks?" spluttered Zombie, visibly scared by the sudden intrusion of the imposing figure standing behind him on his doorstep.

"I've just come to talk to you," said George with a faintly menacing smile. Patrick's key finally turned the lock and George quickly pushed him through the opened doorway into the bed-sit.

"How many times have I told you to *never* call me by that fucking name in public, you twat?" spat George. "You really should show more respect." Zombie just stared back in fear of his overwhelming visitor.

"Especially since I've gone to the trouble of bringing you a present." George reached a leather-gloved hand into the inside pocket of his overcoat and pulled out a small polythene bag. Instantly Zombie noticed the powdery contents that lay inside the bag. Visibly relieved by the offering, he began to smile warmly at his old friend.

"You'd better come in then Mister Dalmano," said Patrick respectfully.

The contents of the small wrap of cocaine had been a welcome distraction for Zombie. He knew anything that passed through George Dalmano's hands would be of a particularly high quality, so he had eagerly snorted a couple of lines of the white powder to quell his tremor.

George spent the next hour trying to ease Patrick's paranoia by giving plausible reasons behind the recent events. The old gang leader carefully explained that Bullet's death had been a tragic misadventure and Yardy had probably been showing off in a drinking game that had gone horribly wrong.

140

"Even old Razor Fish reckons Crusher's death was an accident. He said the silly old duffer had obviously picked up more weight than his knackered body could handle. If that's what his best mate thinks, then that's good enough for me," concluded George. "But quite why the randy old fuck-wit was stark bollock naked is probably another story."

Both men laughed at the mental image of Crusher exercising in the nude. George took off his gloves and opened the buttons on his overcoat. The nervously shaking Patrick had become calmer; his whole demeanour more receptive to George's measured interpretation of the accidental events surrounding their ex-fellow bikers' untimely deaths. George had begun to convince his drug-fuelled friend that no one was seeking retribution for the fraternity's heinous crimes. Bullet, Yardy and Crusher had all died in accidents. They were simply three unconnected deaths that had nothing to do with the Serpent Sons of Thelema. After all, the three other gang members, Sparks, Razor Fish and Zombie, were all still alive.

George couldn't be sure if he had managed to get his message through to Zombie. He thought maybe the coke-head was still a loose canon that needed to be silenced once and for all. George sensed a small flicker of doubt begin to weave its way through his brain. He knew that if the wrong people took Zombie's paranoid ramblings seriously, then the successful businessman's name could be linked to the disbanded biker gang. The authorities might realise that there had been some credibility in William Weber's version of events from forty years ago. That could lead to the Tracey Chambers murder case being re-examined, the whole can of worms being re-opened. What if Zombie's loose tongue backed-up William Weber's story? As the whole potential scenario began to unravel in George's racing brain, he began to think it wouldn't take the police long to put two and two together and establish that Tracey had once been his cock teasing ol' lady.

George allowed his mind to wander back through four decades to the fateful evening when the course of his life had changed forever; the hell-sent night that would bring with it a turn of events so evil, it would twist the hateful biker's world apart and challenge his understanding of what leadership and true loyalty meant.

#

Following Billy Kiddo's banishment from the Serpent Sons of Thelema at Himley Chase, the brotherhood had driven back to their filthy lair in Lye Heath. Tracey had made food for the returning clan. As she served up plates of egg and chips for the six hungry men, she tried to listen in to their hushed conversations about Billy's ejection from the gang. Tracey knew it was not her place to be kept informed of what happened at such clandestine ceremonies, but she had desperately needed to know what fate had befallen her secret young lover. She did not know whether Kiddo had been allowed to leave and live, or if Sparks and his loyal disciples had ended his life. Tracey knew she was carrying Billy's child and she had become totally consumed with fear and emotion after being kept in the dark about the baby-father's fate. She had planned to meet up with him later that night so the couple could make their escape together; then once in the safety of the West Country she would tell Billy about the pregnancy. But without knowing whether or not he was still alive, Tracey could not run the risk of leaving the biker's den early.

She knew there would be no return for her should she discover Kiddo had not survived his expulsion from the gang; she couldn't afford to burn any bridges. Tracey had to protect the new life that was growing inside her belly. She decided if the biological father was no longer around to support her, then she would have to fall back on Sparks to provide for her and pass the baby off as his. It was the final bad decision Tracey would make.

Later that evening, Sparks had become suspicious of his ol' lady when he had gone to the toilet and discovered Tracey's bulging red leather rucksack hidden beneath a pile of dirty towels in the bathroom. He had seethed with anger as he found that, along with most of her clothes, jewellery and cosmetics, the bag also contained a treasured paperweight that she had owned since childhood, along with a couple of precious

142

photographs that she usually kept on a small shelf in the couple's bedroom. Sparks realised instantly that what he had found was more than a simple 'shag bag' for when he and Tracey had stayed away somewhere overnight. This was different. This was a running away bag.

Vivid memories flooded through George Dalmano's brain. Sparks' gathered entourage had heard the bathroom door slam shut. They had silently watched him storm out of the kitchen into the lounge and drag Tracey up off the settee, before he slapped the bewildered woman hard across the face. Sparks had then unceremoniously emptied the contents of her rucksack onto the living room's sticky carpet and screamed at his cowering quarry; accusing her of planning to leave him.

He yelled that he had already had to deal with one disloyal bastard that evening and he would not put up with another. He lied that Billy had paid the ultimate price for his disrespect; he had not been allowed to live. The gang members had watched in reverent silence as their boss meted out Tracey's punishment; his fists had shown no mercy. The distraught young woman had begged him to stop his beating, as she crawled on the floor to try and gather her precious possessions together. She believed Billy was dead and she would have to salvage whatever she could with Sparks. Eventually a petrified Tracey broke the news to her ol' man that she was pregnant.

She tried to explain to the stunned gang leader that she had simply started to gather a few of her things together so that she could sell them; she knew what a burden another mouth to feed would be and it was the only way she could help pay for the new baby's clothes.

At first Tracey believed her lie had worked well to quell her enraged ol' man's anger, as Sparks dismissed his loyal entourage to enable him to speak with his wife alone. Unbeknown to Tracey, her news had only stoked the flames of Sparks' burning fury. He knew he couldn't possibly have fathered her unborn child, as the infertile commander-in-chief had fired blanks all of his life.

During that hot and sultry night of the summer's heat wave the whole squalid house in Anglesey Street was shaken to its core. Earlier in the evening, Sparks had been unable to vent his seething wrath at Himley Chase; he had already felt betrayed as he had been forced to allow one of his hand-picked soldiers to leave the brotherhood. The violent magma burning through Sparks' veins would bubble to the surface; disloyal Billy Kiddo would become a convenient scapegoat.

Sparks' anger had raged into a violent sickening attack as he accused his woman of sleeping around. Tracey had no choice other than to vehemently deny it. She knew living by the strict biker's code of unwavering loyalty to the leader meant she could never admit to betraying or disrespecting her ol' man. She had protested her innocence as he kicked her hard in the stomach. But it was no use; Sparks simply did not want to believe her and instead chose to accuse her of shagging around with Kiddo.

She had groaned in agony and tried desperately to deflect Sparks' suspicions about Billy, but he would not listen to her. With nothing left to lose, she goaded him, saying she didn't care if he killed her. He could snuff out the innocent life that was growing inside her aching belly for all she cared; after all she could have been carrying the spawn of any one of the lecherous men the gang leader had pimped her out to as payment for his failed drug deals.

Sparks had been incandescent with rage, too furious to even consider Tracey's explanation. He would never accept her pregnancy could be a direct result of his sordid method of paying his debts to rival gangs. His mind was made up. She was a whore and it would be far more convenient to accuse the unfaithful tramp of having an affair with a dishonourable ex-brother instead. Sparks had screamed and ranted at the bloodied and bruised woman. The slut's problem was not his fault and, if she ever managed to spawn the bastard, then he would take no responsibility for the squawking mongrel after it was born.

It was no secret that Sparks had become bored with his ol' lady and he was looking for an excuse to end their tempestuous relationship. He had often fantasised about trading her in for a more compliant younger model, but the strict biker code he lived by made it difficult to free himself of the shackles of having an official ol' lady in tow; their coupling had been set for life. Unbeknown to Tracey, the beguiling gang leader had dozens of other nubile fuck-buddies waiting in the wings, all ready and willing to take her place. Telling Sparks about the pregnancy had simply given him all the ammunition he had needed. He would seize the opportunity to be rid of her.

He had made up his mind to replace her with a new and preferably slimmer chick; someone who didn't have constant mood swings and wouldn't jealously snipe and moan about his salacious behaviour. He now knew the reason behind Tracey's recent weight gain and temperamental nature, her pregnancy would be his ideal get out of jail free card; the perfect excuse for dumping her without it looking bad on him. He would manipulate the situation and claim he was a wronged man. The disrespectful Billy Kiddo would become a sacrificial fall guy. Sparks' unfaithful bitch would be made to pay dearly. The couple's disloyalty would be blamed for the gang leader's cruel decision. They could both rot in hell for all he cared.

The whole biker gang had secretly been in love with Tracey. They all adored the rampant red head with big tits and skinny legs, but the close-knit fraternity only ever looked and never touched. It would have been more than their lives were worth to try anything on with Sparks' ol' lady. They didn't know that Billy Kiddo had broken all the rules and lured the fiery vixen away from her ol' man long enough to get inside her knickers.

Sparks had gathered his troops into the lounge at the bikers' den and sat in judgement, as he delivered his twisted version of events. The men had remained mostly silent, and were stunned by their leader's revelations. After being told the poisonous news that Billy had spread his seed into the filthy lying whore, the vengeful jury were left in no doubt that Tracey needed to be disciplined. Sparks continued to prod the glowing jealous embers of their resentment towards Billy and Tracey's affair, until the whole gang was stoked into frenzy. They unanimously agreed each brother would be given free rein to vent his anger on the dirty little cock teaser.

First of all, Tracey had needed to become the sordid clan's communal property; she would need to be deprived of the look-but-don't-touch status that she had enjoyed whilst being Sparks' ol' lady. The coupling of the gang's leader and his woman was officially annulled by the burning of Tracey's name patches.

The brotherhood decided the sleazy little biker slut would then have to be taught a terrifying gang lesson in any way they saw fit. The terrified young woman was forced to strip naked in front of them, before suffering the humiliation of being hogtied and whipped. Her degradation continued as she was unceremoniously passed around from one gang member to another; each man releasing his pent up sexual frustration in any depraved way he chose, whilst the other brothers watched and jeered. One by one they reaped their revenge on her, until their wanton hunger was finally satisfied.

The final retribution would be for Sparks to empty a bottle of brown ale over the defiled woman's naked body; something he laughingly referred to as her un-baptism from the gang. The fateful act of inserting the neck of the glass beer bottle into the screaming woman would bring a climax to the debauched torture. Crusher, Yardy, Razor Fish and Bullet had pinned down Tracey's hands and feet as Zombie held the bottle in place. Sparks gave a swift kick with the heal of his biker's boot to ram the object deep inside her, sending shards of broken glass ripping through Tracey's skin. The six delinquents had stared in disbelief as blood gushed from the wound onto the living room carpet. Instead of dialling nine-nine-nine, Sparks had then ordered Crusher to "put the bitch out of her misery" with a swift blow of a shovel across the back of her head. They then dragged the unconscious woman to the bathroom and dumped her in the bath, callously leaving her to die overnight.

In the cool dewy dawn of a summer's day, the six guilty men shuffled Tracey's defiled and abused lifeless body into Yardy's side-car to take her to Himley Chase. The evil gang of deadbeats had dressed her in a pair of flared blue jeans, her favourite faded black vest top, black leather platform boots and a tasselled leather biker's jacket. Tracey's head wound was hidden beneath a bandana, her bruised and bloodied face obscured by a large pair of sunglasses. Sparks' silk scarf, which featured an image of the American Confederate flag, was tied securely over her nose and mouth. To any passing motorists on the road at that time in the morning, she would simply look like a sleeping woman sat in the vehicle.

At the woodland clearing, the murderous mob wrapped Tracey's mortal remains in an old tarpaulin sheet taken from the garage at the gang's headquarters. In an attempt to hide the scent of her decaying remains from any passing dogs out for a walk in the woods, the body was rolled in sheets of polythene before being discarded in a hastily dug shallow grave.

Soon after Tracey's death, Sparks had decided to disband the biker gang. Kiddo's departure and his ol' lady's deceit had seemed like an omen to him. He realised that he had tested the loyalty of his brothers to the limit and he was shocked by the power he held over them. They had believed his sordid version of events about Billy and Tracey's affair without question and they had eagerly followed his orders. Sparks knew the depths of depravity his lethal kinsmen would willingly sink to for him. They had become a wild pack of animals with a seemingly voracious appetite for rape and torture and Sparks knew it was his fault. He had lit the touch paper and watched them all blow a fuse. He knew they had gone too far but, as the gang's leader, he had felt totally responsible for their actions. Sparks had believed his luck would soon run out if the gang was not brought back under control, and he needed to prevent any of them being prosecuted for Tracey's murder.

The commander-in-chief had needed to take the heat off his troops, reward their loyalty and protect the fraternity. The easiest way to achieve that would be to demobilise the Serpent Sons of Thelema; abandon the clubhouse, sell the assets, split any proceeds and set the gang members free. Everyone would lose their nicknames and go their separate ways; the evil entourage would disappear without a trace, taking their sordid secrets to their graves. The seedy bikers' lair in Anglesey Street would later be demolished and replaced with social housing; no one would remember them. It would be as if Sparks, Crusher, Zombie, Bullet, Razor Fish and Yardy had never existed.

#

Even though the Serpent Sons of Thelema had disbanded nearly four decades earlier, the murderous motley crew had still remained vehemently faithful to their oath of allegiance. But over the years Zombie had become a loose-lipped liability and George Dalmano had always felt it necessary to look after him particularly carefully. Patrick O'Doyle was a reckless ageing drug dealer who had a habit of sampling the merchandise while bagging up his drugs for sale. As a result of his addiction, George had booked his spaced-out friend into rehab countless times over the years. But the hapless Zombie had always lived up to his name and re-acquainted himself with his favourite little white lines within days of leaving the clinic.

Harrowing images of the fateful night of Tracey's murder burned through George Dalmano's brain as he now sat watching Patrick O'Doyle gleefully snort another line of white powder up his nose. George watched Zombie slowly relax back onto an old dirty sofa-bed. His whole body now appeared calmer. Gone was the coke-head's twitch and constant nervous tremor; gone was the fretful expression that concealed so many salacious secrets.

"The plod found your ol' lady though Sparks," muttered Zombie. "We should have burned the greasy little whore as she lay in the pit, they'd never have ID'd her then," he whispered. "That's what Kiddo would've done man. He'd have set light to the bitch. D'ya remember the night he got his colours?" Patrick O'Doyle chuckled softly at the happy memory of Billy's initiation ceremony, as he lay back onto a sweat-stained dralon cushion and peacefully closed his eyes. He was unaware how those careless words would enrage his old commander-in-chief and seal his fate.

Anger twitched through the veins in George's temples. *How dare the ungrateful junkie bring up Billy Kiddo's method of dealing with dead fuckers?* He was angered by Zombie's inference that Billy would have dealt with the aftermath of Tracey's murder better than he had? *You fucking stinking selfish bastard.* Patrick's drug-fuelled slip of the tongue had made up George's mind for him. He knew Zombie had to be silenced once and for all.

The sinister visitor angrily pulled up his old friend's shirt sleeve and tied a tourniquet around the bony man's arm, just above the elbow. Patrick stirred slightly from his drug-induced doze. "Don't worry Zombie," soothed George, as he put his

148

leather gloves back on. He reached a hand inside his coat pocket to pull out a small syringe, before removing a hard rubber cap from the top of it. He tapped the skin on Patrick's skeletal arm to summon a vein to the surface; he then stabbed the needle hard into the sallow skin to inject an illicit painkilling cocktail into Zombie's body. George discarded the empty needle on the floor and placed a small bag of white powder into Patrick's lifeless open hand.

"That'll sort you out, you grasping little shit-head," spat George. "You'll be safely out of the way now, while all this bollocks blows over."

The imposing businessman walked out of the scruffy bed-sit into the damp air of the ramshackle neighbourhood. He turned and closed the chipped wooden front door behind him before walking back to his car. George removed his leather gloves, placing them safely in his coat pocket, as he sniffed back a small tear that had squeezed from the corner of his left eye.

Zombie was dead.

Chapter 15

Early December 2014

William Weber sat in the small meeting room at Chalmoor Prison, patiently waiting for his visitor to arrive. It was an unexpected break in his day and William was making the most of the tranquillity of the space. It was good to escape the constant background noise of inmates living, fighting, bickering and shagging within the confines of their concrete cells. It was a short respite from the day-to-day protests of angry prisoners who shouted and wailed, as their belongings were unceremoniously rifled through during one of Chalmoor's regular cell inspections. William's unexpected visitor had given him the chance to leave the chitter-chatter of the prison's caged stairwells and escape to the peaceful solitude of the meeting room. The inmate sat alone on his pressed metal chair at one side of the old wooden table. The heavy metal door squealed open as Detective Inspector Richens walked through the doorway ahead of a uniformed prison guard. William Weber felt his muscles fizz as a torrent of anger stung through his veins. His old nemesis had entered the room.

"Good afternoon, Weber;" announced Richens. "It's been a while, but I take it you do remember me?" The detective turned back to nod at the prison guard. The dutiful uniformed man left the room and pulled the heavy metal door firmly shut behind him. Richens took his place on the pressed metal chair opposite Billy and stared intently at the inmate. The gladiatorial battle between these two men was about to commence.

The years spent inside Chalmoor's walls had not been kind to William Weber. The sixty-year-old man was looking frail. The once fiercely proud guesthouse owner now had a sallow gaunt expression; a persistent chesty cough bore testament to his failing health. He had become a broken man.

"Billy," began Richens, his tone softening slightly. "I need to ask for your help with something." William stared at the tiled floor to avoid the intimidating hawk-like stare of the man sat opposite him.

"I heard your legal team is trying to launch a new appeal against your conviction. If you give me some information that I need today, then maybe I'll be able to make sure nothing gets in the way of that," the inspector continued. "I might even be able to help you."

A small wry smile came to William's weak lips. He remembered the piercing glare of the thin-nosed policeman very well. Every single detail about Sergeant Richens had been etched onto the condemned man's brain. He recalled how every piece of information he had given to the young upstart detective had been twisted and chewed-up, before being spat back out onto the interview room table with a substantial seasoning of circumstantial evidence. And now, all William could think was, the same devious fact-twisting bastard who had been instrumental in his wrongful conviction ten years ago, was now asking for his help. William lifted his head up and locked on to Richens' steely glare; firmly staring back into the eyes of his adversary. He wasn't about to let this copper think he'd got the better of him.

"I know who you are Sergeant Richens," fumed Billy as he dropped his gaze back towards the floor.

"Ah yes, but it is Detective Inspector Richens nowadays," he replied.

"You did alright for yourself then, Detective Inspector." Billy raised his fingers into the air to place imaginary inverted commas around the policeman's upgraded title. "Jumped into Chiltern's shoes did ya?" he scowled.

"Yes, something like that," smiled Richens proudly.

"What happened to the fat bastard then? Did he snuff it with a heart attack or something?" asked Billy.

"Err, no. He's retired." Richens was instantly annoyed that he had let slip a piece of personal information about his old boss. "Anyway, as I was saying, I'm now in a position to help you Billy, if you can help me." The detective was trying to steer the conversation away from the subject of his former colleague.

The resentful prisoner stared back coldly at his adversary.

"Ah, I see, now you need my assistance?" snorted Billy interrupting Richens' well-practiced opening statement. He sat back in his pressed metal chair and folded his arms before

151

shooting an angry stare directly into the detective's eyes. His mind replayed the endless barrage of questions he had faced at Hanford police station ten years earlier; how his protests of innocence had not been believed. Billy's heartbeat quickened with every memory of how Chiltern and his eager sidekick had stood in Hanford Crown Court and given their twisted version of events, chipping away every defence to help the prosecution to secure a guilty verdict.

"So now you come in here thinking you can bribe me with some half-baked promise of not getting in the way of my appeal, so long as I assist you with your enquiries. How fucking gracious of you," snarled Billy with a sneer of contempt for the policeman sat across the desk.

Billy's veins began to pump with rage, sending a torrent of hatred fizzing through his body. He knew Richens would not have any opportunity to influence his appeal in either direction. The incredulous detective was grasping at straws. Billy believed Richens must have known he had locked away an innocent man in the prime of his life, and now he was trying to prevent the information coming to light during his appeal. He believed the policeman had realised Chiltern had got it wrong all those years ago, and when the full truth came to light it would damage the retired Inspector's reputation. He concluded it was just the plod's evil plan to stick together and cover up the botched investigation into Tracey Chambers' murder. *That smarmy git is only trying to put things right so he doesn't lose face.*

Richens realised this wasn't going to be the easiest of prison interviews and dancing around the houses wasn't going to get him anywhere. He was a desperate man. There was a serial killer on the loose in Hanford who was systematically targeting the elderly members of Billy's old biker gang and William Weber was probably the only person who could help him solve the mystery. The Inspector would just have to come straight out with it, cut to the chase and ask William the well-rehearsed question he had prepared during his long car journey to the prison.

"Okay, okay, I get it that you're angry with me," started Richens. "But what can you tell me about Peter Crowther, Colin Lawson and Brian Walsh?" The detective's unblinking eyes locked on to Billy's sallow features. "Or perhaps you knew them better as Bullet, Yardy and Crusher?" he continued, trying to catch Billy off guard. The weary prisoner remained silent, staring intently at a small speck of fluff that had floated down from the ceiling.

"These are some of the names of the people you claimed were in your sordid little biker gang aren't they? The Serpent Sons of Thelema?" demanded Richens impatiently. "Tell me! Crowther, Lawson and Walsh. They are the real names of the men you protected all those years ago, aren't they?"

The exasperated inspector stood up from his chair, and angrily slapped both of his hands on the table.

"Come on Weber, tell me. Why are you protecting them still? Surely it'll help your appeal if you give me the names won't it? Damn it man, I can't help thinking we're running out of time here."

Billy coughed and raised his eyes to meet the detective's steely glare once more. How prophetic those last words had sounded; William Weber truly was running out of time, although he knew that his cancer diagnosis was probably not what Inspector Richens was referring to. Billy coughed again and patted his chest. He continued to wheeze fitfully as he pointed towards the intercom button to ask Richens to summon a prison guard.

"Sorry," spluttered Billy breathlessly, conveniently evading the policeman's questions. "I really need to see my doctor in the infirmary."

#

A young police officer sat at her desk in Hanford police station. DC Trudi Jones worked in the cyber unit and she had just finished transcribing a voicemail message that had been left for CID on a police tip off line. The man's voice on the recording had a local accent. He spoke very quickly and had a highly agitated tone.

"All those old men's deaths, they ain't accidents," said the voice. Trudi then heard the man take in a gasp of air, as if he was inhaling hard on a cigarette.

153

"That seventies bird in the footage from the pub," he coughed. "She's come back from the dead. I'm tellin' ya man, she's fuckin' comin' for us all. Tracey won't stop 'til she's killed everyone," he spluttered with a chesty wheeze. The sheer terror in the fretful voice was clear to hear. Trudi replayed the recording numerous times, carefully listening out for any other possible clues on the tape as to who had left the message.

According to the log of the number, the call had been made from a local landline and Trudi's next task was to track down where it was located.

#

Sergeant Duke watched two heavily-set men from the coroner's office carry a black body bag out of a squalid little bed-sit flat on the Lye Heath Estate and carefully place it into the back of a private ambulance. He held a large handkerchief tightly over his nose in a vain attempt to hold back the rancid air that filled his nostrils. For several days, a couple of tenants who lived in a maisonette on the first floor of the building had complained to Hanford Council about a putrid stench emanating from the flat below. A community case worker and pest control officer had eventually been dispatched to check out the premises and report back any problems. They had forced entry through the front door to be met by the decaying remains of a man lying on a sofa-bed.

Sergeant Duke walked out of the filthy bed-sit, its cloying air clung to every fibre of his suit as he removed a set of paper overalls. A squadron of bluebottles swarmed around his head as he stepped onto the path outside the front door and took in a few gulps of fresh air. A young plump woman with a clipboard and pen was perched on a low wall that ran down the side of the path. Sergeant Duke read the details on a plastic laminated identity badge that hung from a pink floral lanyard around her neck. She was Wendy Tatlow, Community Case Worker for Hanford Town Council. The casually dressed woman was nervously smoking a cigarette and hastily writing down a full account of the circumstances leading up to the gruesome

154

discovery inside the flat. Sergeant Duke introduced himself to the social worker.

"Do you know who the dead man was?" he asked. Wendy looked up from her clipboard and took a final long drag on her cigarette, before breathing out a long plume of smoke.

"Well, the bed-sit is rented out to someone called Patrick O'Doyle, but I'm afraid I don't know if that's him," replied the woman apologetically, as she dropped the nub end onto a paving slab and scrunched it beneath her shoe. "It's not my patch really. His usual social worker is off sick with stress at the moment. I was just drafted in at the last minute to help out today."

Duke recognised the woman's reply was a clear attempt to distance herself from the case, and to firmly deflect any of the blame for the man's death away from her team.

"If it is Mister O'Doyle, then he hadn't long been out of rehab for a cocaine addiction. It says in the notes here that he stopped paying his rent a few weeks ago and we were about to review his case to see if he'd fallen off the wagon again." Wendy spoke quite flatly, and Duke realised that dealing with the fallout of drug addictions was becoming an every day occurrence for her over-worked department.

The young sergeant always found it difficult to come to terms with the fact that people could become so anonymous within society. How people like Patrick O'Doyle constantly slipped through the authority's safety nets to end their days alone in a shabby run down bed-sit with no one around to miss them was a sad state of affairs. *Surely people don't ever start out in life alone? How could a mother's son, a person's brother or someone's friend ever arrive at that desperately lonely point in their life?*

"It makes you wonder how people end up like this doesn't it?" said Duke thoughtfully as he blew his nose to try and remove the remaining stench of Patrick's flat from his nostrils.

"There's a lot of it about on the Lye Heath. We simply don't have the resources to give everyone the care they need." It was Wendy Tatlow's careful rendition of Hanford Social Services' official position. Duke knew it was simply their well-worn excuse for failing the town's forgotten souls.

155

The social worker agreed to meet Sergeant Duke at the police station later that day to give a full statement. She would also try to trace Patrick O'Doyle's social security files. The young sergeant smiled at Wendy and handed her his business card. The trill and buzz of Duke's mobile phone interrupted his parting gesture. The detective answered the call and walked back to the clean sanctuary of his air-conditioned car.

"Yo Duchess, what's happening?" It was Inspector Richens.

"Hello sir," Duke winced at the use of his irreverent nickname. "Well, another dead pensioner has rocked up, but this time it looks like a drugs overdose to me. The bloke who rented the flat was a well-known coke-head and there was a discarded syringe and traces of white powder on the body and over the floor," summarised Duke.

"Nothing to do with our cases then?" said Richens dismissively.

"Well, maybe sir, there was one interesting thing," stalled Duke. "When the paramedics scooped him into the body bag I noticed he had one of those hexagon tattoos on his chest."

"What about a condolence card? Did you find a card with his name on?" demanded Richens.

"I didn't see one at the scene I'm afraid, sir, but I'll check with the lab to see if anything was found on the body before I got there." Duke inwardly berated himself for not having made a point of searching for the piece of card earlier.

Chapter 16

Mid December 2014.

A beautiful woman with long red hair had been loitering around outside Dave Corden's tattoo parlour for the past hour. She had nervously paced up and down the pavement while occasionally checking her watch for the time. A shop assistant called Steve studied the woman through a large plate glass window. It wasn't unusual for new customers to behave so nervously and linger for a while before entering the premises, but the tattooist was particularly entertained by the woman's jittery uncertainty. Steve knew that having a tattoo or piercing was a decision not to be taken lightly. Aside from having to suffer the pain of the artist's needle, a tattoo would leave an indelible mark on the skin; a constant reminder of a particular chapter of someone's life, whether it be good or bad. Steve smiled warmly as it appeared the beautiful woman had eventually summoned up enough courage to enter the shop.

"Hi, how can I help?" beamed Steve. *Christ Almighty she's absolutely gorgeous.*

The hesitant woman slowly made her way towards the counter. She had a slightly bohemian air, as if she was from another bygone age. Her vintage flared blue jeans accentuated the fluid movement of her curvy hips as she walked. The woman's long red curly hair billowed beneath an American Confederate flag bandana, as a pair of large-framed retro sunglasses perched on the end of her pert little nose. The beautiful customer placed a red leather rucksack on the floor and removed her matching tasselled biker's jacket, to reveal the tight, figure-hugging black vest top she wore beneath.

"Hello," said the young woman as she anxiously chewed her bottom lip. "I'm thinking about having a tattoo, but I'm an ink virgin and a bit unsure of what to go for."

The shop assistant smiled back at her as he opened up a well-thumbed catalogue of tattoo designs and placed it on the counter.

"Well, we have flowers . . ." Steve swallowed hard. The woman's words had begun to softly dance inside his head. Her casual remark *virgin* just wouldn't leave his mind. ". . . or love hearts perhaps," he flirted. The young woman stared blankly at the designs as Steve professionally flicked through the laminated pages.

"You could have your lover's name beneath," he cheekily continued, in a clumsy attempt to find out whether the woman was single or not. "That's if you have a lover of course," joked the enthralled tattooist nervously. ". . . or maybe a boyfriend? he gently probed a little deeper, carefully studying the woman's expressionless face. ". . . or even a girlfriend?" He finally began to realise his efforts to charm the woman were probably going to go unrewarded. *She must be a fucking lesbian.* He was beginning to get a little annoyed that his flirtatious banter hadn't achieved so much as a flicker of interest from her.

After a few minutes the indecisive young woman looked up towards him, a large beautiful smile enveloped the whole of her face. The shop assistant was momentarily encouraged by her warm response until he slowly realised her gaze was firmly fixed beyond him. Steve spun around to discover she was smiling at an older man who was standing in a doorway behind him. Dave Corden had just come out of the studio at the rear of the tattoo shop.

The seventy-two year old shop owner was a well-built man with a very shiny bald head. He had retired from the day-to-day running of the tattoo parlour, but today he was visiting his old premises to check over the end-of-year accounts. The man stepped behind the counter to retrieve a small bundle of ledgers from beneath the till and smiled back at the beautiful customer.

"I'll have a tattoo so long as he is the one to do it," purred the young woman as she elegantly pointed a finger towards Dave. Steve noticed the woman's braless nipples beneath her vest top had started to harden. She had been instantly attracted to his boss and she had begun to playfully suck the end of one of her fingers between her softly parted lips.

"Who? That old codger," joked Steve incredulously. The woman slowly nodded her head while smiling seductively at Dave. The sultry red head leaned onto the counter; her plunging cleavage almost sent both men into a trance, as she pulled up her vest top to reveal two round plump breasts.

"As it's nearly Christmas, I think I'd like a tattoo of a cheeky little red cherub, just to the side of here," said the woman nonchalantly, as she teasingly encircled the nipple on her right breast with a moistened forefinger. The two men remained motionless, hypnotically transfixed behind the counter, as they took in the bountiful sight before them.

". . . and for your information your boss is not an old codger." The woman glared at Steve as she slowly pulled her T-shirt back down. "He's vintage," she winked.

For once in his long life Dave Corden didn't know how to respond to such an incredible invitation. The mesmerised tattoo shop owner had felt an instant connection to the hippy rock chick dressed in seventies' garb and he immediately accepted the job of inking her breast. It had been a while since he had given anyone a tattoo, but the possibility he would be invited to explore the other delights of this woman's incredible body was beyond temptation. Dave allowed himself to believe the attraction was mutual; she had clearly been giving him the come on. If he was going to indulge his wildest fantasies with her, it would have to be without the possibility of any interruptions.

#

Sharron Chambers allowed a wicked smile to crawl across her lips as she added her latest newspaper cuttings to the ring binder. It was a relatively small obituary for Patrick O'Doyle that simply stated a local drug addict had been found dead in his bed-sit following a suspected drugs overdose. There were no fanfares or articles to commemorate his wasted life, just a small paragraph at the bottom of a column of general news. She remembered him as the fretful bony man whose hands had shakily spilled tobacco over the pub table in the booth at the Huntsman's Arms. She placed a red cross alongside his name in her notepad. He would become the fourth addition to her dossier on the group of men who had attended her mother's memorial service.

#

Later that day, Angel sat astride a long leather couch in the tattoo studio. As she waited for Dave Corden to return from the lavatory, she aimlessly played with a button on the side of the couch that adjusted the height of it. Dave had closed the shop early and uncharacteristically given all of his staff the remainder of the afternoon and evening off. Angel snapped open two cans of strong lager and placed them on a chrome plated instrument table that stood beside the couch. A tattooist's gun cartridge had been pre-loaded with ink and placed on the table, next to a couple of fine tipped felt pens and a collection of assorted ink bottles. Angel reached into her jeans pocket and took out a small piece of folded paper that contained a couple of crushed sedative tablets, before hastily emptying the powdered drug into one of the open cans of beer. She knew Dave was an old school rocker, he wouldn't waste any time on idle chatter; he would eagerly return from the toilet ready to brand her breast before moving onto whatever else he had planned for the flame-haired beauty. She had to act quickly. Dave walked back into the room and picked up a couple of fine-tipped felt pens.

"I thought we could have a beer first," purred Angel, as she handed Dave one of the drinks. She pulled off her small black vest top, lay back on the couch and began to playfully squeeze her naked breasts together; all the time locking her captivating green eyes firmly onto Dave's mesmerised gaze. She teasingly picked up her cold can of lager and rolled it over her ample bosom to gently numb the surface. He noticed Angel's milky smooth skin appeared to shimmer in the soft glow of an overhead work lamp; her hardening moistened nipples looked like two shiny copper pennies standing proud of the pert soft mounds.

"I could give you a couple of great nipple rings through those puppies," offered Dave clumsily, as he stared at Angel's heaving chest.

"Oooh," she teased, secretly wincing at the thought of how painful the suggestion sounded. "It's tempting, but I'll just go for the ink today, thanks."

160

"So what's with the seventies' hippy chic look?" asked Dave, trying to return the conversation to a more professional level. He took a long gulp of lager from his can before sitting down on the couch next to Angel.

"Oh I love all things vintage," she replied.

"Even your men?" he winked, secretly hoping that was the case.

"Oh yes, especially vintage men . . . vintage bald headed men actually." The young woman giggled and sat up to move closer towards him before playfully sliding her hands over his shiny shaven scalp.

Dave took another large glug of beer and placed the half empty can on the floor. He stood up and pressed the button on the side of the couch to adjust its height, raising it closer to the light above. He cupped one of Angel's breasts in his well-practised hands and began to stretch and knead the skin between his fingers.

"You've got a great pair of tits," he remarked casually, as he pulled the lid off one of the fine tipped felt pens with his teeth. Dave started to drag the tip of the marker pen across Angel's flesh to begin drawing the outline of her tattoo. "So, why a cherub? It's not really because we're coming up to Christmas, is it?"

"Oh no, nothing like that," replied the young woman. "It's all to do with my nickname. My real name is Angie, but I get called Angel all the time; and cherubs are like angels aren't they?" she smiled.

"But you seem to be more like a little devil to me," laughed Dave as he picked up his tin of beer and took another swig.

"It's kinda like a tag I suppose," Angel continued. Unbeknown to the enthralled tattooist, she was gently leading him into her carefully planned trap.

Dave shook his head slightly and blinked, as if trying to clear something from his eye. He placed his lager can on the instruments table and picked up his marker pen again.

"Have you got a nickname Dave?" mewed Angel, as he returned to concentrate on his drawing. She peered down to see a thin black outline of a pair of angel's wings was beginning to take shape on the top of her right breast. It was a delicate image that looked as if the cherub had just landed above her nipple. Angel knew before long it could be permanently stabbed into her skin with an unrelenting flow of ink from the tattooist's buzzing needle.

She noticed a fine haze of sweat had begun to glisten on Dave's bald head as he concentrated on his freehand masterpiece. Eventually he perched on the couch and sharply let go of Angel's breast, letting it roughly bounce back to its natural position.

"So, Mister Tattoo Man, have you ever had a nickname?" she asked again, slightly startled by the sudden rough handling of her body, but encouraged that the sedative she had put in his drink was beginning to take effect.

Dave gazed at Angel's heaving bosom as he studied his hand drawn work of art. He drank the remaining dregs from his tin of beer and scrunched his eyes together slightly as he noticed his vision had become a little blurred.

"Yep," he replied nonchalantly. "They used to call me Razor Fish back in the day." Dave was beginning to feel a little light headed. He lowered the couch slightly so he could sit on it to regain his composure. He took a firm grip of Angel's naked flesh again and began to finish off drawing the outline image of a winged cherub.

The ageing tattoo artist began to proudly explain that he had been in a biker gang back in the seventies. He'd earned the first half of his pseudonym from having been the only one in the gang with a razor-shaved head; this was at a time when long hair on men had been the fashion. He was originally given the nickname of Fish, as he had a pretty impressive party trick of been able to hold his breath under water longer than anyone else. Unable to decide between the two dubious monikers, his gang had chosen to use both names. Razor Fish.

"Wow," exclaimed Angel. "I'd have loved to have known you back then. I bet you got up to loads of things that would simply fry the brains of many wannabe rockers these days." Dave smiled back at the young woman's compliment; he was beginning to feel dizzy again as distant memories from his misspent youth flickered through his brain.

When he had read the news reports about Yardy and Crusher's deaths, the woman in the CCTV had reminded him of a long lost conquest from back in the seventies. Somewhere in the back of his confused mind Dave now had a vision of Tracey Chambers' petrified face looking back at him during her torturous ordeal at the gang's headquarters. During the days following Crusher's death, a popular Psychic had appeared on the television news, claiming Tracey's spirit had come back to avenge her murder. Dave had dismissed the article and brushed aside any connection between his friends' deaths. Instead he chose to believe they had all been accidents. He had tried to push the memories of his evil old fraternity out of his mind and he had laughed off the suggestion that a vengeful ghost was bumping off the members of his old biker gang. It would have been ridiculous to suspect every beautiful woman with red hair and retro clothes was a murderer; especially the gorgeous woman who now willingly lay down in front of him. He had no suspicions about Angel. He remembered the TV news reports had said the suspect at Crusher's gym was heavily tattooed with roses and barbed wire running up over her neck. This nubile hotty's skin was clean.

"Ah yes," slurred Dave. He tried to take another glug of lager from his empty beer can and laughed crudely. "All the pussies loved to be licked by Razor Fish; 'cos when the fish went down on them, he could hold his breath for ages."

The sweaty tattooist shook his head again. He realised he was losing control of his words. His old nickname had remained a closely guarded secret that had been locked away for forty years, yet he felt strangely comfortable revealing such a salacious detail to the hypnotic red-headed nymph. He couldn't help but think they had met somewhere before, but he knew she would be too young to have known him during his past life in the biker gang. He wasn't sure if it was simply in his imagination, as his vision had become blurred and it was difficult to focus on her face, but she certainly seemed vaguely familiar to him.

Soon, his arms began to feel heavy and it was too much effort to lift his hands to hold on to the young woman's breast. He closed his eyes and tried to steady himself by grabbing hold

163

of the edge of the couch. Suddenly Dave's marker pen slipped from his grasp and dropped onto the tiled studio floor, as the elderly shop owner slumped down onto the leather bench with a soft thud, before sliding off onto the tiles below. The hazy sight of Angel's tousled red curly hair skimming across her ample bouncing bosom would be the last thing Dave Corden ever saw.

Angel got up off the tattoo couch and lowered it to its setting nearest to the floor, before shuffling Dave's limp body up onto it. She pressed the button to raise the bench back up to working height, before carrying out her final vengeful humiliation of one of the last remaining Serpent Sons of Thelema.

Razor Fish would soon be dead. His debauched soul would burn in hell.

#

Miss Tisserand's elegant stiletto heels click-clacked on the painted concrete floor as she hurriedly followed a uniformed prison guard down a soulless grey corridor. Inside her neat graphite leather briefcase she excitedly carried hopeful news for William Weber: It was eight o'clock in the evening, at the end of a very long working day, but Lin could not wait to break the good news to her client. The Criminal Appeal Office had agreed to consider Billy's petition against his conviction. At the end of the corridor the prison guard unlocked a heavy metal door that clanged open into a small medical ward. Immediately the smell of hospital disinfectant clung to the inside of Lin's nose.

Next to the open doorway, inside the infirmary, were a couple of silver-coloured pressed metal chairs that had been neatly stored beneath a grey metal desk. In a vain attempt to make this room appear slightly less austere, a parched spider plant with dry gangly leaves sat on top of the desk. Opposite were two metal beds that had their headboards pushed against a wall. They were separated down the middle by a long green nylon curtain that was suspended from the ceiling. In one of the beds lay a frail and gravely ill William Weber.

Two oxygen tubes had been placed inside Billy's nostrils to help him to breathe; a cannula in his hand constantly drip-fed a pain-killing morphine cocktail into his veins; a small stack of monitors bleeped softly in the background as they kept a watchful eye over the dying man. Miss Tisserand smiled warmly at her client, as she pulled one of the metal chairs over to sit down at Billy's bedside. She softly squeezed one of his pale thin hands as Billy looked back at her through half-closed eyes.

"We've discovered some new information to help your case," she began. Billy slowly blinked his tired eyelids.

"The police now acknowledge the Serpent Sons of Thelema were a real bikers' gang back in the seventies." Billy's eyes fluttered open.

"Apparently, four old men from Hanford have recently been found dead in four separate and strange circumstances. The police say three of the victims were associated with some of the nicknames that you mentioned during your trial; Bullet, Yardy and Crusher." Lin tried to gauge William's reaction to the news as she noticed his eyes were now wide open. She placed her laptop computer on the bed and opened it up.

"The men's real names were Peter Crowther, Colin Lawson, Brian Walsh and Patrick O'Doyle?" The young legal confidante read the names from the screen with a slight upwards inflection at the end as if to confirm whether William Weaver recognised who they were.

"It transpires that all four of the dead bodies have the same hexagonal tattoo on their chests, which the police now believe was an emblem to connect the members of your old gang together." Lin was relieved to see William had begun to smile and gently nod back at her.

Following his visit from Richens a month earlier, Billy was aware that the police had reluctantly come to accept there was some truth in his Serpent Sons of Thelema claim but, until today, nothing else had come of it. The old man softly chuckled; he was momentarily distracted by a persistent lock of glossy blue-black hair which continually flicked across the young woman's eyes when she spoke.

"Also," added Lin eagerly, as she moved the wayward tress of hair back behind her ear. "More importantly than that, I've discovered a document in your old case files that confirms your DNA wasn't on Tracey Chambers' clothes. It was only found on the shovel handle and on the tarpaulin used to wrap around her body."

Billy's smile began to evaporate. He could not imagine why the young woman thought that this was such encouraging news. He had allowed himself to float in a small bubble of hope on hearing the news about the dead Serpent Sons, but now he felt totally deflated; as if he was back at square one in Hanford nick with the coppers wheeling out the DNA to incriminate him.

"This forensic evidence suggests that the canvas sheet must have been pre-soaked in your urine and dried out long before Tracey Chambers was wrapped inside it," continued the young woman excitedly. Billy looked back vacantly.

"I found a pencil written technician's note about the condition of Tracey's clothes. Basically her clothes didn't have your urine or DNA on them, but Old Hathergood totally missed it. I guess he didn't know what the scribble said, mostly because it was quite faint and written in shorthand," Lin rambled, largely oblivious to her client's confusion.

Billy remained still and silent. Unable to summon up the strength to speak, he simply frowned as if to weakly question the point she was trying to make.

"Don't you see William?" She smiled back at him optimistically. "It means we can prove you didn't urinate over Tracey's dead body, so that backs up your original account of how your DNA got on the tarpaulin and spade. It disconnects you from the dead body. In the very least it kicks some of the prosecution's accusations out of the window. It throws doubt on their argument and I can't believe how that old duffer Hathergood didn't pick up on it."

Billy felt as if his heart would burst with happiness; he allowed himself to believe that, after all of the years locked up behind Chalmoor's cold concrete walls, there was a very real prospect he would once more be allowed to breathe the fresh air of freedom. He managed to smile broadly back at Lin and summoned up a little more strength to slowly nod his head.

"It's taken an absolute age for me to make any progress and get anyone to seriously consider my theory about the shorthand though, but I finally managed to convince one of our barristers to test its significance and the fabulous news is, he has agreed that it's a material fact . . . no pun intended." Lin paused for a second to take a breath. She was painfully aware of the late hour and William's limited attention span. She was trying hard to condense all of her information into as short a timescale as possible, but she had one more piece of news.

"You remember Tracey's unborn baby?" Tears welled in Billy's eyes as he fondly remembered the dozens of times he and Tracey had made love.

"Well, the paternal DNA results established at the time of your court case confirm that you were the father of Tracey's unborn child."

The news was no surprise to William as he had always believed the baby was his, but he couldn't understand why this fact would be so significant in his appeal.

"That golden nugget proves that you and Tracey must have had sex at least a few months before she was killed; which backs up your account of the two of you being lovers at the time. It virtually quashes the prosecution's allegations that you raped her because she wouldn't have sex with you. You couldn't possibly have been strangers when she died." Lin smiled back at the frail old man, mindful of how upsetting the memories would be.

"All my senior colleagues agree that this evidence was positively withheld at the time of your trial and the fresh information undermines the safety of your conviction. We've submitted an appeal notice and we're certain that a date for your hearing will come through any day now," she announced proudly. "Please just hold on in there."

William Weber was a tired and old dying man. His endless days had now become a continual cycle of injections, monitors, tests, catheters and bed baths. He had no dignity; he had no reason to hang on to what his life had become. But then, in the cold beige atmosphere of the disinfected sterile medical bay, the beautiful enquiring mind of the elegantly bobbed Miss Tisserand had unleashed a warming glow of hope within him. Could he allow himself to believe that his appeal would be heard in time? Would he soon be released from this living hell? Would he once again know life as a free man?

Billy couldn't help but notice how Lin's sharp legal brain belied her compassionate demeanour. He smiled inwardly as he knew his crusading young legal counsel was going above and beyond the call of duty to help him with his appeal. He would rest safe in the knowledge that by the time she had finished her investigations, the prosecution team and Detective Inspector Richens wouldn't have a leg to stand on. Billy gently closed his eyes and nodded a contented smile at the young trainee lawyer, before drifting off into a morphine-induced sleep.

Chapter 17

The Next Day.

A heavy shower of winter rain lashed the pavement outside the front of Dave Corden's tattoo parlour. A squadron of police patrol cars with blue flashing lights were positioned across both ends of Hanford High Street, a small army of officers in fluorescent yellow jackets had closed the road to traffic. A group of inquisitive neighbouring shop keepers gathered to watch the scene unfolding before their eyes. Behind them a crowd of nosey passers-by huddled beneath a canopy of dripping umbrellas, as they jostled for a better view. Detectives wearing white forensics' overalls arrived at the scene; they donned white polythene hats with latex gloves and wore elasticated plastic bags over their shoes. Resembling an infestation of giant white ants, their production line hustled and bustled in and out of the tattoo shop. Ribbons of blue-and-white crime-scene tape fluttered in the squally wind and rain, sealing off the whole area. Two PCs stood on guard at the entrance to the shop.

Inspector Richens and Sergeant Duke walked along the pavement. It hadn't gone unnoticed by either man how closely this scene was located to one of Ammo's bike shops, Hunter's Bar and Walsh's Gym.

"Christ, I was only here a couple of weeks ago checking out the vintage biker chick's arm tattoo," shivered Duke. "But no one here recognised the design."

One of the PCs lifted a strip of incident tape that had been hastily tied across the doorway into Dave Corden's tattoo parlour, as the two detectives ducked beneath it. Richens and Duke stepped inside the shop and were immediately greeted by another police constable; he was comforting a shaking shop assistant called Steve Perkins.

Steve had arrived for work at half past eight in the morning and had been surprised to find the shop's alarm system was still deactivated and the metal security shutters over the entrance door and plate glass window at the front of the building were in the open position. Steve explained that he liked to get into work before any other members of staff, as it gave him a chance to catch up on emails and check the company's social media feeds before getting the shop open for business at ten o'clock. The rest of the team usually arrived just before opening time. Finding the tattoo studio half open when he arrived for work that day had been highly unusual.

"Christ, I can't believe it," muttered Steve with a small shake of his head. "I thought Dave was the cat that got the cream yesterday, but now I can't believe how unlucky the old codger was," mused Steve.

"Unlucky?" queried Duke.

"Yeah, I mean he doesn't usually come to the shop. So he was unlucky to be in the wrong place at the wrong time. Well, you see, he's a bit of a slave-driver who leaves all of us minions to do all the real work. He's never here." Duke looked back at him quizzically, unsure where the shocked young man's unfiltered words would lead.

"I mean, we all work really hard here, long hours and everything. Now, I'm not one to speak ill of the dead, but he just swans in occasionally and rakes in the profits." Duke could sense a burning resentment rising in the young man's statement.

"So quite a few of you had a grudge against Mister Corden then?" surmised the sergeant.

"Nah, not really. It was just a regular bit of banter. I mean, I know we all joked about it on social media earlier in the week and announced our *lord and master* would be gracing us with a visit yesterday, but none of us would have a reason to kill him."

"So he wouldn't normally have been here, but anyone who follows you online would have known he was coming in yesterday? Richens raised his eyebrows at the revelation.

"I guess so," replied Steve. "And then on the one and only day he does actually come into the shop, some vintage sort rocks up and starts getting her baps out over the counter. Dave was such a jammy bastard, but it's sad to think how one minute he was copping a feel of some bird's tits and the next he was meeting his maker." Duke frantically wrote down Steve's garbling account.

170

DI Richens couldn't help but think it wasn't just a case of the killer striking it lucky. More likely the murderer had tracked the victim's movements. He left Sergeant Duke to take the rest of Steve's statement.

Richens pulled on a set of paper overalls and plastic shoe covers, before making his way through to the rear of the shop into a small room. The tattoo studio at the back was a tiny private space that, over the years, had witnessed hundreds of customers stoically bear the pain of tattooist's needles and piercing guns. In the centre of the room was a long black leather couch; next to it stood a chrome instrument table that had a tattooing gun and a collection of small ink bottles and felt tipped pens on the top. The heat from an overhead lamp illuminated the whole area.

Dave Corden's naked dead body had been discovered by his shop assistant. The owner of the tattoo parlour had lain backwards across the bed in the tattoo studio; his legs dangled astride the black leather couch. A black bin liner had been pulled over his head and gathered tightly around his neck with duct tape to cut off his air supply. Dave's wrists had been bound together with more silver duct tape; his lifeless hands cupped around his genitals that had been shaved with a razor. On discovering the body, Steve Perkins had frantically torn into the plastic bag in a vain effort to resuscitate his boss, but he had been too late to save the shop owner's life. Dave's head now hung limply over the end of the bed; pieces of shredded black bin liner fluttered on the floor beneath him.

Razor Fish was dead.

"So was he found like this?" asked Richens.

Kath Cooper, a forensic medical examiner was busily dictating a few notes into her voice recorder. A scene of crime photographer laden with a myriad of cameras, tripods and silver coloured flight cases began snapping his flashing camera at every possible angle over Dave Corden's lifeless body.

"Apparently he was," replied Kath. "The shop assistant found him lying on the couch and ripped open the bin liner around his head before dialling nine-nine-nine."

171

"What are your first thoughts?" enquired Richens, as he watched two officers from Kath's forensic team carefully turn the dead man over onto a black body bag.

"Well, it looks like he most probably died from suffocation."

"Did someone do this to him or could it have been a solo sex game?" asked Richens as he surveyed the scene.

"I've seen similar cases before when auto-erotic asphyxiation has gone too far, but I can't confirm anything until I've properly examined him on the slab. And before you ask, I can't give an exact time of death yet either as the heat from that thing could have kept him warm for a long time after his demise," replied Kath as she pointed at the overhead work lamp.

"Maybe we'll get a better idea when we look at the CCTV?" queried Richens hopefully, as he turned to face Sergeant Duke who had just entered the room.

"I'm afraid not sir." Duke hastily zipped up a set of paper overalls over his suit. "The shop assistant says the recorder has bust, there is no security footage . . . and get this, it looks like a red-haired woman in vintage biker clothing was his last customer."

Inspector Richens and Sergeant Duke watched as Dave Corden's lifeless body was zipped into the body bag. The two men exchanged a knowing glance as both of them had noticed a small faded tattoo of a unicursal hexagram positioned on the dead man's chest, just above his left nipple. Almost instinctively both men looked up onto the top of the black leather couch, their eyes searching wildly for a small piece of cardboard. Both men gazed around the room, peering above and below the bench. Sergeant Duke moved around to the end of the bed to glance over the contents of the chrome instruments table.

"Here it is," he exclaimed. Tucked beneath the pre-loaded tattooist's gun lay the small condolence card they had been searching for. Duke carefully picked it up with gloved fingers and placed it into a polythene evidence bag. On the front was a faded picture of a lily. On the back a pre-printed line of text read: With deepest sympathy. Beneath, printed in dark black ink was the dead man's old nickname, Razor Fish.

172

"That's another one of the names from the Tracey Chambers' court case," announced Richens. "It's looking like he was a member of Billy Weber's old biker gang."

"There's another thing that connects them too," said Kath as she began to lock up her silver flight cases. "From my initial alkaline test, it appears that all the surfaces have been wiped clean with surgical alcohol, similar to that which was present at Brian Walsh's gym and on Colin Lawson's underpants."

#

The stale air inside Richens' and Duke's small office felt as if every breath of oxygen had been sucked out of it. A small window had been snapped open in a vain effort to freshen the heavy atmosphere and a blast of icy air shot through the opening. DI Richens stood in front of his white melamine incident board as he flicked through his notepad. He began to summarise the pathologist's report and his own notes from the scene at Dave Corden's shop.

The dead tattooist had traces of Flunitrazepam in his blood and had died from asphyxiation. Inspector Richens strongly suspected that he had been given the date rape sedative to incapacitate him while the perpetrator had stripped him and laid his naked body on the couch, before shaving his genitals, duct taping his wrists together and securing a black bin liner over his head.

Steve Perkins had given the detectives his description of the last customer of the previous day; a beautiful woman with red hair who had visited the tattoo parlour in the afternoon. He didn't know her name, but it was possible that she was the last person to see Dave Corden alive. His boss had sent the staff home early at three-thirty and the young woman was still in the shop when they left. No one had gone back to work that evening. They had all made the most of the unexpected time off and gone Christmas shopping before spending a boozy night at the pub. The awe-struck shop assistant knew his most vivid memory of the customer had been her wonderful bohemian breasts that had bounced out from beneath her vest top. The features of her beautiful face had largely faded into obscurity, but Steve happily filled in the blanks and listed the alluring woman's long red hair, American Confederate flag bandana and vintage clothes as being the most prominent details. He remembered she had asked to have a seasonal tattoo of a cherub or angel. He hadn't really paid close attention to what the beautiful woman had said and assumed her choice of design was because Christmas was only just around the corner.

Afterwards, down at the police station, the nervous shop assistant had viewed the grainy CCTV footage of the red head seen entering and leaving Colin Lawson's loft apartment. He had also been shown a black-and-white print of the woman caught on the security camera from the foyer of Brian Walsh's gym. Steve said the customer who had visited Dave Corden's shop looked similar to the women in the video and photograph, as all of them had worn the same style of seventies' garb; but without a clear view of the faces on the screen, he couldn't be absolutely certain either of them were the same person as the hypnotic beauty who had mesmerised him and his boss in the tattoo parlour. Also, the woman who had been at Dave Corden's shop that day was an ink virgin, she didn't have any tattoos at all; let alone a sleeve like the one on the woman in the monochrome footage from Brian Walsh's gym.

Inspector Richens pulled the lid off his marker pen with his teeth and began to write on the melamine incident board. He added two extra columns to his list of victims, by writing the names of Patrick O'Doyle and Dave Corden at the top of the board alongside the names of the other three dead men. Beneath the extended list of names he jotted down the corresponding pseudonym written on the card of condolence found at the tattoo studio. Post mortem photographs of the chest tattoos from each of the two recently dead men were tacked underneath the two new names. Beneath the horizontal dividing line across the board Richens wrote the description of Dave Corden's visitor and the name Cherub/Angel Tattoo, followed by a large question mark.

Richens and Duke noted that condolence cards had been found near to or on four of the bodies, but the detectives had not found one at Patrick O'Doyle's bed-sit. Social workers' notes supplied by Wendy Tatlow had revealed that the dead drug addict was known locally by the nickname of Zombie. He had died from heart failure after taking a mix of cocaine and morphine; a deadly cocktail known as a Speedball.

Background checks confirmed Patrick had been a regular visitor to Colin Lawson's pub. Richens also realised that Zombie's nickname was another one mentioned in the Tracey Chambers case; he had studied his old notes taken during William Weber's interviews, when the hotelier had listed the names of the bikers in the Serpent Sons of Thelema.

In isolation each of the old men's deaths could have remained on the coroner's log as five separate accidents or deemed to be the tragic results of misadventure; but all five men had the same vintage ink tattoo on their chests; they all drank at Hunter's Bar and three of them started their businesses in buildings adjacent to the drinking den. Richens firmly believed it was safe to theorise the tattoos definitely connected the men while they were alive; the condolence cards tallied with the nicknames of the gang members William Weber had given during his trial, and partial fingerprints from all of the dead men were on all of the cards. They had all been members of the Serpent Sons of Thelema and, if they were connected in life, it was possible they could somehow be connected in death. Richens felt sure that would be the case.

"Did the boffins in the Cyber unit ever manage to get a lead off that crank voicemail about the killer being a ghost?" asked Duke with a wry chuckle, as he searched through the files on his laptop.

"Is it some sort of old codgers' suicide pact? Or is someone seriously going around systematically bumping off all the members of a defunct seventies' biker gang just for kicks?" mused Richens, deep in thought. "To be honest mate, I wouldn't be quick to dismiss any theory at this point; ghost or no ghost."

Duke discovered that Trudi Jones had traced the phone number to a landline in the betting shop in Lye Heath. Trudi and the cyber team had managed to synch the audio file of the voicemail with a CCTV security video that had been recorded inside the bookies at the time of the call. Richens quickly opened up a copy of what the technicians had created.

175

The shop's CCTV recording had clearly shown Patrick O'Doyle using the phone at the time the fractious call had been made. From the footage, it was obvious that Patrick was very frightened as he constantly looked around him to check none of the other people in the shop were listening in on his call. The fretful old man hung up the receiver and made his way out of the bookies onto the path outside.

As the two detectives listened to the terrified wheezing voice on the tape, Richens felt it would simply lead to another dead end.

"... *she's fuckin' comin' for us all. Tracey won't stop 'til she's killed everyone,*" Patrick O'Doyle's words ended. Richens stopped the video. He knew that he was grasping at straws. The fact that he had momentarily entertained the preposterous theory that a ghost could be the serial killer meant the case was in danger of falling apart. Duke clicked away the file.

No one had noticed the remaining frames on the grainy CCTV recording featured a tall imposing figure in a heavy black overcoat that followed Zombie along the pavement outside, a couple of seconds after he left the betting shop.

"Well, someone's got a murderous vendetta against the biking pensioners. I reckon Patrick O'Doyle knew more about it than he was letting on," suggested Richens. "And who exactly did he mean when he said *us*? Was it all members of the biker gang or what?"

"Well, it's difficult to say really, 'cos according to his social worker, Zombie, as he was known to his friends, was so spaced out most of the time that it would have been hard for him to know what was fact and what was in his imagination," replied the sergeant ruefully.

"Yes, Duchess, but if they are murders and not some weird coincidence, then this sort of shit has taken some careful planning; just look how ironic the deaths have been."

It hadn't escaped the inspector's highly analytical mind how the gruesome nature of each man's death had encapsulated the very essence of each gang member's nickname. Bullet had shot off at high speed on his bike to lose his head; Yardy had drowned in two bottles of whiskey from his famous yard-of-ale glass; Crusher had been crushed beneath his own gym weights

176

and Zombie had become the ultimate space cadet by filling his bony body with an overdose of cocaine and morphine. Richens shuddered at the thought of how Razor Fish must have flapped like a mullet on the quayside as he held his breath and suffocated inside a black plastic bin liner. The inspector was convinced that only someone who knew these men's nicknames and reputations would be able to meticulously plan such irony.

"That still leaves William Weber in the frame then," suggested Duke. "But he's still tucked up in Chalmoor at her Majesty's pleasure."

Billy had not given Inspector Richens any further information about the Serpent Sons of Thelema during their meeting at the prison. He had refused to confirm if the dead men on Richens' list had once belonged to his sordid brotherhood. Billy had still felt the cold shudder of Sparks' threats should he ever break his oath of allegiance to the fraternity. Chiltern and Richens had failed William a decade before by not believing his innocence. The anxious prisoner simply could not trust the police to protect his estranged family on the outside.

The only new information that Richens had managed to acquire was from the dying man's medical team at the infirmary. They had confirmed William Weber also had a small tattoo just above his left nipple. It was described by one of the nurses as being a six-sided open star; a design that Inspector Richens realised was a unicursal hexagram.

"But why won't the weasel Weber squeal? What has he got to lose?" asked Duke.

"Maybe he's still scared of something . . . or someone," offered Richens. "Either that or he thinks the police failed him before so he doesn't owe us anything now," added the inspector in a contemplative mood.

"What if he's taken matters into his own hands and got someone on the outside to carry out a vendetta on his behalf sir," suggested Duke.

"Nah," replied Richens dismissively. "There are a few faces that would sit nicely in the frame for this one Duchess, but Weber simply isn't one of them." Richens perused a short list of names associated with the case that were written at the edge of the white melamine incident board. He believed it was highly unlikely that William Weber was involved with the murders.

During his time on remand Billy had been a loner. His ten-year prison record so far documented largely solitary behaviour. Since his incarceration he had made no friends on the inside. Furthermore he had no contact with family or friends on the outside; no letters, phone calls or social visits. The only people he had communicated with were those in his legal team.

At the beginning of his sentence, when his first appeal against his conviction had been unsuccessful, William's faith in the justice system had been firmly crushed. He had withdrawn into his cell, resigned to the fact that he would never escape the cold grey concrete walls of HMP Chalmoor. Nearly a decade later, when his health began to fail, he was transferred to the medical wing. The only visitor he had seen recently was someone from his solicitor's office who was trying to launch a fresh appeal in a last ditch attempt to get the ailing man released.

"Yes, Weber definitely holds a grudge against his old fraternity but there's no way he could be behind these deaths," announced Richens. "Also he might not be the only member of the old gang with a grudge that's still alive. What about the leader of the Serpent Sons that Weber mentioned at his trial . . . the one whose name Falcon McBride took the piss out of . . . some bloke called Mister Sparks?" he mused.

The two detectives were baffled by the nickname and began to brain storm the wildest of theories behind why anyone would have such a pseudonym. Was he an electrician? Was he a welder? Had he had any connection with fires? An arsonist maybe? Had any of the dead men on Richens' list of victims been associated with anyone convicted of pyromania? Were any of the regulars at Hunter's Bar electricians?

Seemingly endless lists of ideas were scribbled on the back of Richens' incident board as they tried to deduce the mystery man's identity. All suggestions were carefully cross-matched with a long list of businesses that had occupied any of the buildings on Hanford High Street during the past ten years. More officers would have to be seconded to help track down anyone who would know the identity of the unknown Serpent

178

Son of Thelema. Sergeant Duke set up an automated alert on the police information system to immediately let him know of any newly reported local incidents that involved a host of keywords including flames, sparks or electrocution. His inspector was willing to try anything that would help establish the identity of the elusive old biker. Richens knew it would be an extensive search for an elderly wannabe Hell's Angel who was either an accomplished serial killer or someone who could become the vigilante's next victim.

Richens' leaned back into his leather swivel chair and rubbed his hands over his tired face before bringing his index fingers up towards the fine pointed tip of his thin nose. He tucked his thumbs beneath his chin to adopt his familiar prayer pose. Deep in thought, Richens closed his eyes and allowed his searching mind to wander. It seemed as if every path taken in the sprawling maze of brainstormed ideas had led the frustrated detectives to nothing but dead ends.

No one had believed William Weber ten years earlier, when he had protested his innocence and given Inspector Chiltern the nicknames of his old biker gang; no one had considered the chain of events that Weber's old barrister had offered in his client's defence. Richens had been quick to twist the scared guesthouse owner's words to make them conveniently fit his boss's scenario; he had eagerly pounced on Billy's early admission that he was at Himley Chase at the time of Tracey Chambers' murder. Now, the ailing William Weber lay quietly dying in a prison infirmary while ageing rockers with old names from the past were turning up dead. Richens knew that no one but William Weber held the key to cracking this case. Only Billy Kiddo knew Sparks' real identity and it now appeared the old lag's silence was reaping his ultimate revenge on the frustrated inspector.

"Maybe we've been going at this from the wrong angle," announced Richens. Duke looked back at his boss with an intensely quizzical expression. "What about the dead woman's daughter? Sharron Chambers would have a pretty good motive for wanting to bump off anyone associated with her mother's murder." Richens retained his prayer pose.

179

"Revenge killing maybe? Ah, I see what you mean," offered Duke. "How old would she be now?"

"Dunno exactly Duchess, probably early forties, something like that; but with the right bit of Botox, a boob job maybe and large sunglasses, I bet she could pass herself off as someone younger."

"But why wait until now? And hasn't she made a shed load of dosh off the back of selling her story? I mean, it was a book and a film. She must be raking it in, sir."

"That's what I'm getting at Duchess. How much do you reckon she'd get for a sequel?

"Ah yes, I see where you're coming from. And she's got auburn red hair nowadays," added Duke supportively.

"I wonder if Sharron Chambers has a daughter? Maybe the new generation is bumping off granny's old biker gang members?" mused Richens. The trill from a telephone on his sergeant's desk broke his new train of thought. Duke answered the call and looked across at his boss with a frowned expression.

"It's bad news I'm afraid, sir. William Weber passed away in prison just over an hour ago."

#

A tearful Lin Tisserand sat in her car and started the engine. It was late in the evening and a light flurry of December snow had landed on the windows. William Weber was dead. He had lost his final battle and Lin had dutifully been there to hold her client's hand as he slowly ebbed away.

As she waited for the windscreen to defrost, Lin switched her mobile phone back on. Immediately she could see she had a missed call and a voicemail message. She clicked the message open and heard a man's voice.

"Miss Tisserand, this is DI Richens from Hanford CID. I am very sorry to hear the news about William Weber passing away. I understand you were working on his appeal and I wondered if we could meet up for a chat about the case?" The inspector gave his direct number where he could be reached and asked the young woman to contact him as soon as possible.

Lin stared at her phone in disbelief. A fat salty tear trickled down her right cheek as she shook her head.

"What the hell?" she screamed in anger. "What could he possibly think I would tell him? Fucking cheeky bastard!"

The car's heater fans whirred as they fought a valiant battle to clear away the last of the thin white veil of ice on the windscreen. Lin angrily shoved her car into gear and drove out of the prison grounds; the unyielding walls of HMP Chalmoor towered above her in the rear view mirror.

#

A photograph of Dave Corden stared back at Sharron Chambers as she sat at her dining table and carefully cut around a newspaper report about the tattooist's unusual death. Her ring binder was filled with dozens of plastic wallets that safely housed a growing dossier of the local businessmen whom she had met at her mother's memorial service. She took out her notepad and wrote a cross alongside Dave Corden's name. Sharron noticed the only name left on the list without a cross was the imposing George Dalmano. She shivered at the memory of how uneasy he had made her feel at their brief introduction in the Huntsman's Arms all those years ago.

During the past few months, following her meeting with Lin Tisserand, Sharron had come to the unwelcome conclusion that there was a distinct possibility William Weber had been telling the truth and his conviction was unsafe.

A couple of local newspapers had keenly reported the leaked information that the group of recently deceased men in the town had the same chest tattoo. This connection had led Sharron to believe that Peter Crowther, Colin Lawson, Patrick O'Doyle, Brian Walsh and Dave Corden were all members of a biker gang. Could the men who had been at her mother's wake be the Serpent Sons of Thelema? The gang of wannabe Hell's Angels that William Weber had so adamantly blamed for Tracey's murder?

Sharron had reluctantly begun to accept her mother had been killed by the lawless biker gang, but such a revelation would need delicate handling if the author was to retain the public's affection for her gym-slip mum in any sequel to her story. Tracey's involvement with the gang would have to be carefully edited with a very creative piece of writing.

Sharron smiled to herself as she imagined what her free-spirited mother must have been like. How strong the draw of the open road must have been for the young impressionable woman, to leave her whole life behind and take up with a lawless gang of bikers. She thought about the utter shame her grandparents must have felt when Tracey had made her bad decision to leave home and give up her toddler to start a new and exciting life. It was no surprise that Sharron had been brought up on a much tighter leash.

Sharron sniffed back a small tear that was threatening to squeeze out of her right eye as she realised how much she had missed out on while growing up. She had never known the touch of her mother's hand; she had been too young to even remember her mother's voice. Instead she had been raised by embittered grandparents who had only ever given her a carefully edited version of events behind their wilful daughter's disappearance. Someone had robbed Sharron of her mother's love and she was determined they would be made to pay, whoever they were.

#

Miss Tisserand sat in front of DI Richens in his office. She studied the hawk-like stare of the thin-nosed man as he spoke. Lin smiled inwardly as she fondly remembered the way William Weber had described his nemesis; her mind wandered back momentarily to how her client had given an accurate impersonation of the steely detective. She wondered what the policeman expected to achieve from their meeting that day, as she had only agreed to attend out of curiosity. Lin had absolutely no intention of divulging any of Billy Kiddo's carefully guarded secrets.

"Is there anything that Mister Weber was going to use in his appeal that would confirm the real identities of the Serpent Sons of Thelema; evidence that they really existed?" asked Richens. "It's just that I'm investigating a spate of recent deaths and the victims all appear to be associated with the names of William's old biker gang. Now, I need to be able to rule out once and for all if the gang really existed, or if it's just a coincidence that the names have surfaced again?" Richens had carefully phrased his well rehearsed question. Lin took in a deep purposeful breath and stared directly into his eyes.

"As I'm sure you're perfectly aware Inspector, I am under no obligation to give you any of the information that Mister Weber shared with me to help secure his appeal, it is a question of client confidentiality you see," she began, her answer equally well-practised. Richens started to feel a little deflated that the young woman was playing her cards very closely to her chest.

"However, I am sure William would have wanted Tracey's murder to be solved and the perpetrator brought to justice." Lin tucked back an annoying lock of black glossy hair behind her ear. A small glimmer of hope fluttered through the detective's mind. Maybe this wasn't going to be a totally fruitless meeting after all.

"Our main evidence for the appeal pointed to the fact that the shroud used to wrap Tracey's body had been pre-soaked in William Weber's urine. The fact that her clothes were not stained in piss never saw the light of day in court," continued Miss Tisserand. Richens was surprised by the astute young woman's frank description but was unsure where her declaration was leading.

"Basically, that could prove William had not urinated over Tracey Chambers' dead body," she explained. "Secondly, William was the biological father of that poor dead woman's unborn child, which disproves the prosecution's claim that Billy was a stranger who raped her. That's just another fact that was not mentioned at the trial." Lin sat back in her seat, happy that she had been allowed to deliver her findings without interruption. "But quite how Mister Weber's appeal relates to your recent string of unexplained deaths is beyond me I'm afraid."

Richens looked back at her quizzically, gently clasped his hands together and brought his fingers up to beneath his nose, to adopt his prayer pose. *She definitely knows a lot more than she's letting on.*

183

"So what did Weber tell you about his old biker gang? Why did he hold back so much information at his old trial and take the rap for a murder he didn't commit?"

Lin tried to escape the policeman's stare by looking at her watch to check for the time but she knew her attempt to dodge the probing question was futile. Her client was dead. There was nothing to be gained by withholding all of Billy's secrets. However, she was irked by the policeman's attitude and his irreverent use of her client's second name without saying mister before it. She believed William deserved more respect. Lin took in another deep breath and pursed her lips together before carefully thinking about how to phrase her answer.

"Well inspector, *Mister* Weber told me that while he was on remand he had received numerous threats from his old gang leader's acquaintances."

"Would that be someone called Sparks?" interrupted Richens.

"I believe so," replied Miss Tisserand dismissively. "Anyway, William was told what those vile delinquents had done to Tracey, and he lived in fear that his own family would meet a similar fate if he divulged the Serpent Sons' real identities to the authorities."

"So, did he ever divulge Sparks' real identity to you?" asked Richens.

"You've got to understand Inspector, William Weber was a very scared man indeed, and he took those names to his grave." A small tear squeezed out of Lin's right eye.

#

Sergeant Duke sat at his desk in his home office. He had spent most of his evening poring over the names of people who had worked at Dave Corden's tattoo parlour during the two years prior to the shop owner's death. He had initially wondered if a disgruntled ex-employee may have had a grudge against the old tattooist. The names were now being cross-matched against a list of people who had been associated with Brian Walsh's gym, Colin Lawson's pub and Peter Crowther's bike shop. Unfortunately for Duke it was only an informal list of names that had been jotted down during routine enquiries at the business premises following the suspicious deaths. None of the businessmen had kept accurate books and many of the staff had been transient part-timers who were drifting between jobs. Suddenly an unusual name caught the sergeant's eye. He quickly picked up his phone and punched in his boss's number.

"Hi Duchess, how's it going?" announced Richens amid a hubbub of background noise. The inspector had taken a rare night off and had been enjoying a meal in his local pub with Kath Cooper when Duke called. Kath was fully aware that Richens' conversation with his sergeant could take quite a while, so she casually picked up the puddings menu to make it less awkward for her dinner companion.

"Sir, I think I've found something. There was a girl called Angel who worked at Ammo's Cycles just before the owner died; she used to help out in the shop. I dunno if she's anything to do with the woman looking for an angel cherub tattoo, but I'll run a check to see if Peter Crowther ever told the tax office about his employee. We might be able to get an address for her or something."

"Yeah, good plan Duchess," Richens smiled back at Kath as he mimed a small winding-up motion with his right hand.

"Sir, are you in the pub?" From the uncharacteristic short reply, Duke sensed his boss was eager for him to end the call, so he quickly finished his update and hung up.

"Ooh, that was quick. Everything okay?" asked Kath, relieved that Sergeant Duke hadn't hi-jacked their evening. This was the couple's first time alone together outside of work. Kath had warmed to Alexander Richens the very first moment she had met him. His cool measured demeanour had been a most attractive quality; however his delay in asking her out on a date had, for a long time, made her wonder if the attraction was mutual. It had taken weeks of Kath's flirtatious chatter before Alexander had allowed himself to think of her in anything other than a professional capacity. But tonight, she had finally got him all to herself in the pub and things had been warming up nicely until Duke's phone call. Kath had overheard some of the conversation on the phone and reluctantly thought she had

185

better show an interest and ask if there was anything she could help with.

"Well, we seem to be making a bit of progress on stuff, but sometimes it feels like we take one step forward and then two steps back." Alexander picked up a bottle of wine off the table and re-charged both of their glasses.

"I met up with Weber's new brief earlier," Richens' mind switched back into professional mode. "You know, the one who was working on his appeal." He took a sip of wine. "Well, she seemed ever-so cagey, playing her cards tight to her chest. Rather than spill the beans about the old biker gang, she just went prattling on about no one at the trial mentioning the piss stains weren't on any of Tracey's clothes, they were only on the tarpaulin apparently. But there was something about her that made me think she knows a lot more than she's letting on."

"Well, I don't suppose you can blame her really Alex." Kath nodded back at him and lifted her wineglass in appreciation of it being re-filled. "Her poor old client pops his clogs before she's had a chance to clear his name. She must have put in a lot of work on the case and she's bound to feel quite protective about anything she's unearthed, I suppose," she added ruefully.

"Hey, I didn't bring you out on a date to talk shop all night, you know," said Richens, suddenly aware of the change in mood at the table. He smiled warmly at Kath. After months of hesitation, he had finally managed to summon up the courage to ask her out to dinner. He didn't want to waste the evening talking about work.

"Is that what this is then? A date?" chuckled Kath.

"Well, if we're both thinking about dessert, then I should bloody-well hope so," laughed Richens with a wink as he picked up the puddings menu.

Chapter 18

George Dalmano flicked a switch on his Jacuzzi to drive the hot tub bubbles to massaging power. He slowly lowered his silver-haired torso beneath the rippling water. In his mind he deserved the rewarding pleasure of the warm frothy water soothing his leathery tattooed body; after all he believed he'd just given his latest squeeze the best fuck of her life and that had taken stamina. He was convinced the sultry cock teaser had an insatiable appetite for rough sex that constantly needed to be satisfied. The arrogant lothario firmly believed the woman was always gagging for it, always ready; even on the rare occasion when she had said no, he knew she had really meant yes. George needed to re-fill his glass with fresh champagne to help wash down another blue pill. He could then recharge his spent batteries ready for the next performance.

The woman he was so eager to service was a beautiful flame-haired woman called Angie, or Angel as she was nicknamed by her friends. She had always been a keen little devil in the sack and George had become fond of lengthening her name to give him more to grab onto during his moments of ecstasy. The four syllables of Angel-Baby was always a perfect fit to accompany his final thrusting jerks of torrid sex. It had become George's predictable method of announcing he would soon be finished with his conquest; it would be Angel's cue to dutifully crawl away and loyally wait for the old fiend to recover.

George Dalmano believed his Angel-Baby was everything he had ever searched for in his ideal woman. She was a perfectly compliant fuck slut who would obediently do anything he told her to do. The alluring concubine with captivating green eyes and long red hair had playfully wriggled beneath him between the satin sheets of five-star hotel bedrooms, at all times of the day and night. She never answered back; she never asked awkward questions, instead she had eagerly responded to every depraved demand and taken his pumped-up cock inside her in any debauched way George had invented. Angel-Baby had never complained about the tight buckles and straps that had burned into her soft skin, or the stinging spank marks and bruises that had followed seemingly endless bondage sessions in a merry-go-round of anonymous luxury penthouse suites. The once fiery red head had been tamed; she silently obeyed any command George chose to fire at her and she had now become his full time fuck-buddy of choice. Today, as a special reward for her months of sexual servitude, she had been allowed to visit the millionaire's opulent home and play with him on the pool party deck.

George closed his eyes and let out a small self-satisfied sigh of contentment. The foam of hot-tub bubbles frothed over his body, a small wave of caressing warm water lapped over his leathery torso. He didn't see the slender hand that pushed the patio heater over the edge of the sunken hot tub. He had no warning of the thrashing electrical torrent that was unleashed when the three kilo watts of power hit the water. He had no escape from the cascade of burning current that would furiously extinguish his sordid life.

Sparks was dead.

Angel got dressed quickly. She knew she only had an hour or so before the gardener would arrive to cut the lawns. Although this was only the first time she had been invited into the millionaire businessman's home, she knew every small detail of the grounds man's routine. The proud George Dalmano had often bragged that he never needed to lift a finger to maintain the expanse of gardens that surrounded his plush mansion. His team of carefully selected housekeepers and handymen ran a very tight ship. They were under strict instructions to visit the house each afternoon at two-thirty sharp and work their magic for three hours only. This arrangement meant minimal intrusion on the millionaire's lifestyle and he knew he would not be disturbed outside of the timeslot.

Slowly and purposefully Angel pulled on a pair of latex gloves. She washed out her empty champagne flute and placed it next to the other glasses on the neatly stacked bar. Next she reached into her rucksack and pulled out a cleaning cloth and small bottle of concentrated surgical spirit. Angel thoroughly wiped over the coffee table and sun loungers. She gathered all of her belongings together and walked along the edge of the garden towards the front of the house. The young woman paused before turning around to take one final look at George Dalmano's twitching dead body that lay in the electrified Jacuzzi. She smiled inwardly, knowing that her work was done and the last member of the Thelema brotherhood would soon be crawling through the burning gates of hell.

#

Lin Tisserand sat alone in her office. She stared across at a tall stack of manila-coloured folders that had been arranged in a neat pile on one corner of her leather-clad desk. For over a year, every spare moment in the young trainee lawyer's daily life had been consumed by the overwhelming need to win William Weber's appeal. She had spent hours before the start of each working day checking over any new details that had come to light; long evenings had been spent alone with her laptop computer as she typed up her latest findings. The stack of beige cardboard files had become such an integral part of her daily life. The determined Lin had embarked on a one-woman crusade to secure the release of William Weber from Chalmoor Prison before he lost his own valiant battle against ailing health. Now her dream of victory, standing triumphantly shoulder-to-shoulder with her suited-and-booted client outside the Court of Appeal lay in tatters. It was too late; she had failed in her mission. William Weber was dead. Today would be her last day in Hanford, before she took up her new position in the company's Bristol office.

Miss Tisserand leaned on the desk and rubbed her tired eyes with her hands. The persistent lock of glossy blue-black hair flopped in front of her face. She smiled inwardly as she remembered how often her client had playfully teased her for having such a boyish short hair cut; how William had laughed each time she pulled her long fringe back behind her ears, for it to then promptly spring forward again across her eyes.

Lin heard a soft beep on her phone to alert her to a new message. It was an email from the clerk at the Land Registry

189

Office that confirmed the pebble-dashed bikers' den on Anglesey Street had been owned by a man called George Dalmano until the end of nineteen-seventy-six. The paperwork had been difficult to trace as the building had since been demolished when it became the subject of a compulsory purchase order in the early eighties. The land was taken back by Hanford Council and developed for a new social housing scheme.

This was a welcome piece of news for Lin, but it had come too late to help her client. Miss Tisserand knew that Godfrey Hathergood had never made any enquiries into the property as Billy had insisted at his trial that the clubhouse was a squat. Godfrey had agreed that, as there was no official tenancy agreement back then, it would have been an expensive waste of time establishing who owned the house. But now it would have been another crucial piece of evidence to secure William's successful appeal. It would have at least confirmed the existence of the biker gang's headquarters that had been so easily dismissed by Fiona 'Falcon' McBride at William's trial.

Lin stood up from behind her desk and picked up a large cardboard archive box that had her client's name written on the side. With tear-filled eyes she neatly placed the stack of manila folders inside the carton and secured a lid to the top with twine. She took a black felt pen and wrote the date beneath William's name, followed by the word 'deceased' in brackets. Lin knew one day she would start a fresh appeal to get a posthumous pardon for her client, and today's news about the house would help with that. But, for the time being, the case was on hold. The large cardboard box of carefully gathered evidence and memories would now be consigned to the bulging shelves in the archived storage facility across the other side of Hanford town centre.

#

DI Richens raced his car along the dusty winding road. Duke sat in silence in the front passenger seat. He realised his boss was deep in thought by the way that Richens was biting hard on his bottom lip and gripping the steering wheel firmly in both hands. As the car snaked through miles of narrow country lanes, Duke gazed out of the windscreen and watched the summer sunshine wash over a patchwork quilt of farmers' fields that were edged with neatly manicured hedges. The detectives had been called out to the scene of a suspicious death at the mansion of a local businessman. The dead body had been discovered by the estate's gardener.

During the past six months since Sergeant Duke set up his automated alert on the police information system, there had been numerous reports of deaths and near fatal accidents associated with sparks, electrocution and fires; but nothing had connected any of those victims to the Serpent Sons of Thelema. All the detectives knew was their latest hapless victim had been electrocuted by a patio heater in George Dalmano's Jacuzzi. Could this be the final piece of the William Weber jigsaw they had been searching for? Or would it be just another one of Duke's dead ends?

The wheels of Richens' car swung onto the gravelled driveway in front of a large cream-rendered Victorian manor house, before braking to a shuddering halt on the Cotswold stone chippings. Richens and Duke climbed out of the car and were greeted by the heady aroma of freshly mown grass. The two men followed a waiting police constable down a narrow footpath to one side of the building. The small entourage made their way around to the gardens at the rear of the house. Richens and Duke peered down towards the end of a long lush green lawn and, in the distance, saw the familiar site of Kath Cooper wearing white paper overalls and plastic shoe covers. The forensic examiner was kneeling down beneath a large white canvas structure, next to George Dalmano's Jacuzzi pool. She beckoned the two detectives to join her behind the gazebo's billowing muslin drapes.

"Hello Alexander," said Kath, giving a small soft smile to Richens as she pulled off a pair of latex gloves. "It all appears to be accidental at the moment. An accurate time of death is difficult to establish because of the temperature of the water, but as soon as I know anything you'll be the first to hear." Kath had anticipated the detective's predictable questions.

191

"The deceased has been identified by that chap over there as being George Dalmano," added the medic, as she nodded in the direction of a bewildered-looking elderly man who was being comforted by a police officer. The startled pensioner was Derek, the gardener. He had visited the property to carry out his usual methodical maintenance of the grounds, starting with mowing the vast area of lawn next to the house, before making his way down the long wide runway of grass towards the pool area.

"Our victim had a fair bit of dosh to his name then?" observed Richens as he surveyed the scene and pointed at the dead body in the Jacuzzi.

"Yes, he was the owner of Dalmano's Motors?" she replied, with an upwards inflection at the end, as if to ask whether Richens was familiar with the company. "He was a bit of a shady character by all accounts. I nearly bought a new Merc from his dealership last year." Kath began packing away her silver flight case.

"You changed your mind then?" Richens had only ever seen the pathologist drive a Lexus.

"Yep, basically Dalmano was a bit condescending and he had a load of cheeky chappies working for him. I don't think any of them had much respect for women. Anyway, everything was friendly in the showroom, but I sensed an underlying menace that I'd end up in the foundations of a fly-over if the car was faulty and I asked for a refund."

Richens glanced around the carefully laid-out decked party zone. He imagined how often it could have been the scene of raucous parties with scantily-clad young women giggling as they frolicked with dirty old men in the pool. Despite his rough diamond reputation, George Dalmano had never graced the cells at Hanford town nick. Even in his misspent youth he had always managed to slip beneath the radar of any serious criminal investigations, but his reputation as a slightly dodgy car dealer and wild party animal had preceded him. Richens could only stare in wonder at the decadent trappings of the millionaire businessman's lifestyle.

The opulent surroundings were extremely comfortable. The decked hot-tub area sat beneath a semi-permanent gazebo that was next to a long rectangular swimming pool. The whole party section was sited away from the main house, at the end of the partly mown sumptuous runway of grass. Out of sight of any prying eyes, the Jacuzzi deck would have been a perfect secret haven that could have enabled the homeowner and his acquaintances to indulge in unimaginable levels of perversion, and no one would ever have known. Derek's hastily parked ride-on lawnmower was positioned at the end of the grass, it had been abandoned by the shocked gardener as he was about to make his first turn back up towards the house.

Could this ageing pony-tailed car dealer have been connected to the other five dead men? wondered Richens. The inspector shook his head as the seemingly ridiculous thought withered to the far recesses of his mind. Even though George Dalmano was a dirty old man, Richens thought there was no way anyone with his amount of wealth and business acumen could ever have been involved with a gang of delinquent bikers. The steely inspector was beginning to doubt this death was associated with the other five investigations.

It had been six months since William Weber had lost his battle with Cancer. Until today, there had been no other unexplained deaths of old men in Hanford since then. When Billy died the killings stopped. Inspector Richens was beginning to regret his crusade to find the elusive man called Sparks. He had rushed head-first down another one of his sergeant's dead-end alleys and a brick wall had hit him firmly between his tired eyes. He believed George Dalmano's electrocution would be just another coincidence that matched the sparks alert signal set up by his assisting officer. Another one of Duke's dead-ends.

"Sir, he's got a tattoo," shouted Duke, rudely interrupting his boss's contemplative mood. Inspector Richens walked over to join his colleague at the side of the Jacuzzi. Two officers from Kath's forensics team lifted George Dalmano's body out of the water. The short silvery blanket of hairs on the dead man's chest glistened in the hazy evening sunlight to reveal a small faded tattoo of a unicursal hexagram located just above his left nipple. Richens and Duke nodded a knowing glance at each other. The inspector inwardly chided himself for having earlier

193

doubted his loyal sergeant's diligent work. They had found the final member of William Weber's old biker gang.

The inspector turned to face Kath Cooper as she finished off packing her instruments into a silver flight case.

"Have you lifted any decent prints from anywhere?" asked Richens.

"Not as many as I would have expected there to be. It smells as if the scene out here has been wiped clean with some kind of surgical spirit again," replied the medic.

Duke watched a policeman gather up a white fluffy towelling bathrobe from a sun lounger by the pool. The officer lifted the robe by the collar and began to roll the garment into a large polythene evidence bag.

"What's that?" shouted Duke. A small piece of cardboard had dropped out of the pocket of the bathrobe and fluttered down onto the decked terrace below. Duke pulled on a pair of latex gloves and bent down to carefully pick up the piece of cardboard. On the front of the card was a faded picture of a lily. On the back a pre-printed line of text read: With deepest sympathy. Beneath, in neat smudged handwriting was the nickname 'Sparks'.

#

Sharron Chambers stood in a short queue at her local newsagent's shop. The woman in front had a small sleeping child with her that was strapped into a baby buggy. The young mother was busy arguing with a shop assistant, claiming she had been given the incorrect change. She was blissfully unaware of the increasing line of customers patiently waiting behind her. The stroppy young woman tried awkwardly to turn her baby's pushchair around in the confined space at the counter, before carelessly running one of its wheels over Sharron's foot. The bounce of the buggy awoke the child inside and she began to cry.

"Sorry," apologised Sharron, even though the encounter hadn't been her fault. The young woman glared back accusingly before pushing her buggy and squawking toddler back through the queue and out of the shop. Sharron shook her head and stepped up to the counter to pick up a newspaper. The shop assistant smiled warmly as he rang up the sale in his till.

"It's amazing how people can be so rude, isn't it?" he said, as he held out his hand for Sharron's payment. "Life's too short to be moody. You should live every day to the full, that's my motto. I mean just look at that poor old sod." The chatty young man pointed at the headline on the front page of the Hanford Recorder.

Local Millionaire Businessman Found Dead.

The article announced that the successful car dealership owner, George Dalmano, had been electrocuted in his Jacuzzi. The police had said the death was unexplained, Detective Inspector Richens had declined to comment on whether they were treating the incident as suspicious.

"No matter how much money you have, you never know when your number's going to be up, do you?" continued the shop assistant. Sharron paid for her newspaper and smiled warmly back at the philosophical young man.

"Yes, I guess you never can tell," she replied with a wry smirk.

Chapter 19

January 2016 – Six Months Later.

Inspector Richens studied his old chaotic notes written on the white melamine incident board in his office. The names and pseudonyms of six dead men were still written across the top of the board, photographs of their chest tattoos still tacked underneath. In Richens' mind there had been plenty of evidence to suggest George Dalmano met his fate at the hands of the same person responsible for at least four of the other deaths. A condolence card had been discovered at the scene and traces of isopropyl alcohol had been found on the coffee table and sun loungers on the party deck. However, those pieces of evidence did not prove foul play.

Richens impatiently tapped the end of his marker pen between his teeth. During the past six months he had become increasingly frustrated that he had no further information to add to his notes underneath the horizontal dividing line. There had been no further sightings of the red-haired woman in vintage clothing associated with Dave Corden's death; the mysterious beauty that Richens and Duke now referred to as The Scarlet Angel.

Duke's hopeful lead of a young woman matching that name who had worked at Ammo's bike shop had been fruitless. There was no record of her at the tax office and no other contact information at the shop. She had been a casual member of staff paid in cash from the till. Another former employee had remembered Angel was at Peter Crowther's funeral, but that was the last he had seen of her.

The detectives' other possible theory that Sharron, Tracey Chambers' daughter, was the perpetrator had been quickly dismissed. They believed avenging her mother's death would have given Sharron a strong motive for committing the murders, but the middle-aged woman had little means to carry out the crimes; she simply did not match the suspect's appearance. Sharron's slightly over-weight frame and older face would not have seduced the men or lured them to their deaths. She also had water-tight alibis for the times of each incident. Duke had once suggested that Sharron may have had a younger accomplice, but further investigations had revealed she had no obvious relatives or associates that would fit the bill. The police could not establish a strong enough connection between the woman and the dead men.

Kath Cooper's pathology report said George Dalmano had taken a sexual stimulant shortly before his death which suggested he had been anticipating a close encounter with someone; yet no one had seen anyone enter or leave the randy old car salesman's home on the day of his death. Derek the gardener was adamant that, while he had been mowing the lawns, he had not seen anyone else at the property; there had been no one else there apart from George's dead body lying in the Jacuzzi.

There had been no CCTV footage from over the garden or pool area at George's house. Although the presence of solvent cleaner had been suspicious, and the condolence card was a common element shared with four of the other deaths, the rest of the scene around the secluded hot tub suggested it was nothing more than another tragic accident. At George's inquest, the coroner concluded there had been a distinct lack of evidence to prove foul play. It was assumed the old man had consumed a few too many glasses of champagne and drunkenly pulled the electric patio heater into the sunken Jacuzzi pool himself.

"There's got to be something that I'm missing here," mused Richens. Duke looked up from his desk. He completely understood his boss's frustration but felt powerless to help. Little bits and pieces of the puzzle had seemed to fit into place so easily, but there were too many gaping holes throughout the whole case. Apart from knowing Patrick Zombie O'Doyle drank at Yardy's pub and he had a hexagram tattoo on his chest which linked him to the Serpent Sons of Thelema, neither of the detectives could find anything else to positively connect the old drug dealer's demise to all of the other men's deaths. Additionally, despite an exhaustive search, no condolence card had been found at Zombie's bed-sit; however Patrick's partial fingerprints were among those on the five cards found at the other scenes.

"Let's just take the coke-head out of the equation for a moment," said Richens in an almost defiant last ditch attempt to breathe life back into the flagging investigation. "Maybe Patrick O'Doyle's death *was* an accident." The inspector's racing mind continued to run through all the data as Duke watched his boss frantically scribble over the incident board one more time.

"Okay, it could have been murder, but I don't think the same person who was bumping off the rest of the gang was responsible for Zombie popping his clogs; otherwise we can assume they would have left a condolence card, right?" Richens looked over to Duke who nodded in agreement.

"Whoever did this wanted us and the victims to know the deaths were all connected, that's why they left the calling cards. They wanted us to know the Serpent Sons of Thelema were being systematically picked off one-by-one, whilst making all the deaths look like accidents or misadventure to the outside world," mused Richens. "It was a stark warning to all the bikers in the gang; almost as if our Scarlet Angel was saying you can't escape, sooner or later I'm coming for you all."

The terrifyingly vengeful undertone had been clearly understood by the detectives. If she had been a vigilante serial killer, then she had pulled all the strings in this case and, six months later, the police were still dancing to her tune. They were no closer to unveiling the perpetrator's identity. Richens knew he had lost control of the investigation, as everything in it had begun to unravel.

The men's chest tattoos were the only common theme to link all six deaths. The pseudonyms on the five cards matched the nicknames given by William Weber at his trial, but the wrongly convicted man had been unable or unwilling to confirm the true identities of the men who had been in his biker gang.

Public appeals to help identify the woman seen in the grainy security footage taken from the landing outside Yardy's loft apartment and the foyer at Crusher's gym had been fruitless. Subtle small changes in her appearance had created enough doubt in the minds of witnesses that they could not confirm the woman at the bike shop, pub, gym and tattoo studio had been the same person. The elusive red-haired woman who had wanted an image of an angel inked onto her breast at Razor Fish's tattoo parlour was nowhere to be found.

The detectives' only other lead had been from a rambling phone message left by a male caller just after the third death. The voice claimed the woman in the CCTV from Hunter's Bar was the ghost of Tracey Chambers who had returned to avenge her murder. The detectives had later established it was Patrick O'Doyle who had made that terrified call from a payphone inside the bookies shop, but they had never had the opportunity to speak to the old biker, as those fretful cries would be the last phone call he would ever make.

Richens had reluctantly come to believe that William Weber had been telling the truth about the Serpent Sons of Thelema and he had not been involved with Tracey's death. He had initially believed that if Billy was an innocent man, then surely the old lag would have wanted to reap his revenge on the gang? But Lin Tisserand had divulged the sad fact that the old biker had feared for his family's safety; his faith in the justice system had been shattered and he could not risk any reprisals. He could never give the authorities the true identities of his old brotherhood.

The man whom Richens believed had the ultimate motive for committing the series of gruesome murders had been in prison at the time of the first five deaths; he had passed away six months before George Dalmano's electrocution.

The late William Weber had been a loner on the inside and he had received no visits from friends or family at any point during his ten years in prison. The wrongly convicted dying man had cut himself off from the outside world; he would not have had the opportunity to arrange the murders from behind the concrete walls of HMP Chalmoor.

William Weber had died in prison one year ago. Richens firmly believed Bullet, Yardy, Crusher, Zombie, Razor Fish and Sparks had all been murdered; all six deaths made to look convincingly like accidents. If that was the case, then the seasoned detective knew he was dealing with a serial killer who was still very much at large. He only hoped to God that, now all of the members of the old biker gang were dead, the vigilante had reaped her revenge and no more of Hanford's old men would suffer a grisly end.

Sergeant Duke watched his dejected boss reluctantly remove the six photographs from the incident board before wiping a dampened rag over the white melamine. He hated to see his team lose. It felt as if most of the last couple of years' work had been for nothing. Richens grudgingly handed the photographs to Duke for filing into six separate folders. The inspector had fought desperately with his superiors to keep the files open as one large case; clinging on to any loose thread of hope that he could find. But due to a lack of any new evidence, Richens and Duke had been instructed to wind down the investigation. Despite the inspector's firm belief he was dealing with half a dozen connected murders, the six deaths could not be unequivocally linked and they had each been officially recorded as accidental or misadventure. The two detectives would be assigned to new cases in the morning.

The mysterious perpetrator would remain at large, proud of having rid Hanford of a sleazy gang of sexual predators whilst avenging the murder of Tracey Chambers and the wrongful imprisonment of William Weber.

Inspector Richens left his office early and got into his car to begin the slow crawl through rush hour traffic. He joined a meandering snake of stop-start cars on the High Street and allowed his mind to wander through the facts of the all-consuming case he had failed to solve. It had been one year since William Weber had passed away in Chalmoor Prison, and it had been six months since the last discovery of a dead body with a unicursal hexagon tattoo. The contemplative inspector sorely regretted not being able to quell the nagging realisation in his mind about Tracey Chambers' murder; the awful truth that he been instrumental in the conviction of an innocent man. Had the reclusive vengeful William Weber become a successful serial killer from behind the prison's walls? If so, how had he got away with it?

What a fucking mess. Richens thought if only he hadn't blindly followed Chiltern all those years ago, maybe he wouldn't have been so quick to put away the wrong person. He wondered what drove his old boss to be so convinced that Billy

Kiddo was a murderer in the first place? *Maybe old boy Chiltern could give me his perspective on things now.*

Richens knew DI Chiltern had retired many years before, but he still regularly attended social events with CID and kept in touch with old colleagues; but would his old boss be up for a chat about the historic case?

#

The Granary Mill Hotel was a mock Tudor building at the end of a long stone-chip driveway. The site had once been part of the Himley Estate and its owners had capitalised on its geographical location to re-brand it as being part of a stately home. A chill wind blew into Sharron Chambers' face as she quickly made her way to the entrance doors, crunching the kitten heels of her leopard print shoes on the honey coloured gravel driveway. A smiling concierge gave her a familiar welcoming nod as she entered the wooden-beamed reception hall.

This was a favourite location for Sharron to visit when meeting with her publisher. It was a moderately sized hotel that offered a certain degree of anonymity for its guests yet it still retained a warm homely atmosphere. She loved the private nooks and crannies in the residents' bar; the medieval wooden booths that kept secret conversations totally confidential. The elegant middle-aged woman ordered a pot of coffee for two before walking over towards a large inglenook fireplace and sitting down on a comfortable chaise longue. A young studious man was sat on a sofa opposite. He was reading a printed manuscript and seemed to be absorbed by its contents, as he didn't bother to look up to see who had joined him by the fireplace. He was Sharron Chambers' literary agent, Tarquin Flanders.

Sharron had been keen to take full advantage of the renewed media interest in the case of her mother's murder. It had been a few years since her first novel and the subsequent film had captivated its willing audience. The Royalty cheques had long since depleted but Sharron's expensive lifestyle still needed to be funded. Media speculation had been sparked by the deaths of

201

six local men and many of the tabloids referred to them as members of the gang suspected of Tracey's murder.

Following the deaths of Peter Crowther, Colin Lawson and Brian Walsh, Sharron had started to collect her large scrapbook of newspaper clippings. She realised all of the dead men had attended her late mother's memorial service. The writer's interest had been further aroused on hearing about the deaths of Patrick O'Doyle, Dave Corden and finally the imposing George Dalmano.

Once the information about the dead men's chest tattoos had leaked out, the press had associated all of the deceased ex-bikers with William Weber's infamous Serpent Sons of Thelema and the Tracey Chambers' case. Some newspapers had gone so far as to suggest Hanford had a brutal serial killer who was hell bent on avenging Tracey's murder. The vintage appearance of the red-haired young women featured in CCTV footage from two of the murder scenes had added another interesting dimension to the unsolved cases.

Steve Perkins had deliberately described the young woman who visited Dave Corden's tattoo parlour as 'other worldly' and that she appeared to be from a bye gone age. Steve's carefully chosen words had brought him numerous lucrative television interviews and fuelled an urban legend that the vigilante who was killing the ex Serpent Sons of Thelema was the ghost of Tracey Chambers. Scores of paranormal investigators had contacted Sharron, all keen to offer help in contacting the lost spirit of her murdered mother.

A waitress delivered a fresh cafetiere of coffee, two bone China cups and a small jug of cream and placed them on a table in front of the sofa. Sharron silently poured herself a cup and settled back into the chaise longue as she patiently waited for Tarquin Flanders to give his critique on the sequel to her story.

Eventually, Tarquin looked up and acknowledged his client with a smile. He turned over the last page of his manuscript and placed the bundle of papers on the coffee table.

"What do you think then?" asked Sharron excitedly, as she nervously bit her bottom lip. Tarquin poured himself a fresh cup of coffee and relaxed back onto his sofa.

"So, what you're saying now is that your mother was killed by the Serpent Sons of Thelema; She was abducted by the gang and slain in the woods. William Weber was an innocent man convicted of the crime and now all the guilty men that were really responsible for Tracey's death have been bumped off by a vigilante serial killer." The young man gazed back at his client in feigned disbelief. "Alternatively you think it could be your mother's ghost committing the murders?" Tarquin allowed a wry smile to grow across his lips. This was an explosive and captivating sequel to an otherwise dead-in-the-water story that had long passed its sell-by date.

Tarquin did not believe in the super natural; however he did allow himself the delicious indulgence of imagining Sharron Chambers had arranged for the killings herself. Such notoriety would certainly add an interesting dimension to his client's saleability, but would she do such a thing simply to keep interest in her mother's story alive?

#

DI Richens sat at a breakfast bar in the kitchen at his former boss's house. Inspector Alan Chiltern had been instrumental in securing an early trial for William Weber ten years previously. Richens had always wondered why his senior colleague had been so sure that he had the right man in the frame for Tracey Chambers' murder.

"You've got to remember I'd not long left the vice squad before coming to work out my last couple of years at Hanford before retirement," said Alan casually, as he poured tea into two mugs that were sat on top of the work surface. "Christ, when I think back to all the dregs of humanity I had to deal with back then; all those holier-than-thou do-gooders on local councils who were no better than the squalid thieves on the streets." He handed a mug of tea to Richens before opening a tin of biscuits.

"Most of them were lining their own pockets with as much filthy money as they could lay their hands on; poncing about in posh motors, quaffing down champers, cutting shady deals at their secret society gala dinners . . . and, at the same time, looking down their snooty noses at honest Joe Public," ranted

Alan, as he dunked a custard cream into his steaming hot tea. "Believe you me, there is plenty of lowlife in high places Alex."

Richens couldn't help but wonder if the embittered old man sat in front of him had allowed his vast work experience of dealing with corruption to cloud his judgement. He remembered that his boss had taken an instant dislike to William Weber. Chiltern's hackles had risen when he discovered the hotelier was a freemason. Although William's membership of the organisation had only ever been an innocent networking tool, in Chiltern's mind this conjured up images of clandestine deals and the painful memories of when untouchable dignitaries in the past had enjoyed immunity from prosecution; an occupational hazard the curmudgeonly ex-copper had been faced with throughout his long career.

Richens took a sip of his hot tea as he listened to his old boss wheel out his list of other reasons he had for believing William Weber had murdered Tracey Chambers; from the incriminating DNA on the shroud to the condemned man's refusal to offer up the real identities of his former gang mates, it had been an open-and-shut case in Chiltern's eyes.

"Come on man, you remember Weber's cool-as-a-cucumber response when we showed him the photos of the shovel that was used to stove in that poor girl's head don't you?" prompted Chiltern, trying to back up his old theory.

DI Richens left the old inspector's home that afternoon and climbed into his car for the short journey back to the office. He was feeling ashamed that he hadn't asked more questions at the time of William's arrest; to try and get beneath the accused man's skin. Instead, the awe-struck newly promoted sergeant had blindly followed his boss's lead, but now, ten years later, the older and wiser man firmly believed it was Chiltern's preconceptions of William Weber's lifestyle that had driven him to ferociously pursue the innocent man.

The pulsing snake of rush hour traffic stopped sharply, bringing Richens' car to a halt outside the imposing wrought iron gates of Hanford Town Crematorium. Instinctively Richens turned his car into the car park of the memorial grounds and switched off the ignition. Slowly the inspector took in a deep breath and brought the palms of his hands together. He raised his index fingers towards the fine pointed tip of his thin nose and tucked both of his thumbs beneath his chin. He rested his elbows on the steering wheel to pause for a few moments, before slowly getting out of his car. Richens walked through an open pedestrian door in the wrought iron gates and made his way through to the garden of remembrance. Eventually he stopped and knelt down beside the sun-bleached engraved wooden plaque that bore Tracey Chambers' name.

"I'm so sorry Tracey," whispered Richens.

Out of the corner of his eye the remorseful detective suddenly noticed a small baby robin had landed on the grass nearby. The little bird hopped around on the ground for a short while, before fluttering up to perch on the top of the memorial plaque; its scarlet chest feathers in full view.

"I know the wrong man paid the price for your murder Tracey." Richens watched the little bird skip across the top of the piece of weather-beaten wood. "I promise I'll try to put it right." The inspector stood up slowly and smiled at his new feathered friend before walking back to his car.

Chapter 20

In a peaceful West Country graveyard, the crisp afternoon air was filled with pretty birdsong. An attractive young woman sat at William Weber's graveside. The ever-efficient Miss Tisserand wore a smart red leather two-piece trouser suit and cherry-red cowboy boots. Carefully she leaned a large floral arrangement against a newly positioned granite headstone, taking care not to sink her feet into the soft earth beneath. She smiled at the simple wording that had been etched into the ebony coloured granite. The smart gold lettering, that gave William's name and the dates of his birth and death, bore testament to the existence of the client she had fought so valiantly to save. It was such an anonymous looking epitaph that gave no hint of the bravely stoic man he had once been. Today would have been his birthday, and it was only a month following the first anniversary of his death.

The newly qualified advocate brushed back a chopped lock of fringe that persistently fell across her eyes, as she tenderly remembered the gravely ill client who had given her so much encouragement to carry on with her dream of becoming a lawyer.

Lin stood back from the grave to fondly look down at the flowers she had just laid there. It was a large floral display in the shape of a motorcycle. She had attached a small piece of card to the flowers, a carefully hand-written note that simply said 'To my Daddy.'

Angelina Tisserand turned to walk away from her father's graveside.

The elegant young woman paused for a moment among the gravestones. She cast her mind back almost twelve years to the time when, as a young plump schoolgirl with plaited strawberry blonde hair and freckles, she had attended Tracey Chambers' memorial service. She had watched a group of six middle-aged men arrive; each carrying a small bunch of flowers. George Dalmano had handed out a pack of pre-printed condolence cards for each man to sign. They were passed around the group before being tucked inside the posies.

Angelina had stood in Hanford's garden of remembrance and spoken to Sharron after the memorial service for Tracey Chambers. The young girl had wanted to take up the woman's invitation to join her at the Huntsman's Arms, but her impatient teacher had insisted there was not enough time for the party of schoolgirls to attend the wake; Miss Winbrook had worried that she would get the blame if her pupils missed their afternoon train back to Oxford.

The astute Angelina had pulled on a pair of silk gloves before quickly collecting the pre-printed cards of condolence that the six guilty men had scrawled their nicknames onto. She removed them from the flowers beneath the murdered woman's memorial plaque, taking care to only handle them around the edges, before slipping them inside her notebook for safe keeping. The schoolgirl had recognised those nicknames as the men her father had adamantly blamed during his trial. She returned to her Oxford boarding school and began to craft the perfect plan to avenge her innocent father's wrongful imprisonment.

Angelina's newly married mother and French stepfather had moved to Switzerland to open up a mountain retreat and yoga centre. Soon after, Angelina graduated from the academy in England and the young forensics student began to study law at the University of Lausanne. She had been eager to re-take her father's Germanic surname of Weber, but instead chose to use its French translation; Tisserand.

Ten years later, Angelina learned the sad news of her father's Cancer diagnosis. She knew she needed to help him before it was too late to set the record straight.

Angelina managed to secure an internship with the large organisation that had taken over Godfrey Hathergood's old legal practice. She gave a convincing claim that she wanted to become a defence lawyer and cited William Weber's case at her interview. The enthusiastic student demonstrated how she would relish the opportunity to try and get the guilty conviction over-turned. The law firm largely felt the infamous case was a lost cause, as their client had been rather uncooperative during his trial, so they had nothing to lose by allowing the spirited young woman to test drive her methods. If Angelina succeeded with the appeal, then it would bring free publicity for the law firm; if she failed, then it would have been an ideal project for her to cut her teeth on.

Wearing a glossy blue-black wig and with her first name suitably shortened to the more professional sounding Lin, Miss Tisserand had visited her father in prison.

It had been extremely painful for William to confess to his daughter that he had chosen not to pursue his old biker gang for Tracey's death. He revealed in graphic detail the threats he had received from Sparks whilst on remand; the gruesome account of how Tracey had died and how he had been left with no doubt in his mind that a similar fate would befall his daughter should he ever reveal the gang's details to the authorities. William knew his fateful decision had given him a life sentence and robbed the young girl of her dad, but at least it had kept her safe. Angelina knew her father's selfless act was a large debt that would be almost impossible to repay. In the very least she needed to clear William's name whilst reaping revenge on the Serpent Sons of Thelema.

William and Lin decided at the beginning of their mission that the police could never know about their true relationship. The Webers simply could not be sure who they could trust; for all they knew George Dalmano could have had Inspector Richens in his back pocket and they could not risk the old gang leader being tipped off that Billy Kiddo's daughter was back in town.

Angelina learned all about her father's former sordid brotherhood. How they had systematically raped and defiled Sparks' ol' lady as they had roughly passed Tracey around the gang; bruising her flesh, breaking her bones and shattering a glass bottle inside her, before crushing her head with a final swift blow of the shovel. William had given his daughter all the ammunition she needed to avenge the death of the first woman he had loved; dates, places and the real names of his old fraternity.

Angelina successfully tracked down the men who had conspired to frame her father for their heinous crimes. Armed with the information William had given to her in the cold sparse meeting room at Chalmoor Prison, she knew all of their dirty secrets; their filthy perversions; their unrequited lust for Tracey Chambers and penchant for red heads with big boobs and skinny legs.

The young law student had been keen to meet with Sharron Chambers; after all, the author had profited so handsomely from William Weber's case. Angelina believed if she could convince Tracey's daughter of Billy Kiddo's innocence, then maybe any forthcoming sequel to her book would set the record straight. Angelina had known it would be a risky manoeuvre as there was a very small chance that Sharron may recognise her as once being the young schoolgirl at Tracey's memorial; but there was a second motive to her meeting with the author and it was a risk she had been willing to take. Angelina knew if the police ever discovered she possessed a list of the true identities of the Serpent Sons of Thelema, then it was of paramount importance Inspector Richens did not know William Weber had given her the list of names. If she could get Sharron to mention the names of the local businessmen who had been in the Huntsman's Arms at Tracey's memorial, then Angelina would have a legitimate second source for the information should detectives ever question her about it.

The vengeful biker's daughter had then systematically ticked off every man's name from Sharron's line-up, with a fitting tribute to each of their ill-gotten pseudonyms.

William's wife, Juliette, had also been a fiery red head and Angelina had inherited her mother's genes. With her naturally long red curly hair and wearing green contact lenses with figure-hugging seventies' clothes, the young law student had transformed into slutty Angel; an idealistic image that her targets simply could not resist. Only Zombie had escaped Angelina's direct line of fire. But Angel-Baby had drip-fed George Dalmano so many poisonous doubts about the coke-head's loose lips, that the millionaire car dealer had been driven to murder his old loyal friend out of fear of being associated with Tracey Chambers' death and the Serpent Sons of Thelema.

William had never known the full extent of his daughter's exploits, nor the depths of sexual depravity she had been forced to sink to in order to snare her prey. Angelina was grateful that she had been able to hide the catalogue of sordid details from her ailing father. She had been completely focussed on the vengeful outcome. The initial planning of her sleazy activities had never included sex, but sacrificing her innocence to two of the dirty old men had been an unavoidable means to an end.

Angelina had researched her victims well and initially devised each man's demise with absolute precision. She had never envisaged a small lapse in concentration on entering Brian Walsh's gym would lead to him brutally raping her; that would be the last time she would allow herself to become complacent. Nor had she ever intended to become George Dalmano's fuck-buddy of choice; but planning his perfect demise amid an electrocuting shower of sparks had taken time.

The gang's leader needed to be the last to die. He needed to be made to suffer the mental torment of knowing someone was picking off his old gang members one-by-one. George had hidden the fact that he had felt terror fizz through his veins each time another one of his old timers had met their maker. After Razor Fish's death, George had come to a slow realisation that he had to be next; there was no one else left. It would only be a question of when it would happen.

It took many months of Angel teasingly wriggling between satin sheets in hotel penthouses before George felt comfortable inviting his compliant little fuck-slut into his own home. Even though she had born a startling resemblance to the women associated with his friends' deaths, the old lothario was too arrogant to even contemplate that his sleazy concubine could be capable of such crimes.

Unbeknown to the ageing businessman, and just like the rest of his sordid fraternity, he would die on his own turf, surrounded by all he held dear; in a place where he had felt most comfortable and could safely let his guard down.

Worryingly for Angel, she found that the longer her depraved filthy charade continued, the easier it became to adjust to her alter-ego's lifestyle. Now her mission was complete, she prayed to God, in time, her depraved sexual exploits could become a buried memory.

Angelina slowly walked along a narrow path away from the graveyard; her newly-trimmed auburn hair glinted around her shoulders. She opened her red leather rucksack and retrieved a short black wig from inside. How useful that prop had been whilst starting out in her new legal career. But now it was time to confine the efficiently bobbed legal assistant with glossy blue-black hair to history; a more mature woman had risen from those embers. Angelina scrunched up the hairpiece and dropped it into a waste paper bin by the side of the path. She started to zip her rucksack closed but noticed a small familiar looking piece of crumpled card was inside, caught in a fold at the bottom of the bag. She pulled out the condolence card. On the front was a faded picture of a lily. On the back a pre-printed line of text read: With deepest sympathy. Beneath was written the nickname 'Zombie.' The young woman smiled and let out a small laugh.

"Well, I won't be needing you either, will I?" she snorted, before tearing the card into shreds and throwing it into the bin with the discarded wig.

She climbed astride her father's crimson-red Norton Dominator motorcycle, tied an American Confederate flag bandana across her face and pulled on her crash helmet. The young woman had carried out her father's last wishes and successfully avenged Tracey's murder. With one swift thrust of the kick-start, the vintage motorbike roared into life. There was now only one thing left for Miss Angelina Tisserand to do. She would seek to clear William Weber's name. It was the only right and proper thing to do.

Epilogue

The function suite at the Granary Mill hotel had been festooned in bunting and banners in celebration of Detective Chief Inspector Richens' career. A couple of long tables groaned beneath the weight of a sumptuous buffet and bottles of chilled champagne, as a team of waiting staff buzzed in and out of the room to check everyone had fully charged glasses. Richens had enjoyed a long and successful career in the police, culminating in his promotion to DCI a few years earlier. Many of his old colleagues were present at the retirement party, along with specially invited members of the legal profession. The recently promoted Inspector Duke and his wife Trudi had organised the reception for their old boss. They had recently returned from their honeymoon in the Canaries and the sun-tanned newly-weds now stood side-by-side to welcome their guest of honour. Richens arrived with Kath Cooper on his arm. He had been dating the pathologist for eight years and the couple now intended to retire together to enjoy a slower pace of life in the Dordogne. Richens immediately made his way over to Duke and gave him a hearty man hug. Kath gave Trudi a small peck on the cheek before both women left their men alone to talk shop one last time. Richens and Duke had become best friends over the years and today mark the end of an era for both of them.

"Any regrets then?" asked Duke as he took a small sip of champagne.

"What? About leaving all of this behind?" laughed Richens. "You must be joking mate. Me and Kath are off on a jolly tour of French vineyards next week, and then after that, who knows?" he added with a wink. Duke and Richens clinked glasses as the younger man quickly surveyed the room. He was looking for one specially invited guest in particular.

"Oh blimey, there's the spectre at the feast then," said Duke as he caught a glimpse of Lin Tisserand at the other end of the room.

Following the successful acquittal of the late William Weber, Lin had bathed in the limelight and gained great notoriety from media interest in the case. Her career had rapidly progressed and she was head-hunted by Hanford's most successful legal chambers that specialised in fighting miscarriages of justice. She now enjoyed an enviable reputation as an accomplished defence barrister. Over the years the young advocate had demonstrated fastidious attention to detail, she had managed to get a couple of other historic convictions over-turned, and was well-known as the successful defender of hopeless cases.

Lin was a formidable force and she knew her successes had become a thorn in the side of Hanford's hard working CID, so she had been a little surprised to receive an invitation to DCI Richens' retirement party. Now sporting an elegantly chopped long auburn bob and her trademark grey suit, the young woman smiled over at Richens and Duke before raising her champagne glass in acknowledgement that she had been spotted.

"Perhaps my only regret was not proving that Hanford had a serial killer all those years ago," said Richens ruefully. "Because I'm even more sure about it now; in fact I'm positive that all of those old bikers' sticky ends were connected."

Duke knew the catalogue of deaths from almost ten years previously had remained classified as accidental deaths or misadventures. He thought back to how deflated the whole team had felt when the cases of the dead biker gang members were re-filed as separate incidents and Richens' major investigation was closed down.

"It's a shame, but you can't win 'em all though boss," said Duke supportively. He knew Richens had one of the best clear-up rates of all time at Hanford CID and he wanted to ensure that today would be a day of celebration of his friend's long and distinguished career. None of the gathered guests would be allowed to dwell on any unfinished business from the past. Duke stood up on a chair and tapped the side of his champagne flute with a fork to get everyone's attention.

"Ladies and gentlemen, I would just like to say a few words about the man we are all here today to say farewell to," began Duke. Richens feigned embarrassment by covering his eyes with the palm of his hand, but he was truly delighted by the turn-out of familiar faces that filled the function room.

"I'll certainly miss the old curmudgeon and his bloody brain-teasers," laughed Duke. "But seriously though, I will be forever thankful for his guidance and I'd just like to say how much I have enjoyed learning this old craft that we call policing from perhaps the best teacher anyone could ever hope for."

Richens looked up at his prodigy and mimed a small thank you.

"To DCI Richens; the best analytical mind in the crime fighting business," added Duke as he raised his glass into the air.

"To DCI Richens," chorused the audience, as they all began to clap and demand a speech from the guest of honour. Duke grabbed his old boss's hand and pulled him up to stand on an adjacent chair. Richens cleared his throat and thanked Duke with another hearty hug, as the gathered crowd waited to hear his fond farewell speech.

"As many of you know, me and the lovely Kath Cooper have worked together very closely over the years." Most of the audience giggled and nodded their heads as they were all privy to the open secret that the couple had been in a relationship for the past eight years. Duke graciously climbed down off his chair to give everyone a clearer view of his old boss.

"I am very pleased to say that one thing has lead to another so-to-speak and err, well, can you believe it, Kath has only gone and agreed to take me on and become my wife." The whole room erupted into glorious cheers as everyone raised their champagne flutes to toast the happy couple.

"But that's not all," added Richens. "I'd just like to say that, as you all know, I have had another loyal and hard working partner in my life over the years, and I can't leave here today without mentioning my great admiration for Inspector Duke." Everyone gave a quick cheer. "Let me just say that I have every confidence I am leaving Hanford in a safe pair of hands." The gathered entourage all laughed and clinked glasses, with shouts of *hear, hear* in agreement.

"So, that just brings me onto the serious bit," interrupted Richens in an attempt to quieten the boisterous crowd. "These retirement things can't happen without some sort of reflection on the ones that got away." The room became quiet as most guests fully understood the direction Richens' speech was about to take.

"As many of you know, my biggest regret was my failure to track down Tracey Chambers' killer. Also, not solving the Serpent Sons of Thelema deaths is always niggling at the back of my mind. I suppose some would say they are destined to remain an unsolved mystery," Richens looked around the room for his old superintendent who had closed down his investigation eight years previously.

"But I'm sure Duke hasn't just got you all to come here today to hear me waffle on about my career and how blissfully happy I am going to be in my retirement with Kath. Nah, I'd like to let you all in on a secret." The audience hushed again as they stepped in closer to hear Richens' closing anecdote. Duke had begun to move towards the back of the room as he knew exactly what bombshell revelation his friend was about to unleash.

"Those unsolved cases have driven me to write my memoirs, especially after all the hard work me and Duchess did on them." Richens chuckled as he knew that this would be his last opportunity to jokingly rile his friend by using the irreverent nickname. "So, with that and the other research I've done over the years, I couldn't let it all go to waste now could I?" The merry group of revellers were all silent, transfixed by the old man giving one last sermon. Lin Tisserand stood motionless at the rear of the room, carefully analysing every word.

"You see, when the whole world came to a shuddering halt with Covid, we weren't quite so run off our feet in CID. I had a bit of spare time on my hands so I went back over a few old case files. Also, my ever-astute fiancée ran a few more forensic tests on some of the old samples we had from back in the day." Kath had returned from the bar with Trudi and gazed up lovingly at her fiancé, giving him a supportive smile.

"Amazingly, something called Touch DNA evidence has come to light, and that positively connects most of the old biker gangs' deaths together."

215

Lin felt her body freeze to the spot, as if the lifeblood in her body had drained out through her stiletto healed shoes. Vivid memories of the close contact she had with her victims just before their deaths shot to the front of her mind. Being kissed hard on the lips by Bullet; squeezing the cheeks of Yardy's face around the funnel; slapping the brutal Crusher across the face; his fingernails scratching across her chest; sliding her hands across Razor Fish's shiney shaven head before suffocating him; the rasping burn of George's bristly chin scratch across her delicate skin as he climaxed in the Jacuzzi, and finally, her wearing the fluffy white bathrobe. Lin knew back then it would have been impossible to get a positive DNA match from such little skin-to-skin contact, but she felt a sudden flutter in her chest. Could those touches now provide trace evidence to link her to the scenes?

She slowly placed her champagne flute on the table and began to step away from Richens' gathered well wishers. She turned around and clumsily bumped into the familiar tall frame of Inspector Duke.

"You know, it's a funny thing, one person's DNA in particular kept cropping up when we did the tests," continued Richens, as he delivered his parting speech. "So, me and Duchess did a bit more digging on my suspect's history, just to put my mind at rest." Duke laughed along with the crowd at the irreverent use of his nickname. He was thankful that it would be the last time he would hear it at work.

"It turns out the perp had been right under our noses the whole time." Everyone in the room looked around accusingly at each other. All of the party guests started to quietly chatter among themselves, wondering where the old DCI's revelation would lead? Lin Tisserand was only too aware that a long-awaited time bomb was about to explode.

"He's very good isn't he?" whispered Duke to Lin, sensing the scared young woman's urgency to leave the room.

"Yes, he is," she replied hastily. "But I'm afraid I have to go now."

"Ah yes, you've probably got to catch the train back your father's old guesthouse in the West Country, haven't you?"

Lin stepped away from him as if she had stood on a bolt of electricity. *How does he know anything about my father?* Adrenaline fizzed through her body as she scanned the room for an escape route. She knew she had to get away. Lin realised immediately that the police must have continued their very thorough investigations behind-the-scenes, and she was no longer in control of the situation.

"I think you'd probably best hang around for the next bit," said Duke, as he casually took a hold of Lin's wrist.

The whispering audience went quiet again as the retiring chief inspector remained standing on his chair. He took a glug of wine and resumed his speech with a small tap of his champagne flute.

"Right then, just imagine, all of that time goes by and the advances in forensic techniques now mean that the slightest touch on the skin from one person to another all those years ago can be detected. Who'd have thought it? There was an audible gasp of anticipation from the crowd, as they all waited patiently for the punch line.

Lin felt physically sick, as she tried to compose her thoughts. She knew she was about to become centre stage of Richens and Duke's elaborate production, but maybe there was a small glimmer of hope that the steely old detective was bluffing. It was a common tactic very often used as a final throw of the dice. *Don't be stupid woman, pull yourself together. He's got nothing substantial on you.* Lin tried to calm her nerves by convincing herself no one back then would have been so fastidious to collect the samples. The old swabs could have become contaminated anyway, and she could soon throw enough doubt over the evidence to disprove she had any connection with the murders. Her breathing became steadier as she pulled away from Duke's grip to defiantly pick up her champagne flute.

"Unfortunately though, you can only be sure of a Touch DNA test working if you were thorough enough to gather the evidence at the time of the original investigation," sighed Richens as he resumed his monologue.

217

Lin allowed herself a small self-congratulatory smile and a gasp of relief. *See, I knew you were bluffing, you twisted bastard. I just bloody knew it.*

"Mind you, one thing is for sure." Richens took a final sip of champagne. "The wonderful lady in my life was perhaps one of the most thorough collectors of swabs, slides and samples that I'd ever met," he chuckled. "She used to drive me up the wall with how long she'd take with her test tubes and sticky tape before letting me and Duchess anywhere near the body." Everyone turned to clap their appreciation at Kath Cooper's foresight, as she stood there blushing at Richens' side. Lin felt a wave of vomit well in her stomach.

"But some of you know all too well how strong forensic evidence can be invaluable in a cold case," continued Richens.

"Yes, especially our esteemed Miss Tisserand over there." Richens pointed at Lin, as the now trembling woman stared back in stunned silence. All she could imagine in her mind was if the case went to court then her vengeful dirty secrets would be unveiled; the whole of her life and career would collapse around her.

"You know, don't you? Especially after all of those miscarriage of justice reviews you have been successful with over the years." Richens raised his glass in feigned honour of the popular defender. "Oh yes, if anyone can appreciate the advances in forensic science to catch killers, it's you, isn't it, Miss Tisserand?"

Everyone turned around to clap again, however their enthusiasm quickly evaporated as they noticed Duke placing a set of handcuffs on the lawyer's wrists.

"Or would you prefer me to call you Miss Weber?" added Richens. The whole audience drew in an audible breath as Inspector Duke began to caution her, before leading the startled woman out of the room to a waiting police car.

The old inspector had always felt a slight unease around Miss Tisserand. He had always felt since their first meeting that there was something crafty about her which he couldn't quite put his finger on.

Kath Cooper had been able to establish there was a link between the trace evidence found on most of the biker gang's bodies and the white bathrobe found at George Dalmano's house. The only victim who didn't share the same contact was Patrick O'Doyle. However, his results had shown traces of George's DNA on the tourniquet around the injection marks on the junkie's arm. The cyber team had also enhanced the CCTV recording from the bookie's shop. The footage showed that as soon as Patrick had left the premises after making his call to the police, he had been followed along the footpath by a man who bore a strong resemblance to George Dalmano. Richens and Duke both had a strong suspicion that it was George Dalmano who had murdered Patrick with the lethal cocktail.

The pathologist knew the unidentified trace DNA found on the five other men was from a woman, but the profile was not on the national database, so Kath carried out a familial DNA search to try and identify potential relatives of the alleged perpetrator. It was then William Weber was found to be a paternal match to the unknown samples.

Richens began a new line of enquiry into any children that William had. It didn't take long for him to discover what had become of William's daughter and how the young Angelina Weber had changed her name before taking up her law studies. The mere fact that Lin Tisserand had concealed her family connection to the man she had fought so valiantly to get acquitted, confirmed in Richens mind that he was onto something with his new line of enquiry. But he had wanted to play his cards very close to his chest and make sure he had all bases covered before arresting one of Hanford's most eminent lawyers. He couldn't afford for anything to go wrong.

It had been relatively easy for Duke to set up a casual meeting with the young barrister to discuss another historic case that she was working on. After the meeting, her discarded coffee cup was swiftly retrieved by the detective and sent for DNA analysis. The results were a match to the unidentified profile and firmly linked the lawyer to five of the dead men. With the final pieces of the puzzle slotted into place, DCI Richens created his elaborate plan to arrest Lin Tisserand. It would be a momentous parting gift to his old team.

"You enjoyed that little bit of amateur dramatics, didn't you Alex?" laughed Kath as she helped Richens down off the chair.

"Yep, I've been waiting quite a while to get that one off my chest. I feel a bit sorry for her in a way though 'cos she did the world a favour by bumping off all of those lowlifes. I'm guessing she'll fight it to the bitter end and jump through all kinds of legal loopholes to try and get off on a technicality. She'd probably claim we got her DNA without her consent or something. Or maybe she'll be able to explain why traces of her DNA were found on five of the corpses. Who knows? But for now I suppose you could say that touch DNA business is a bit of a slap in the face for Miss Tisserand." The couple clinked glasses as Alex drew Kath towards him for a celebratory kiss.

Kath Cooper couldn't help but feel a little uneasy knot begin to unravel in her mind. She knew she had been one of the technicians who had worked on Tracey Chambers' remains when they had been brought in to the lab from Himley Chase. Kath had written an observation of the condition of Tracey's clothes in short-hand and had meant to type it up at the end of that very busy day. It was not lost on Kath that if it had been clear in the forensics report at the time that no urine had been discovered on Tracey's clothes, then it would have been more difficult for the CPS to connect the woman's murder to William Weber. Kath lamented that it had never been mentioned in court that William was a paternal match to the foetus found in the remains. Had she been able to share that information, then that would have disproved the prosecution's stranger rape theory. Maybe the innocent William Weber would not have been found guilty of Tracey's murder; maybe then his daughter would not have been driven to kill six old men. It was a secret the retired pathologist would have to live with.

THE END

Printed in Great Britain
by Amazon